WILLINGTON

SEAN.J.LAVERY

Willington

By Sean.J.Lavery

ebook edition published 2016

A Northern Town Publication

Back cover photograph by Alice Evans

For Ginny, Peggy,
and those who cared to listen.

Contents

Keep your feet still ! Geordey hinny,
Let's be happy for the neet,
For aw maynt be se happy throo the day.

Joe Wilson

THE BEGINING

The driver followed the moons cats-eyed reflection, with
squint eyes. He'd forgotten his glasses, left them behind with
what remained of his other life. And her, she sat impassively
beside him. Devoid of her usual emotional ticks. There was
no euphoria tonight, just a bone crushing, understanding of
their predicament. The signpost read Bamburgh One Mile,
but they weren't going there. They were just stopping off to
admire the scenery. Making one last pilgrimage, before the
arc of their journey headed south. Fragments of the
intervening years lay scattered on this barren
Northumberland beach; yet this was no sentimental journey.

They had time to climb the dunes and revisit a few
glittering memories; he with a bottle of vodka, she with
vermouth. Round a makeshift fire they would drink, while
the ocean chipped in its chorus of moans. On a night like this,
with the full moon risen – Lindisfarne and the Farne Islands
were visible. Ghosts of long dead monks followed wooden
crosses along the waters edge, carrying the ancient bones of
St Cuthbert to safety. And the cries of seals, flapping their
flipper arms; and sea-birds ever present – scavenging for
scraps. And the smell of a makeshift fire; burning driftwood,
a family allowance book, a hospital weight card, smouldering
with small items of children's clothing. She could see his face

illuminated by the flames. Pushing out of the darkness, like a study in light by Rembrandt or Caravaggio. He touches her hair, moistened by sea air and flaked with debris from the wind. He smiles a wide open grin; an unexpected flash of happiness.

The details are important to her, his Sacred Heart lapel badge, the shine of his grey tonic suit. His hair growing long at the back, curling and unkempt. A large gold signet ring, it had belonged to his father, and had rough edges that scratched. He had a dimple on his chin, like Kirk Douglas; but that's where the resemblance to Spartacus ended. He was no champion of the underprivileged and underfed, he was the champion of him. And if you were to ask him how things were, he would say champion, as a reflex.

"How are you," she wanted to say. But instead she concentrated on keeping her legs still. They had started shaking under the table at St Vincent's, while port and lemon poured themselves down her throat. People had noticed her silence, she could feel the rumour circulate the dance floor and bar. A sideways glance here, a stare from above the foamy head of a pint. All that attention was making her sweat; making her nerves twist, and her legs shook in reaction.

Halfway through the evening, a singer took to the club's ramshackle stage and belted out a passable Matt Monro impersonation. The PA being what it was, barely rose above the conversation noise, but the singer kept on going regardless. Between gulps of alcohol, she was mesmerized. Fixated on the intricate frill of his evening shirt; following the pattern as it twisted and turned in wild flamenco. And what started as a smile became a snigger behind her cupped hand. She was making a show of herself and getting even more of those looks and glances. And she could feel his eyes boring channels across the dance floor, hitting her like a punch to the solar plexus.

She took herself away to the toilets and splashed water on her face. Reapplied a dab of powder and lipstick to her mouth. She brushed her hair with a steady hand, and returned back to the crimson velveteen seat. And her eyes followed; she watched him drift between groups of men, who shone when he arrived and looked downcast when he was gone. She felt a tinge of jealousy as they swooned when their shoulders were squeezed. And there were the glances across St Vincent's heaving lounge; clandestine but with a suggestion of more to come. And the hole the size of Liverpool, scooped out of her heart. And the road to Bamburgh: empty and dark, leading to extinction. And the sea rising and falling, when night gives way to day.

The shaking pursued her through St Vincent's car park. It was with her in Hopper Street, and in the back lane, where she slipped into his waiting car. So she held her legs together and apologized for the show she'd made, and he passed her a cigarette that shut her up. A new beginning is what this was. An escape– once and forever. He made it sound so easy, so matter-of-fact, that it sounded like something people did every day. He shrewdly left out all the complications. And there was no question there would be complications. She could hear them rattling behind, like tin cans on a wedding car. They were over there in Seahouses, eating a fish supper by the harbour; they were inside his wallet where a picture was stuck and refusing to move.

The details are important. He tasted of carbolic and disinfectant when she kissed his cold neck. And his skin had a waxy, dead, texture. In the dark of his car, he was silent. All red-raw hands, and bitten down fingernails. And his shirt looked new, a crisp sea-island white with French cuffs. He had the look of a frightened bridegroom; cornered at the altar, waiting for someone to shout stop. And she, with her shaky legs, and bottle of vermouth, felt impervious to everyone, and everything, but him. At Seahouses he adjusted the momentum; shifting down a gear, the car shuddered.

Memories, locked up inside closed restaurants. Moored down at the harbour. Standing by the water's edge, posing for a photograph. A chance meeting, a shared cigarette, sex standing-up behind the public toilets. He lingered; crawling along the closed main-street, eking out the pain.

To the left, a new church cross jutted out – stark and white; and they both made the sign-of-the-cross. She felt compelled to ask for god's forgiveness, with an unspoken De Profundis; and all the while the bric-a-brac of Seahouses

10

passed them by. The butchers offering Northumberland lamb. Kendal mint cake a hundred miles from Kendal. Children's toy buckets, fishing nets and tiny Wellington boots. The silence was filled by the sound of absent day-trippers and children at play. And she longed for different sounds, for music, for the hubbub of conversation, for the sound of his tinny radio and the light programme.

"Let's have some music," sounded reasonable. But it hung pregnant in the air. He made no movement towards the dashboard, and his expression remained fixed. And she was ready to ask again, but he began to sing in a low menacing baritone. It was the threat of violence, lurking round a familiar collection of notes that stopped her from interrupting. He was singing the way men do, when they work; a droning counterpoint, to the task at hand. The words seemed to be fashioned by despair, and melancholy.

Listening to him sing, she felt an accomplice, an accessory after the fact. And she thought again about a wife and the sound of children at play. She listened, impassively beside him, while the moons reflection danced about his face. And she tried not to shake, or give her fear away.

The details are important. He had dabbed on cologne to hide the stench. Changed his shirt, to a crisp sea-island white. He had arrived at St Vincent's, the back-way. Past beer crates and kitchen waste. There were no witnesses, save for the missing entry in the doorman's book. And it was her mistake not to ask, why tonight and not in the morning. Her

11

mistake, to slip into his car drunk and dressed for summer. And it was the cold North East wind, cutting through chrome and glass that chipped away at the alcohols warmth. At Alnwick, she was sober, and aware of her predicament.

He brought the car to a halt. In the distance, Bamburgh Castle jutted out to sea. Heavy dunes hid the beach, salt tinged the air, and everything was still except for the tides ebb-and-flow. She listened to his laboured breathing; it reminded her of an athlete, post-race. Gulping down the air in huge mouthfuls. Oh the sharks.....

THE PARISH

The parish of St Vincent's is situated on the north bank of the River. To the east is a rumbling sea. To the west; a neat suburban sprawl. For people outside the parish, the area is simply Willington. But for those who observe mass every Sunday. Who have God on their side; then St Vincent's is an entity. A country, within a country.

In this country of the soul its inhabitants are descended from settlers. Migrants who found work in Mining, heavy industry and shipbuilding. Some are converts who married into the faith. A few are Anglo Catholics; survivors of the Reformation. The parish is no ghetto; it's inhabitants no strangers to the important transactions of this small Northern Town.

Down by the river, cranes droop over the skeletal shapes of ocean going vessels. Men from the parish work as Platers and Welders; they fuse great steel panels together. Electricians fit out ships, threading cables insulated with asbestos through hulking shells. In the drawing office; the location of each and every rivet is documented by pen and paper. By men in grey flannel suits, who work in shirtsleeves.

Women assemble garments in factories, backing on to tributaries that snake into the great river. They thread ropes and assemble cakes in the Co-Op bakery: hair scooped up into a white headscarf; hands gloved and white. They teach children in St Vincent's Infants, where the parish offspring are instructed in the ways of god. Where the Catechism is learnt by rote and play in the schoolyard is wild and free. Their small voices ring out true and loud; with the confidence and certainty of those who have a lot to learn.

A teacher stands in the playground of St Vincent's Infants ringing a wooden handled bell. Calling in the children from play. Her hairs tied back into a bun; dinner time is over. Children run this way and that. An idea for the afternoons activity, brews. Her lessons: planned and re-planned for three years of training now occupy the part of her brain reserved for reflexes; for autonomic responses. She can dump out an afternoons activity, in the same way a memory man recites a list of Derby winners. She remembers, that's what she does. The faces of strangers and those with names attached. Every child she had taught is stored and filed away for future recognition. And like the people she encounters outside of school; they were reduced to a set of simple attributes. Hair colour, eye colour, the slant of a nose, and the looseness of teeth. The whiff of armpit and body odour. A tendency towards alcoholism. A love of too many sugary things. The gap between two tombstone teeth; a set of bitten down fingernails. The colour of socks, men's socks. Her memory stretches way back; back through long summer holidays spent with the women and men of her parish. The bell tolls, and her arm swings.

PILGRIMS

The Penitential Rite:
As we prepare to celebrate the mystery of Christ's love, let
us acknowledge our failures and ask the lord for pardon
and strength.

He smelt of freshly cut ham and pease pudding sandwiches.
Of pickled onions and dark brown beer. He smelt of a
cigarette, smoked, just before they boarded the coach. There
was none of the incense and altar wine. No mothballed
vestment smell about him; just the smells that make up a
man.

Judith Pemberton, patted down her summer skirt, so
her exposed knees were no longer visible. She allowed
herself an idle thought about Father Flannery, a thought so
unusual, she put it away. She let the passing French
countryside take her attention to a safer place. Broken down
buildings, beautiful fields, full of yellow and green. A farmer,
a town, a church clock stuck on quarter past three.

Father Flannery, read, his arms jogging with the
buses motion. His body, neat and compact, remained still.

She caught his reflection as they passed under a railway bridge. His angular face, half shadowed had the look of an existential poet. Or how she imagined such a person looked. Swap his dog collar for a black roll neck, his brilliantine for natural, his neat trilby for a floppy hat, and the transformation would be complete. Then the thought came back, just as her face turned to his.

But he was lost in the book, unaware of her gaze. Deep in spiritual concentration. She imagined only a serious act, like an act of god would break that concentration. An ordinary girl like her had no chance. After all what would she do with that attention: flirt, flutter her eyelids? He was a priest, a man married to god.

As the bus slowed, his jittery hands became still. Small speeding cars flew past like fireflies. Pilgrims stood up to stretch their legs. Mrs Mac adjusted her headscarf, and applied a thin emulsion of lipstick. With the bus slowing to a halt, it's insides filled with cigarette smoke, no longer able to blow out the top window. Each pair of seats had a silver orange segment ashtray, and each ashtray a collection of butts. Father Flannery had emptied his pipe in hers, and when a little ash dropped on her leg, she never let on. Instead she brushed it away, while he returned to his book, Justine.

A funny book for a priest to be reading she had first thought, a book about a woman. But then nuns were women, and Mary was a woman. And St Bernadette had only been a girl like herself when god came calling. And now here she was, on a pilgrimage to the site of that miracle. Where the old and infirm of St Vincent's were going to be fixed. Where she was going to spend five days, sipping French coffee and eating croissant.

There were other distractions of course, French men: a species so rare and exotic; she could barely imagine having one close like Father Flannery. A glimpse from the coach window, the man who served coffee at the last stop, just fuelled her interest. They were both old, at least thirty and not particularly handsome. But they were exotic as mermen, film actors and Jack Kerouac.

The coffee shop man had responded in French to orders given in English. He showed no sign of understanding anything but his own language, then the order came and everything was as it should be. She toyed with the idea of speaking French fluently, the way English people abroad do. She wondered if the man had a son, closer to her age, with better looks and a fancy for English girls. Maybe a devout, church-going boy, who just happened to be visiting Lourdes for the cure. She imagined until her coffee became cold, and it was time to board the bus.

Now they were getting off at another small café, this time it was a stop for tea, and a rest for their driver. Who would sleep in his seat, while they ate. "Back in one hour," he shouted as they trailed off the bus. But one look at his heavy lids and you would know one hour would stretch into two.

Father Flannery stood to let her out. A gentleman she thought. He gave her that happy look, reserved for outside mass and socials at St Vincent's. Except this time, he opened his mouth as if to say something, and his face momentarily looked troubled. But whatever happened to be on his mind, was interrupted by Mrs Mac pushing through. It passed into the place reserved for words unsaid and unfinished thoughts. It followed behind her along the isle, until she was out in the fading French sunlight; shading her eyes with a milk-white hand.

Then he was lost in a crowd of pilgrims, vying for his attention. A small black speck surrounded by summer bonnets and cream panamas. And there was no reason for her to join the crowd; she could follow those drifting into the café. Order her tea before the crush. Flirt with a waiter; before the busybodies locked into Father Flannery passed through its door.

There was reason for Judith Pemberton to take out a mirror and add some life to her lips, but only starlets did that. And there was no complaint when she pushed past Mrs Boyle, McKenzie and Brown; to within an inch of his priestly nose.

"Father, Father," she said. A little too breathlessly, interrupting one of his Lourdes anecdotes.

"Peace you see, was all he was after. Peace and ...."

Eyes swivelled in her direction, and ears pricked up to hear what she had to say. She felt like finishing his over familiar sentence, but "the love of a good woman" sounded like a proposition. So instead she blurted out the second thing that came to mind.

"Can I sit next to you Father at tea. It would be a great honour."

Some of his audience managed a bemused expression, while others furrowed deeply. Father Flannery's malleable face quickly reassembled itself into that good-natured, after mass look. He patted her shoulder gently, making contact for the briefest of moments with bare flesh.

"That would be a pleasure Judy. You can order for the both of us, in that excellent French I heard you using earlier today."

Night had already happened as their bus skirted its way down the narrow country road. Leading to The Petite Hotel; a soft cotton wool dream of a place, hidden behind a hundred tall poplar trees. A single light shone out from its first floor, guiding their way into a darkened reception. A crudely written note welcomed the midnight guests. Father Flannery led the way, with a torch produced from his brown mountaineering knapsack.

"This way Mrs Mac, that will be your room Mrs Boyle," interrupted the sound of shoes echoing down the hotels corridor. Then before she knew it, her turn came and Judith Pemberton was tucked into a strange single bed. With a snoring Mrs Brown, a foot away.

20

Soon the rhythm of the woman's breathing passed into her dream. It became the rhythm of the sea as it lapped against a familiar shore. She was ten years old again, watching the tide come in on Tynemouth Long Sands. Her mother, dressed in a one-piece bather, wetted a richly painted toe in the surf. She beckoned Judith to join her, but something pulled her back. Down into the coarse grain of the sand. Her mother's gestures became more frantic, until they resembled a spastic semaphore. But there was nothing she could do, the quicksand held her tight.

The image of her mother waving on the horizon, merged with the sound of an old woman snoring, and the saline sting of her tears. She pulled the bedclothes tight and closed her eyes. The sound of the old woman breathing, dropped down an octave, and in her mind his heavy presence was there in the room. She imagined the back of his head, sleek and groomed; even in sleep. His shoulders broad and exposed had her arm draped across them. He wore no pyjamas, just his own skin and the smell of shaving soap. She stretched to the limits of her imagination, and viewed his shoes: polished and neat beside the bed. His trousers draped over a chair, his suit jacket hanging like another person over the chair back. The rhythm of the sea returned as she approached the far reaches of her imagination, and then the woman's snores, like the soft purr of a cat, came back.

The Petite Hotel had notepaper where she wrote her first letter home. Addressed to Grandma and Uncle Pete; it described her first taste of French food, and the Channel crossing where many turned green at the gills. She let them know Father Flannery was taking care of her and Mrs Brown. She let them know about the mysterious relationship many had with the French language.

While her roommate slept, Judith wiped her face with the monogrammed hotel flannel. She let herself out, walking on tip-toe to breakfast. Where she sipped a wide bowl of hot chocolate and munched through soft brioche. Afterwards she walked through the hotel grounds, past the one hundred poplar trees. Outside in the still morning, she closed her eyes and let a ripple of tiredness flow through her.

And that's where the priest found her. Where his hand moved to hers, and held on for longer than was decent. Where she let those unusual thoughts run away with themselves. It was only much later. When sunlight gave way to another dark hotel corridor, that the thoughts of the morning intruded. Had she actually kissed Father Flannery? Held his mouth against hers; long enough to taste his breakfast and morning cigarette.

Had he squeezed her hand, before withdrawing, so the space between their faces was appropriate. He had certainly helped her up; maintaining the grip started just minutes before. And he only let go when they were in sight of the hotel, and the rest of their party were boarding the bus for Lourdes. And on and on; to another dark corridor, and another shared room. Where the morning would disappear, along with popular trees and The Petite Hotel.

Mrs Brown's breathing once again became prominent in her mind, taking on the sound of a small paddle steamer; skirting a distant shore. It put, putted about the room, as Judith Pemberton lay with her eyes open. It followed small dainty hands as they moved below thin cotton blankets, and rested on her pubic mound.

For a while she kept her hands still. Warming them up. Getting used to the sensation they brought. And when her head was emptied of everything but his priestly nose, pressed against hers; she began to stroke. Slow luxuriant movements, against her inner thighs. Then bold incursions, deep inside her. With each infinitesimal change of pressure. With each brush against her clitoris, came a different image. The slow strokes brought him close; his thighs touching hers. Brushing gently as he allowed the urge to finish himself subside. Breathing urgently, but without effort. Then his breath would quicken, and so would her fingers. Rubbing from left to right. Synchronising with his ever-deepening thrusts.

His hair a messy mop; fell over wide, excited eyes. His arms, pushing deep into her mattress. Traversed by great prominent veins; engorged with blood. There were no words, just movement and thought. Exquisite thoughts. A great jumble of feelings piled one on top of another. Until nothing

23

could stop the involuntary jerk of her pelvis, and the great shout that ripped out of her chest.

His face receded, drawing back and back, until all she could see were dark wooden shutters. It drew out the tingling sensation from between her legs, and replaced it with sleep. And she could hear the sea calling, pulling back from Tynemouth. Revealing a dark strip of moist sand, and rock pools teeming with life.

Her dead mother was now beside her, holding her hand. She smelled of salt water, turning stagnant in the sun. And where her eyes had once been; there were shells, bleached white. They watched the tide go out, she through pale blue eyes. Her mother through pale white shells. They watched until the horizon and sea became one.

"Do you see me during the day," flowed from thought to mouth and into the cool sea air. It was something, she'd never voiced. There were moments in the confessional dark when the question formed in her mind. Moments with her grandmother. When they lay in bed, reminiscing about her mam. But the thought always passed silently away.

So her imagination filled in the spaces, where a vast celestial audience tracked her most mundane activities. But mostly there was her mother watching alone, from above. Someday, they would meet again. And she would atone for all those sins committed in full view of dead aunts and uncles.

"Can't you see my eyes, nothing passes into them; nothing but the salt of this sea air, and the smoke of

24

grandads cigarettes. I saw you last, as a little girl, holding onto my hospital bed, like it would fly away. I saw the back of your head as you walked out of my sick room. A pink ribbon in your hair, and a slight skip in your step. And I remember the last words you said to me: Mam, when are you coming home. That's where the pictures end and feelings take over."

And there was no hint of regret in her voice, no sadness or pain. Judith Pemberton supposed all those things just passed away with the body. Disappeared with the ping of a bell and a whiff of incense: the sound of a makeshift mass, happening out of earshot, as life was extinguished.

The image of her mother's face was there with her as she woke. Mrs Brown was gone and the shutters open. Her dishevelled sheets, spilled over and onto the floor. There was something of that tingling sensation remaining. It accompanied her on the bus into town, increasing in intensity as she crossed and uncrossed her legs. And she was glad when the journey came to an end, saving her the embarrassment of a stifled orgasm, on a bus full of pilgrims.

Profession of Faith:

He smelt of croissant and chocolate, of a cigarette smoked before breakfast. He sat next to her once again, as they took the bus into town, and read the same page he had been reading since Dover. Deliberately avoiding her gaze; while turmoil raged inside, like a stormy sea. It felt hotter, twenty degrees hotter, and his dog collar cut into his neck. Beneath the book, he counted folds of thick black worsted cloth. So suitable for draughty confessionals; so unsuitable for Lourdes on a sunny day.

She was looking out of the window, her blond hair cut in a childish bob. And she smelled of the same food as he. Consumed in silence, on separate tables. A simple prayer before bed. A round of the rosary as he knelt; stripped down to his underclothes. A biography of St Ignatius Loyola, open on his bedside table. All failed to ward off those thoughts. In the dark of his special room; he was carried aloft like a triumphant general, on the shoulders of lust and desire. And at some point in the night, his self-control crashed. And he ran through the same scenario, again and again, until he let go.

Now looking again at the innocent by his side, he felt uneasy about those thoughts popping uninvited into his head. They soiled his picture of how a priest should be. Like shit on a pair of shined-up shoes. Or those yellow urine stains that never washed out of white underpants. And there was something more than impure about having those thoughts right here, right now. Right next to such milk white skin and clean smelling hair.

So he looked away and into the eyes of Mrs Mac, who was smiling, revealing wonderfully loose false teeth. And it was then his thoughts exploded into cinemascope; shooting off in the most inappropriate of directions, until he was finally down on his knees.

"Father Flannery, don't you think Lourdes is just the most wonderful place on earth," said Mrs Mac. And he found himself nodding in agreement, his face a picture of sated serenity.

And out the window, a trail of pilgrims followed other pilgrims through town. They stopped occasionally, lighting candles at makeshift shrines. Others walked foot long crosses, singing hymns to the blessed Virgin, the ocean star. But rather than subside the turmoil grew stronger, filling every idle moment. When his mind was not being dazzled by a hundred faces; by great effigies of the Virgin, and Jesus Christ. He was on his knees. And no amount of dipping himself in the holy waters was going to cure that desire. So when the bus stopped to let them out; he lost his party and himself in the crowd. Taking one step for their two; until the headscarves and panamas, were those sported by strangers.

He watched as the blond childish bob walked arm in arm with Mrs Brown; he watched until their heads became pinpricks, surrounded by a hundred others. A living tapestry moving this way and that. And with a lightness of foot, he retreated and let the crowd take him in.

The night was hot, so he removed his jacket, and rolled up his white shirtsleeves. And with his dog collar detached; he moved with ordinary people as a new man. He followed their ebb and flow; stopping to gawp at shop windows, as they did. He watched a man play find the lady with passer-by's, and left some francs in the outstretched cap of a flute player.

And he drove like a dynamo, through streets free of pilgrims, shedding his priestly skin, streetlamp by streetlamp. His dog collar and cross followed a sacred heart pendant into the gutter; while his body found itself huddled in the shadows of a back street bar. A place where people like he - may spend some time at peace.

Doxology and Great Amen
Priest: through him, with him, and in him, in the unity of the Holy Spirit, all glory and honour is yours almighty Father, for ever and ever.
All: Amen!

Jean Paul listened to the man peeing. He smoked a cigarette and let the post coital emptiness wash through him. His limp dick leaking a little on his thigh, left a cold sticky feeling. But he was too comfortable, too in the moment to move. He thought of an automobile travelling fast down a long, straight country road. The woman passenger, a blond, let the wind blow through her hair; the driver covered his with a cap. They were heading for a horizon, of white clouds and blue sea, and they acknowledge him with the blow of a horn. The man in his bathroom broke wind, and he was back in a dank bedroom. One hundred miles from the coast; with a stranger, and a half smoked cigarette.

The stranger called himself Jim, and spoke English with a thick, impenetrable accent. This kept their conversation succinct; heightening every other sense. So like blind men, they felt, and smelt, and bit their way round each other. The Englishman could well have been Scottish or Irish. He had the thick wild hair of a Celt and pale pale skin. His arms were those of a labourer, while his hands felt like girls. And like a girl or adolescent boy, his chest was hairless and stretched tight across his ribcage.

But it was his heavy, ridiculous suit that marked the man out as a tourist. And the abrasive feel of its cloth, reminded him that English men were not just bedroom masochists. This was his hair shirt. Taken out and worn every day. A suit woven from the birch branches of flagellants. It was the suit, and the suit alone, that had first caught his eye. Its owner: sweating underneath heavy worsted cloth, was just another pilgrim straying from Jesus. A composite, of a hundred others he had met in this bar and that. And how could Jean Paul resist such a suit, with its thick, thick cloth. Black as a Priests cassock and nuns wimple. Black as the dirt underneath his fingernails, black as the thoughts turning themselves over in his head and the sleek dark hair of the suits owner.

And now the suits owner was naked and peeing in his
bathroom, while his unusually shined-up shoes, were neatly
stacked beside his bed. And over the sound of his piss
waterfall, he whistled a tuneless tune.

Communion Song:
[During the reception of Communion, an appropriate song
is sung, or at least a short "Communion Antiphon" recited]

The sound of pilgrims, heading to morning prayers, clicking
their heels against cobble stones. The metallic thump of his
water heater, igniting. Water flowing from the faucet,
splashing against hand and face. A stranger, getting himself
ready to leave. Scraping a razor across his face, dampening
down his unruly, wild hair. Jean Paul removed this from his
head, and replaced it with a more acceptable vision.

There was the bottle of oil, laid out on his bedside
table like a sexual condiment. And the towel. White and
freshly laundered; still smelling of the washerwoman's soap,
lay spread out on his bed. A sip of white wine commenced
the ritual, and he would let the stranger drink from his glass,
before the man lay prone upon the towel.

They were both naked, and the room in darkness.
And he would drip small round circles of oil, at regular
intervals, down the man's spine. Jim the tourist would slowly
dissolve. And in his place there would be a pair of lily-white

shoulders, and a broad peasant back. Soft sallow skin; a mole on his left shoulder. An oval brown blemish. And there would be no stopping that car, as it sped towards the horizon. Sounding its horn in abandon.

The man lay still, and his fingers, moved down the freshly oiled spine; inexorably moving down and down. Causing the stranger to moan, to move his hips from left to right. To splay open his legs; exposing a crumpled testicular sac, and the beginning of an erection.

It caused him to shout out loud, "Body of Christ," and he found himself replying instinctively with an "Amen". With the swift insertion of an index finger, he applied more oil, inserted another fingers. And soon he found the prostate, and the moaning dropped a low guttural octave. He worked the stranger with his free hand, massaging until they were both ready.

But inevitably the screwy water heater intruded, and he was right back there on a warm Easter morning. With the sound of Pilgrims shoes clip-clopping down his narrow street. Jim no doubt would join them. Meeting-up with his saintly pals, and lighting candles for the blessed Virgin.

He felt like punching the man. Cutting his lip; drawing ruby red blood. But stranger Jim had those powerful arms. And there was something about his eyes, and the humourless way he carried on: that said, leave me alone. And that was the great shame; the waste of a perfectly good man. And the shame was he was not a weaker man. Who

31

would have taken his penance, like a man. Allowing him to wipe away the blood, with a damp handkerchief. And maybe steal another kiss, another squeeze.

It was always in the moment of leaving. The second before they crossed his door, that the truth pushed its way to the surface and demanded a hearing. It was there on his lips as he said goodbye, and they waved; leaving for a wife, a girlfriend, or to confirmed bachelordom. Jean Paul, their Frenchman, had taken them to a place never listed on a pilgrim's itinerary.

Transubstantiation

Jean Paul smoked a cigarette after Jim had gone. He adjusted his hair, so his fringe was swept back. This simple movement transformed the man's face, making him at once younger and more serious. The small dabs of rouge, wiped away with a damp towel. And so did the kohl dark of his eyebrows. He folded away the light blue Italian cut trousers and seersucker jacket, and suede tie. He toyed with the idea of taking them out again, to remain as he once was. But time was tight, and soon Madam Mernier would be there, demanding her landlady's rent for the night. And with her upturned nose, she would sniff round her apartment and ask him if anyone else had stayed the night. He naturally would act shocked, and she unconvinced. And the scene would be played out until a crisp few francs passed from his hand to hers.

He laid out his other clothes, in neat impersonation of a body reclining on his bed. And flipped a coin to determine his mood for the day. Austere felt right and fitting for an Easter morning. It went well with the cold white bathroom tiles, and silver steel fittings. A round sink and toilet bowl manufactured in Lyon. A bath green with age ornately finished with lion's feet. A bar of soap: used by a hundred others; whittled down to a grey slither. The cold steel of his cutthroat razor. All dovetailed perfectly into his act.

Even the water heater, exhausted by the shaving stranger, chose to dispense cold water. Closing up the pores on his face, causing the shave to take off skin and hair.

"Forgive me father for I have sinned," felt like the appropriate words to accompany this ritual. And so did the thoughts of suicide, and the vision of his ragged throat, gurgling out everything that was bad. Until all that was left would be him, and that counterfeit Jean Paul, would be gone, gone, gone.

Outside, at the end of the alleyway he could see pilgrims moving; filing past with candles waiting to be lit. And the warm Lourdes sun was already creeping into the shady doorways; marking the entrances of rooming houses and hotels. By twelve the sun would reach his door; peeling away small flecks of blue paint with its intense rays. While he pushed wheelchair bound parishioners, to healing pools of holy water.

As the sun travelled down to the stone step, and disappeared at a point between pavement and doorframe. He would take a well-earned rest. And in the anonymity of dusk, his eyes may follow the long shadows of strangers. Lingering for a time on a strong pair of shoulders; on a thick muscular backside. He would sip the golden head of his beer, and shiver as the cold liquid collided, with the warmth of his soul.

Blessing:
Bow your heads and pray for God's blessing.

She linked arms with him, on their way to evening mass. Darkness giving her the confidence daytime took away. And the looks from other priests; sitting at tables, drinking beer and wine, hardly seemed to matter. Mrs Mac and Brown, were shapes walking with other shadows. Hardly real. Hardly worth bothering about. His hat was missing, and so was some of that brilliantine. Without the oil and grease, his hair curled over his collar.

"Father Flannery you know I would just love to join you for a drink. But what would the others say."

And he would say:

> "don't worry yourself Judy. Those things happen all
> the time. At the bar of St Vincent's; over here in
> Lourdes. Look over there; a priest is drinking with a
> woman. Do you see heads turning, do you see a
> crowd gathering, no? And if the others complain. I
> will ask them to consider what they would do, with a
> poor motherless girl, alone in France."

She worked over these conversations in her head, as
they walked in silence. Wearing out her imagination, until
there was just the sound of their footsteps, and those of a
thousand others. The sound of hymns drifted out into the
night air. An old man played a flute tunelessly, and he held
out his cap as they passed. They stopped, while Father
Flannery fished in his pocked for change. Over in the square
a lone priest drank beer. He looked well shined up, like a film
star. And his eye followed their performance, taking in
Father Flannery's outstretched hand. He made contact with
her eyes a second later, and held her gaze with the ferocious
certainty of a man who knows what he wants. The good-
looking priest raised his glass; nodding his head in
acknowledgement of her, Flannery and the beggar.

Later, Judith Pemberton left mass before the blessing.
She left with the half-formed idea of spending some time
with the good-looking, beer-drinking priest. But instead she
walked through quiet streets, while pilgrims celebrated the
last mass of the day. She walked until a small bar found her,

and a glass of Dubonet found itself un-drunk in front of her.
And when she finally sipped the drink: it tasted of
communion, and reminded her of vestments, and incense,
and the fact that Priests were nothing like Montgomery Clift
in I Confess.

THE FIGHT GAME

I

He was only six years of age in 1951. Nobody owned a TV set back then, everyone went to the pictures if they wanted moving images. Otherwise they listened to the radio, or they read. But a six year olds options are more restricted. The radio was pretty rubbish. Reading was something he'd yet to master. But the pictures, they were everything; a place of possibilities. October 26th, 1951, was a Friday. Friday night was the night men went out together. Saturday they stepped out with their wives and sweethearts. His dad, Bob Henderson was no different; except on October 27th, 1951.

He deviated from his usual routine that day. Because in America, in New York City. Friday night was fight night. And on October 26th, 1951, Friday night was a World Championship fight night. Two of the greatest boxers the world had ever witnessed were going to be slugging it out at Madison Square Garden. Some clever fellow had decided to show the Fight in its entirety, at the Ritz on Saturday, the day following the Fight. Patrons were advised not to read their usual Saturday paper so as not to spoil the excitement.

Bob Henderson preferred the word ruin. Saturday afternoons were the strange interlude between the Kidda's Pictures and the big hitting A and B features. They were a halfway house between childhood and adulthood. A frustrating time for all.

The clever fellow surmised that a good portion of the audience would be men. He also surmised that a trip to the cinema would also work with the wives. Eating into the usual round of club, betting shop, football match, pub. There was no need to cook an elaborate tea, because the big eater was going to be out. The only losers in this equation were those in-betweens. The Kidda Pictures would still run, although the clever fellow had also surmised that there would be a smaller demand for ice-cream and orange juice that day. Instead Dad was going to be buying tabs from the cigarette girl to calm his shredded nerves.

Something: a premonition, a piece of childish wisdom, told him that going to see a fight with dad was going to be much more exciting than two dimensional cartoons. Bob Henderson liked cartoons. He would laugh a wide expansive laugh at the silliness of Bugs Bunny and Roadrunner. Become sentimental during Snow White, and hysterical with Laurel and Hardy. Saturday afternoons at the pictures always bested afternoons in the club or at the match. Except on special days like October 27th, 1951.

He'd heard Dad mention the fight was going to be on at the Ritz as an early evening feature; but made no connection between their habit and this new thing. All the schedules were cleared. There would be no time for tea. Instead there would be Ham Stotty's.

Keith Henderson was too young to know the nuances of persuasion. Instead he used the oldest trick in the book. He fixed dad every day with sorrowful eyes. He fixed his dad with that same expression, until the man buckled. There would be no cartoons; but their Saturday tea would still happen, just five hours earlier. A fry-up of Black Pudding, Bacon, Sausages, Fried Bread and Pan Haceldy; topped with brown sauce and a large brimming mug of tea.

"It won't hurt you to miss the cartoons one Saturday lad. Think of how excited you'll be next week, "said Bob Henderson, three days into their war of attrition.

"But I don't want to see the cartoons Daddy."

"Aye, tell me another."

"But I don't, honest."

His little voice breaking on the word honest.

"So tell me lad, what's your plan?"

He had no plan of course; six year olds don't make big plans. They make small plans.

"I want to go with you to the fight."

"What."

"To see the men fight in America."

"You're too young."

"Why."

"Because you're too young."

39

"Boys and girls fight at school, and the boys club."

A look of puzzlement appeared on his dads face. A first. Normally he said yes daddy to everything, and that made dad happy.

"Aw. Has someone put you up to this son," he said, shaking his head. So he shook his head too, with vigour.

"Well if you think I'm a difficult customer, go ask Mam, see what see says."

She said:

"You can't take a six-year-old to a boxing match, have you lost your mind man."

Then she started laughing and everything was ok.

"Now I'm going to have to teach you everything about the fight game."

II

Joe Louis v Rocky Marciano. The Garden, October 26th 1951

Jersey Joe Walker, Edward J Hoover, Robbie Goldstein – referee. Joe Louis balding and bulky eagerly answers the bell. The big question tonight, can the ex-champion come back – he's the slight favourite. Round one, Louis keeps flicking in that left Jab. But he's not able to put together those famous barrages of his.

Grey Easter drizzle hitting hot skin. The cotton fibre of his tee-shirt is sodden. Plimsolls make a slap slap sound against wet pavements. A whiplash of an angry North Sea wind, buffets his cheeks. Arms moving freely, cutting upwards, like a nimble fighter, making light of his opponent.

Rocky Marciano, hits your arms, he works his gloves into your torso, takes a swipe just under the ribs. Grey April evening, running the piers length then turning back. Looking out at the great rivers mouth and thinking about Mairi.

Marciano refrains from sex two weeks before a fight. He rarely sees his wife. Instead he runs gym-shoes ragged, in the Catskill Mountains.

On the opposing river bank, a second pier juts out. An identical image, protruding from the south. A male and a female. He thinks of her, over on the South Side, a ferry's ride away. She's spending the night in her family's house. Mairi's only seventeen, but he imagines her man is older: maybe twenty-one or twenty-two.

He's older, heavier, has a better reach. Like Joe Louis: six one in his stocking feet, weighing in at a hefty two hundred and twelve ponds. Marciano is a mere strapling at One Hundred and Eighty-Four, and possibly only five ten. But the big fellah is 37 maybe 38. And the Rock, with his piston-like right, his Susie Q, is twenty-eight. Marciano is not the meditative type; he's not on the bench head-in-hands, or saying a prayer to St Anthony and St Sebastian. He's sleeping, curled up like a baby, resting before his fight. Cool, calm and collected.

A boat bobs out on the ocean. Waves curl up, with white tips, falling violently against the piers wall. In the distance St Mary's lighthouse, winks at him. A shiver tells him he needs to be on his way; back to Willington, back the bottom way. He throws a final punch, then he's gone. And She's receding from view, like the boat, the lighthouse and the river's mouth.

Halfway home the smell of oil and noxious chemicals caresses his nostrils. Darkness closes in. The Syndicate, Harrison's, Adaptor Engines, and Creasy Components are quiet. Only the huge engine sheds of Bonds remain open. Men move like ants around giant-sized turbines. A stolen glance into the world of heavy engineering. A world devoid of trivial things.

He takes a route down by the waterline. One of the many slipways is occupied, ready to give birth to another steel-child. Ready for launch day when tools are downed, and riveters silenced. When office boys, like he, wear their Sunday best. When everyone shares a common purpose – until the crack and smash of champagne, and the scream of a ship hitting the slipway.

The Yards roll on to Willington, following the rivers bend. Illuminated cranes keep shipyard housing in permanent daylight. A constant reminder of work for those who would prefer to forget their daily grind. People living in shadow and light.

Shadows of hulks under construction and buildings coated with corrugated iron. The railway noisily carrying coal and construction materials. A white-walled pub and an adjacent figure lighting a cigarette; a dark skinned face revealed by his flame. The orange light fades and the man is swallowed by night.

Keith Henderson crouches low, shadow boxing along the bottom road. Red-raw skin and matt-black hair. Thick with moisture; thick industrial air. Snarling and grimacing; and muttering fuck you's. The smiling faces of his tormentors who casually step aside as punches fail to connect. And then there is work. Thick tea monotonously stirred. A pile of letters and a trickle of trivial jobs to be done. Be double quick Keith.

Seconds out round-one:

Mairi bending over in a yellow dress, playing dookie-apple. Sitting in a wigwam down her back lane. Kissing boys at the bottom of Crow Bank. The shape of her breasts inside a soft cotton bra. A whole adolescence worth of wasted ejaculations. All those moments alone that never materialised. Her changing from a girl into a woman, he standing still. Forever a little boy, never quite getting the Marciano crouch right.

Seconds out round-two:

Mairi drinking tea, delicately nibbling on fondant fancies and marzipan slices. Pursing her lips and making his heart swell. Those moments, while his mother brewed more tea, when they were alone. Moments when he was struck dumb; when his hands grew to twice their normal size and fidgeted wildly. Where his eyes would involuntarily scan the contours of her body – locking like a magnet on those soft breasts. And she, drinking her tea, oblivious to his discomfort.

There were days when sunshine filled the front room. Where her body and face were obscured by the hazy light. When something approaching dialogue happened. But mostly he invoked the inarticulate spirit of James Dean during those mumbled attempts at conversation.

Joe Louis lies splayed out over the ropes. He is assisted by supporters and sports journalists sitting at the rings edge; they hold his body, so he doesn't tumble over the apron. Two minutes, thirty-six seconds into the eighth round, the flat footed and tired Brown-Bomber's fight career is over. In bars frequented by fight-fans, there is a hushed silence, as the television camera pans over the splayed figure on the ropes. The big fellah was their man, now he is no more. Time marches relentlessly on.

And Keith Henderson, he had the peaceful dreams of a child that Saturday night in 1951. He was still not grown the year Marciano retired, less than a year after his messy fight with Archie Moore. By the time he had his first amateur fight, Floyd Patterson had become the youngest Heavyweight Champion at twenty-one years and ten months.

Another wet evening snaking through the back-lanes of Willington. Station Road, Hawthorn, Woodbine, then home – Oakfield Avenue. A three foot wall and a privet hedge. Front-room, scullery, backyard and bedrooms. An outside toilet and an indoor bath. Superficial concessions to modernity: gas fire, gas fired hot water, electricity, TV set and radiogram. Axminster carpet laid wall-to-wall. Lino in the scullery, tiles in the hall.

"You'll catch your death," his mother said. Throwing a towel in his direction.

"I've left you out some luncheon meat, and there's tea in the pot. But dry off first Keith, and don't go trailing those sodden shoes through the house."

She returned to the front-room, where a TV audience clapped noisily and a grateful performer repeated "thank you" over and over.

The rough over-washed fabric felt good against his skin. Abrasive, painful, a penance. In the narrow wardrobe mirror it was only possible to view a small section of his body at a time. First he flexed his left bicep, then moving sideways, the right. He pushed fists together and pushed out his pectorals. Next came the barbells, three repetitions of fifteen arm-curls. Followed by the same number of tricep extensions.

Sweat drips from his forehead. On the wall a Sacred Heart of Jesus extends his bloodied heart; newspaper and magazine pages of Miles Davis, Elizabeth Taylor and Rocky Marciano form a collage above his headboard. A clipping from Life shows Joe Louis splayed out over the ropes. He is assisted by supporters and sports journalists sitting on the rings edge; they hold his body, so he does not tumble over the apron. Two minutes, thirty-six seconds into the eighth round, the flat footed and tired Brown-Bomber's fight career was over.

He tenses the muscles of his stomach and exhales until the gagging reflex has him gulping in air. Sit-ups follow press-ups, follow one hundred expansions of his Charles Atlas Chest Expanders. And when he's done, he relaxes. Sitting naked on the side of his single bed, he masturbates: eye to eye with Liz Taylor.

He lights a cigarette and inhales rapidly; burning down the Embassy to its filter. The TV noise rises upwards through floorboards and rug; distorted and metallic – the sound of circuits and diaphragms, and distant other worlds.

Sleep, gives respite from the day's turmoil. Time to switch off the brain and give in to subconscious desires. In the dream world of sleep and stupor he exchanges Willington for the city. A cramped cubby hole next to the mailroom, for a tower of concrete and glass.

Sleep is a time for sex without consequences. Sometimes with Mairi, sometimes not. No need to worry about his virginity, no need for rubbers or tissues or concealment. Pure physical pleasure. Release then oblivion.

On Easter morning he lays his suit shirt and tie out on the bed. Arranged so they resemble a flattened version of how he would look. Neater and less wrinkled. Winkle-pickers with a Cherry Blossom shine. Sea Island cotton shirt and a button down collar. A silk two-tone tie fastened with silver pin. Three buttoned Burtons suit, six-inch side vents and cut-away pockets. Trousers with tapered bottoms. Hair combed to a side parting. Face neatly shaved and Old Spice sparingly applied. A carnation fresh and fragrant, pinned to his button-hole.

Keith Henderson assembled his costume with loving care. He paid particular attention to the small details. The creases on his French Cuffs and the amount of sock exposed. The polish on the back of his shoes, inspected along with the sole.

"You look lovely Keith," his mother said. She has bags beneath her made-up eyes; they'd been hanging there for as long as he could remember. Her housecoat is a little frayed and her best skirt, peeks its indifferent shade of blue from beneath. The matching jacket hangs on a hook, with the pinnies and the aprons. It is short, so would not cover up the frilly cream blouse. But what she lacked in sartorial finesse, she made up for in swagger. Her presence filled the room. Yet there was no denying, she looked terrible.

"So do you mam," he replied. Looking down at his feet so she wouldn't see the lie in his eyes. Suddenly all the pain stored-up; shot through his constricted feet, and he winced. But she was already busy making a breakfast, so his facial contortion went unnoticed.

"You're the perfect son," she said to a collection of sausages spitting grease. If there was sarcasm in that remark, it was hidden by the cooking, and the turn of her back. But he knew she was lying all the same. And she probably knew about his forlorn obsession with her from over the water.

Joe Louis fought Rocky Marciano to pay his back taxes. He was terrible with money; the stuff flowed from his hands and pockets, and into other peoples. He earned over Four Million Dollars during his career, a hefty sum. Bought his family cars, houses and a comfortable life. There was talk of mink coats and diamonds, of tables in expensive restaurants that would accept money from coloured people. He invested in businesses that eventually failed. His former opponent in the thirties, Max Schmeling, remained his friend, despite all the furore about the Nazi and the African American. Schmeling never supported the Nazi party, but he was Germany's champion. On the night of his second match with Louis, he recalled the ambulance journey following his defeat:

"As we drove through Harlem, there were noisy, dancing crowds. Bands had left the nightclubs and bars and were playing and dancing on the sidewalks and streets. The whole area was filled with celebration, noise, and saxophones, continuously punctuated by the calling of Joe Louis' name."

He sent Louis money; when his need was great. Cradled him like an older brother. Schmeling and Louis were unlikely friends; the defeated supporting the victor; the white supporting the black.

Inside St Vincent's Parish Church ten to twenty murmured conversations were happening simultaneously. Echoing from marble clad pillar to pew. Voices distinctly male and female. But indistinct – their words transmuted into pure sound; reaching the lower and higher ends of the sound-spectrum.

The churches acoustics are particularly good. Somewhere out in the public domain there exists a recording of St Vincent's organ. A recital performed by the man now seated high above the congregation. Soon his gloves will be removed and his thick stubby fingers exercised once again. Keith Henderson sandwiched between his mother and Uncle Anthony listened to the rise and fall of voices; the renewal of acquaintances. The direction of altar boys, and guests being greeted by ushers with a hymnbook and order of service.

He watched his relatives take their places. Wood and leather, fancy hats and stiffly fitted shirt collars. Lace mantillas. Smiles and po-faces. The young, old and very old.

All St Vincent's regulars. Faces squared by genetics and the elements. Hirsute and bald; ginger haired, dark and blond. Distant cousins linked by a common culture. At the very front sits a big fellah, the potential husband-to-be, maybe? Holding himself with a mature dignity; not a million miles away from a heavyweight boxer. His broad muscular back dominates the front right-hand pew, and beside him stands an equally large man, a brother, a cousin, they looked identical. Both wear jackets cut in the Italian style. Their hair fashioned into free-standing pompadours, has been cut rather than clippered.

Before a fight Rocky Marciano's mother prayed to the Virgin Mary; and each time her prayers were answered. His Susie Q never gripped the ropes like the sprawling Louis; instead it pounded opponents into submission. After retiring he sensibly turned down a match with Floyd Patterson. Rocky was good at making money; he acted on TV, made personal appearances and endorsed products. A shining example of the Italian American dream. He never trusted banks, stashing bundles of cash here there and everywhere. He kept a couple of hundred miles between he and his wife, but remained a doting father – albeit at a distance. And his mother continued praying to the Virgin. The world turned and he rolled with it.

The toll of an offertory bell, and they all knelt down to prayer. Black and white figures faced the priest and tabernacle. Incense stung his eyes; and a riot of prayer, communion and hymn singing followed. The sound of his father's voice rose above all. He saw her at the altar as she took communion, saw her survey the big fellah, for so long it ripped through his heart.

By the fourth round Rocky's nose was bleeding, in the fifth a cut above his right eye was bleeding profusely. But his Susie Q kept hammering away.

Back in his pew he leaned into his mother and whispered,

"you didn't tell me our Mairi has eyes for a knuckle scraper."

"Keep your voice down Keith," she hissed.

But it was too late, the lamp had been rubbed and the genie was out. The appearance of Mairi's men hardly mattered when they'd been merely an offstage presence. But now the men without a face, name or physique had been made flesh and blood. Her type was blessed with good looks and the swagger of a riverboat gambler; he was the type of Rock Hudson hunk swooned over by teenage girls the world over.

Willington like any small town had its feudal hierarchy. Its pecking order of trades. At the top were the skilled engineers; the top earners. Men who earned more than white collar workers. And with this position came a way of being. A way that involved expensive suits lined with silk. The Big Fellah had declared his intent; sending out a fuck you to anyone who could understand his signal. He was giving the two fingered salute to the McMenemy's, Pemberton's and Henderson's. To Keith Henderson and all the other scrawny runts of St Vincent's.

But there was still hope:

Round eight, Rocky's crowding Louis leaving him very little room to punch. Marciano's short arms, normally a handicap, are an advantage at close range. He throws another right. Louis flat-footed and tired is driven back to the ropes. Marciano's hard left hook sends Louis sprawling to the canvas; but he gets back to his feet. Rocky tears in to follow through the advantage. A left, another left, crumples Louis. Then a blazing right and Joe falls through the rope. The ex-champion is finished for the night, two minutes and thirty-six seconds into the round.

GLASGOW FORTNIGHT

Grey slate roofs and a space-ride spinning. The top of the waltzer is as green as algal bloom. Dodgems circulating, pink and blue and yellow and girls in summer dresses, screaming as they crash. A woman in white, has her back to the crowd. Hen's and horses ride the carousel, and for a shilling you can have chills and laughter in The House that Jack Built.

The fairground is packed with Glasgow fortnight holidaymakers; they ride the Big Wheel or sit nervously in Ghost Train seats. Faces are sticky with candy floss and toffee apples. Children have broad grins, and milk-teeth missing. The din of Rock n' Roll is all around: a distorted mutation of the sugar coating endorsed by television; it's volume is a notch below the pain threshold. The high-pitched wail of a Musitron Organ: *I'm a walking in the rain*, sings Del Shannon.

Standing a head and shoulders taller than their younger siblings are teenage girls, acting the part of grown women. And older boys and men, in skinny ties and suits: hovering on the edges of the waltzer; riding the dodgems, reckless and fast, deliberately crashing into the prettiest girl they can see. The girls scream with delight as their insides shudder.

The smell of fish and chips, winkles and vinegar pervades. A gaudy delight of one-arm bandits and shove-hapenny extrudes through the windows of Duncan's Amusements. Something sweet is sticking to Mairi's lips; she passes her tongue around the circumference of her mouth, making eye-contact with watching men. The Big Wheel descends to street level. And then it moves upwards, tentatively: as if its engine has taken on board some of the nervousness infecting its human cargo.

She opens her legs slightly, giving the watchers a glimpse of underwear and thigh. A shiver of excitement passes through her body; ground zero is situated somewhere deep in her. She rubs herself against an imaginary thigh, and wishes for something more solid, more abrasive than air.

Del Shannon segues into the Everly Brothers, who are saying bye bye to love. She closes her eyes and catches their dreamy faces, and their flying saucer eyes, moist with tears. Their cheeks are as close as lovers. She watches them kiss violently, their tight compact bodies locked in a lovelorn embrace. Both are wounded, dripping in hair-oil, pushed to a pit of despair by the same girl. So they settle for each other. They harmonize, consumed by the sex that's eating them alive.

Her eyes open and the change boy, in denim jacket and turned-up jeans, comes into focus. His arms drape over the barrier like James Dean. He's adsorbing each and every female on his ride; consuming their flesh with his twinkling eyes. Imagining not a single, but multiple scenarios.

At night, the girls who stay late become bold. They distract him from his voyeurism with snippets of conversation and come-on's disguised as jokes. At night he may have half a dozen pouting Brigitte Bardot's, Jane Mansfield's, Marilyn Monroe's. Pushing heavily perfumed flesh close to his; making inaudible small-talk. In the dark they don't see the darkness behind his eyes. So blue they look like a saints; like the magnified eyes of a film star, fifty feet high on the screen.

Sweet Jesus, sweet Jesus some shout as he grinds his crotch into theirs. As denim connects with cotton and silk. In the dark, between shifts, behind the candyfloss stall, he takes them up against a shuddering generator.

The grey slate roofs of Whitley Bay come into view again. In the distance St Mary's Lighthouse, winks. Already night is descending on The Spanish City, creating dark corners and opportunities. Creating a brutal gaiety from neon and plastic and multi-coloured glass. She wills the wheel to move on, to take her down: so she can look into those deep blue eyes; those Phil and Don saucers, glistening and moist.

Later, after her fifth ride on The Big Wheel, he takes her to the candyfloss stall. He's a mix of tobacco smoke and brown ale; of body odour and sweet Brylcream. And there's no attempt at conversation, no sweet-talking man. No there's him, raw and naked underneath his oily clothes. An underneath she can't wait to feel.

He bites her lip and she begins to bleed, her mouth is filled with sweetness again. He pushes her head down, and unbuttons his fly. His cock is thick and unclean; it's taste at first makes her baulk. She sucks as he thrusts and she closes her eyes and sees Phil and Don. Phil, Don and him. She feels the jerk as he orgasms, and descends to wet earth. Vomiting while he strokes her hair. He mutters something, but his voice is gravel and mud. An eagle flutters before her face. And when she's done, he holds her close.

"Don't feel bad pet lamb, it happens to everyone the first time. You'll get a taste for it. If you want, I'll teach you. Come back, I'm on Thursdays, Saturdays and Sundays. The rest of the time, is the rest of the time."

And then he was gone, back to his barrier and grandstand view of a hundred Fannies a minute. Mairi cried, strange, easy tears. She came back on Thursday and he turned up at twelve o'clock: there were nicks on the side of his face, where he'd cut himself shaving and a few patches of stubble that he'd missed (small outcrops of the night before). He carries his jacket over one shoulder and struts. Then she sees his limp. She'd not noticed the deformity on Saturday. He'd felt whole when they made love. Now she could see through the illusion, see his twisted left arm. The muscular right had a tattoo of Jesus Christ. Christ with a warm orange face and both hands outstretched; his sacred heart is detached and throbbing. Then he leans against the barrier, and is reconstituted.

It gets dark before the crowds come, surging-in after their landlady's tea. Thursdays are not Saturdays. There's a subdued atmosphere. Everything is quieter including the music. But the big wheel keeps on turning. Girls ride high in the Whitley Bay sky and he looks upwards, admiring the view.

Mairi watches as he smokes his cigarette; slow like a cowboy. He throws the burning tab-end to the ground, where it continues to smoulder. A small halo of flickering light, combusts at his feet. He should have a comb and be combing back his hair she thinks. Instead he wears a fisherman's cap, the type she'd seen on a seamen long long ago.

She took her turn on the big wheel at three. With the sun high in the sky, he had to shield his eyes to catch a glimpse; but he did. Her dark hairy mound floated over Whitley Bay. And he, with his eyes as wide as Phil and Don's, smiled. There was no biting this time, but he asked her to put a finger up his arse and she complied. It felt messy and odd, and it made him come extra quick. He stroked her hair while catching his breath, "Good lass," he said, while hugging her close.

"No more hoying-up."

And he kissed her hard on the mouth.

On Saturday he wasn't there so she played the one-arm bandits. She met a blond Scots girl, a year or so younger than her, and they played the amusements together. At dinnertime, the girl's folks came looking.

"Who's your friend Jennie," the mother asked. And the girl, quick as a flash, said:

"Why this is Mary, she's from around here."

Mairi, rechristened Mary smiled, she let the situation happen.

"Must be lovely living here all the year round," said the girl's mother.

"I've never really thought about it, but I suppose it is."

The winter seasons grim reality, wasn't going to spoil their holiday. Nobody likes to think of their holiday paradise as careworn and cold. Or of the sea crashing over the twin piers, getting perilously close to enveloping the promenade. They don't want to know about the bitter winds and driving rain; or about boarding houses that stay empty for months, and of chambermaids who gut fish in the off-season.

"Would your friend like to come with us for a fish and chip dinner." The girl looked at her, not exactly imploring, but with great expectation.

"I'd love to Mrs..."

"Ahh, what a nice polite girl you are Mary; you're a credit to your Mam and Da."

They sat down to eat, squeezed into a back-room full of chattering holidaymakers. Buckets and spades sat next to bags spilling over with sea-side paraphernalia: rubber rings, gaudy towels, and bathing costumes to change into later.

Pictures of fishing boats and fishermen adorned the walls. Old photographs showed sedate Edwardians taking the sea-air; trussed-up in tweed Norfolk Jackets and Knickerbockers. A sign reads:

The Consumption of food

from outside these premises

is not allowed.

Scots accents, mix with Geordie. Salt and pepper shakers; a vinegar bottle and tomato sauce disguised as a plastic tomato. Cutlery comes wrapped in a white paper napkin. Jennies dad asked if he could have a beer with his fish, but only tea, coffee and pop were available.

"Aye," he said wistfully, like beer was as rare and unobtainable as the wine from the last supper. Aye, she liked the way his Scots accent softened the word, made it a little kinder than its Willington equivalent. They came every July, for a holiday in Whitley Bay. And during July it was impossible to miss their accents and glowing sunburnt faces. The Glasgow fortnight swelled the town and beach population; sweeping aside the coasts stuffier pretensions.

She passed her finger over the Formica tables surface; encrusted with shiny, coloured glass. It glittered like a night sky full of diamonds. She touched a green emerald, a red ruby, a purple sapphire and a clear diamond. Somewhere on the periphery of her mind she acknowledged this as something new, something to be treasured and polished. Eating in a strange café, where parents eat with their children. A four-hour train-ride from their troubles; a four-hour train ride away from the daily grind of work. From the boss, the foreman, the knob in charge. Four hours, feels like four million, atop the big wheel as it begins its climb. Over the heads of holidaymakers. Over the grey slate roofs of Whitley Bay, until you join the seagulls.

She thought of dad; had he ever experienced a day like this man. No such day existed in her fragmentary memories. The waistcoat, the pocket chain and his whiskers. A visitor from another age. And no such day was ever mentioned by her mother. No recollections of them ever spending even a second together in quiet harmony.

"I expect Mary must have wonderful fish every week," he said.

And he was right, she could have fish like the ones they were eating, cheaply and every day - but absent the joy she was having today.

"Aye," she said, trying to sound wistful like Jennies dad.

Sometime between Saturday and Sunday morning, she cried into her pillow. After mass, the crowd is milling on the front steps of St Vincent's Church. Mairi catches sight of Judith

Pemberton, her hair shines like gold in the sun. Grace Kelly gold; wow. The golden girl from school. Girls from her side of the river, never mixed with girls from over the water; it was a voodoo rule, that nobody broke.

"Hollow I'm Mairi, we go to the same school," ran like cement in her mouth. Aye, she said to herself as the golden girl disappeared into the streets of Willington. As arranged she met the McKenzie's at the outdoor pool, close to the Longsands. A chalk sign outside gives the waters temperature, and inside, the noise of children shouting is deafening. Jennie has already changed into her bather. She dances from foot to foot and her plastic-sandals squeak.

"Mary, Mary, "she calls as she spots her new friend. And Mairi feels the joy of yesterday ebb away. Even the name Mary, begins to irritate: it's the name of a child she never was and never will be.

Jennie wanted to race the length of the pool; she wanted throw a ball, and hold her breath under water for as long as she could. Mairi wanted to drape a towel over her shoulders, drink a cup of hot Bovril, take away the shivers and watch the older boys strut about in their trunks. But Mairi at that moment, standing in the pool, surrounded by kids enjoying themselves, felt a hundred years old. She thought of the big wheel, and the change-boy, slouched over its barrier. The juxtaposition of innocence and him, made her feel strange, unsettled, not quite part of everyone else's fun.

At five, she left for home. But somewhere along Front Street, on the way to the station, she turned back and headed towards The Spanish City. She saw him, talking to the girl; his fisherman's cap, pushed back ala Tommy Steel, and his withered limbs, disguised by heavy denim and leather. He flew as he gesticulated, and then the girl punched him. It was weak and ineffectual, and he laughed. She was ordinary, just like her, but less beautiful. About seventeen, just like her. They created enough commotion to attract some bystanders, who watched and licked their candyfloss.

The big wheel kept on turning, but soon it would stop, and he would have to make sure everyone was off safely. That's when she supposed the girl would go away, and lick her wounds in some dark corner of The Spanish City. She hit him again, but this time a finger, or a ring caught his eye, and he recoiled in pain. The amused look on his face disappeared. She could see what was going to happen next, and looked away.

"Mary, Mary what are you doing here, I'd thought you'd gone home," forced her to turn around. She caught sight of the poor girl's body, crashing against the barrier. A group of men, who'd been idly watching, jumped on the change-boy, and began pounding with their fists. His soundless cries, and fists and bodies, and the smiling face of Jennie, intermingled.

"I changed my mind on the way to the station, and when I got back to the pool, you were gone."

She gave no thought to the plausibility of the lie. Instead Mairi concentrated on the action happening a hundred yards or so away. She looked over Jennies shoulder and saw a policeman disperse the gathering crowd. He spoke to the girl first, who looked surprisingly unharmed and composed. Then he turned to the change-boy, who was lying in a crumpled mass on the ground. His attackers were gone, and so was the leather jacket that disguised his withered arm. He looked small and vulnerable, like a child.

"Well now you're here, fancy a go on the Big Wheel."

She wanted to shield Jennie from the fight that she'd missed, and from seeing the change-boy all broken on the ground. But already Jennie was turning round.

"I think its best we go on the dodgems, the man at the big wheels had an accident, so I don't think it's open right now."

"Did he fall off."

"No he just fell over and hurt his head; he'll be ok though a policeman's helping him now."

She watched as the boy raised himself from the ground. His clothes were torn and bloodied, but from a distance, it was difficult to make out the battering his face had taken. He covered-up the withered arm, and leaned to the right. The fisherman's cap was gone, the girl was gone, and the policeman was writing in his notebook.

"Come on Jennie, let's get a car before they're all taken."

The summer of 1961 did not end when the Scots returned to their shipyards and crowded tenements. It kept on running, right through to September. The Spanish City carried on into Autumn, and landlady's held out for commercial travellers and contractors. And Mairi, she kept on going too.

MCMENEMY

It was the beginning of the summer; close to the end of June. He watched their faces open with expectations; marvelling at the long empty days ahead. Schoolgirls on the cusp of adulthood, ran through the streets of Willington. Ribbons streamed from long hair and their legs, bare and exposed, save for white ankle socks, rolled-low, above summer sandals. A vision of an arse, soft and downy, pink like the skin of a peach, entered his mind. Then McMenemy spoke and the vision evaporated:

"So what do you think of the site Alderman."

"A fine view Mr Kane has here, one of the best in Willington."

"One-day people will pay to look out over this part of town. They will see a vision of Concrete and stone, the like of which has not been seen since Roman times," said McMenemy, surveying the semi derelict plot of land, that marked the centre of town. "Willington will have a market square to rival Newcastle, Leeds and Manchester."

"And don't forget St Marks Square, McMenemy. Think of the place teeming with lovely senoritas."

The Alderman winked at Kane, who stood a few paces

to his left. He caught sight of a poster, advertising Saturdays dance: the girls skirt is flared out in motion, exposing a brief glimpse of stocking top. *Let's jive tonight* reads the slogan.

"A meeting place for people on the move," he added. Letting the girls running on the street, combine in his mind, with the dancers on the wall, with a peach ripe and pink, held sweetly in his hand.

"I can now see what you see McMenemy: with your design skill and my builders, we could transform this sad excuse for a town. Out with the old and in with the new. Now all this pioneering is giving me an awful thirst. Shall we retire gentleman, to a welcoming hostelry, and sample something long cold and dark."

The walk through town took them past Marchetti's. A blond and dark haired girl sit at a window looking out. The dark one toys with her hair in an absent minded fashion; she pouts like Bardot. Boys and men who pass the window, are momentarily captivated by her act, their pace slowing, from a stroll to a crawl. And their heads inclined to the left or to the right. Similarly, the Alderman, his mind still full of schoolgirls and stocking tops, stops for a moment to adjust his shoelace. Kane and McMenemy stopped too. And that's when the blond waved, she did it for reasons she hardly understood, and Kane waved back. A question formed in the Alderman's head, as he observed the wave and pout. He saved it for a moment in the saloon bar, when he and Kane were alone.

They walked down to The Ship. The pub opened its doors, out of hours, for the right sort of men. At the bar a ritual that's been acted out a thousand times or more, commenced. It mimicked the ordinary conversations occurring around them. But its theme was not United's latest defeat or the winner of the three o'clock at Gosforth Park.

"Holy Joe has to go and call his missus," was said after McMenemy left to make a call. It cemented the bond, the conspiracy between Kane and his prosperous benefactor.

"Look I've got to keep him sweet. So if that involves getting in bed with the devil, that's what I have to do."

There is a silence at the other end of the telephone, only the sound of his wife's breathing indicated she's still there.

"Flannery's given me his blessing why can't you."

"I can't because of what he stands for. You're everything he's not Maurice McMenemy, and he'll drag you down with him. And as for Kane, he should be ashamed of himself: his poor little boys, what are they going to do when their daddy's in prison."

"Nobody's going to prison pet; the Alderman has half the police force in his pocket, and half a dozen judges keeping them company. He rolls-up his trouser leg, with the rest of them. He'll see that Kane has his

67

wrists slapped and nothing more. "

He tried to think of a snappy way of exonerating himself:

"I'm working with the system pet, I'm not the system – remember that."

"And the system will swallow you whole Maurice, it's an open sewer, and it's going to corrupt you, as it's corrupted poor Jimmy Kane."

"Don't you think he was already that way. Men like Twinkle toes are born that way; all the Alderman had to do was give him a push. Kane's a weak man, it didn't take much to get him mopping-up the crumbs from the big man's table."

"Well don't beg my forgiveness when it all blows-up in your face Maurice. I've seen what people like him are doing to Birmingham and Plymouth, is that what you want for here?"

Deep down, he knew she was right. The Alderman could run roughshod over aesthetic; if it interfered with cost, or upset the planning committee. Innovation was never going to prosper, in a country of backscratchers and get rich quick merchants. He knew his attachment to the Alderman was as precarious as that of all the other nobodies who were caught-up in his scheme.

"No pet, I want a town our children will remember forever. Somewhere that's not just a forgotten footnote when ship building and coal mining go the way of penny farthings and horse drawn carts."

"Come home Maurice, make an excuse. They won't even miss you, those two."

"That's what I'm worried about, not being missed. If I'm that insignificant, the job will go to some city firm, with a thousand secretaries and a fleet of cars. And what you'll end-up with is another nuclear bunker."

"Come home Maurice, you're a good man, I don't want to see you go bad."

It was his turn to pause and to breath shallowly into the mouthpiece. His tongue felt dry and thick, an uncontrollable instrument. He took a long drag from his cigarette, and fed the last of his change into the box. Nothing could take away the bad taste in his mouth.

"I'll be home for tea I promise; now stop worrying. Chops with turnip and mash, that's what will get me home: I'll follow the smell of your cooking with my nose."

"Just be...," *she* said as the pips silenced her voice.

"They're both close to underage," whispered Kane.

"Since when did that matter to you; I thought they were both orphans," said the Alderman. His voice a little too loud for the others liking.

"Technically only ones an orphan, the other has a mother."

"A mother who lets her roam the streets at night, and

lets her sleep wherever she fancies."

"Technically yes," said Kane. He had no idea where the girls slept, but he agreed anyway. Anything for a quiet life.

"So we can dispense with the technicalities of age. By the time they find out real sex has nothing to do with Rock Hudson and Doris Day dressing-up in pyjamas; they'll be in too deep.... Yes"

"Yes," said Kane.

"And if anyone of them were to complain; then it's their word against people who stand for something. "

"Yes."

"All you have to do is arrange the meeting; I'll take care of the rest."

The Alderman squeezed Kane's bicep, only releasing his grip when McMenemy returned.

FERRY MAN

Jack squeezed into the ten-foot square cabin; his window on the world. Where the river stretched out, on undulating tides. Flowing grey and black, bobbing up and down. Meeting the brackish sea at its mouth, wide and ready. Where he watched the twin piers, recede from view. Each day, the metal of his hull, met the ferry landing. Coupling, and decoupling, like frenzied young lovers. And except for the sound of metal, engaging metal. There was the sound of water, lapping against its side. The sound of peoples talk, as they journeyed from North to South, and back to North.

And in between the turning of her wheel, he had time to fill. Thin slithers of a day, when his boat traversed open water. Pushing through the grey on a blanket of foaming white surf. The moments when they embarked and disembarked, taking short steps from ship to ferry landing. Single file, swaying with the tides ebb. Moments when the boy was busy mooring. Fishing for fares. Skiving with a cigarette stub hanging from his mouth. When old Jack had time to empty his bladder, into the ships bucket. To sip strong sweet tea from a thermos cup, and take bites of his bait.

Moments like now, with warm piss echoing inside

empty tin. When he just happened to look out of his window, and into familiar eyes. Pale blue eyes and light brown skin. With a Viking mop of blond hair, yellow like the liquid flowing into his bucket. The man's tall frame stooped as he stepped onto Jacks boat; following him are three nattily dressed gents. A fourth in denim and a corduroy sailing cap, stood apart. His eye welded to the view-finder of a small cine camera. He scanned the boat, nipping here there and everywhere like a frantic seagull. The four suits moved across his deck; officers on parade. Their sculpted presence at odds with the rough and ready shipyard ferry.

Jack, protected by his cabin glass, still managed to feel that uneasy sinking sensation, in the pit of his stomach. He was the eighteen-year-old recruit again; standing to attention, every muscle screaming to be released from its contortion. He could feel the distain exude from their neatly pressed suits and polished smiles. From their unbroken nails, and shoes shined like mirrors. And no matter how much he strained, all he could hear above the engines drone, was the shipyard buzzer sounding.

On the river, time moved with the elegance of a Cunard Cruiser, navigating out of dock. Unlike dry land, there were few surprises floating below its choppy surface. The modern world, sailed in metal boxes; transported to greedy recipients on either shore. Barely touching the rivers inhabitants. The modern world happened when her engine was silent and Jack took his place in The Ship. Where the fingerprints of progress were all over its neon strip lighting. Progress spewed out of TV sets and TV watchers. It brushed against him inside new indoor toilets, giving a wide tooth paste smile as it sucked the life out of life.

Only the corduroy fisherman kept his lips tightly closed, as he circled, like the gulls above. Filming as his friends looked out to the river's mouth, pointing at distant objects. He filmed as they talked in a huddle, as they dispersed, pacing the deck on independent trajectories. His camera tracked the dull grey skies, and the white foam following the boat. Moving among the men, and out to sea, over their heads and up to the cranes on either side of the river. To Jack, all of this moving about had the same randomness as a seabird dipping low to meet the waves, then rising above the clouds. If there was a purpose to all this, it was beyond him. But when the focus of the cine camera moved from landscape and men, to the boy, Jack decided that whatever happened next would be his doing.

But he can't escape that feeling of disgust. The coward cowering in a foxhole, while shells explode all around. A gutless wonder, shitting its pants. The men in suits; they'd only been hero's. Winners in life. Resplendent in victory. He crept his shoulders down a little further.

South Quay ferry landing stood empty, and a few minutes away. It's yellow steel, pockmarked with rust and primitive scratching. On a morning, or at five fifteen it's small deck and inside shelter, heaved with men. Weighed down by tool-bags and heavy industry, they caused the boat to list. And he would always have to remind the boy to move them on, away from the edge. But on afternoons, when his passengers were busy building bigger, more important ships, Jack could afford to play a little with time. Nothing drastic, nothing the Port Authority, or some nosy parker would notice. Just a turn in the river, a detour down to the old coal staiths. Where the coal from long extinct mine shafts would pour into vessels of all shapes and sizes. Where Jack, when he was feeling so disposed, let the boy into a little secret river history. And with the engine off, he would come down from his cabin, to share a cigarette and a nip of whisky.

On a good day they would get away with fifteen still minutes of time, filled with Jack's resonant baritone. Rising and falling with a tide of stories and songs seldom heard on the mid twentieth century river. *Fare thee well my honey* he would sing while turning the ferry away from South Quay. The boy, mesmerised by his new posh pals, failed to notice their change of course. Too busy threading rope for the cameraman. He stared into his lens, acted the fool. Now it's my turn thought Jack, and he belted out the song.

Whether it was the tuneless drone cracking through the cabin window, or a tip of her deck, as the ferry cut through ninety degrees. Whatever it was, caught the attention of those familiar blue eyes. And they were now looking directly at his. There was nothing arrogant or angry about those eyes; nothing more than a suggestion of curiosity. Jack smiled back, and gave the man a wave. An ocean skipper greeting a VIP.

Whatever else was happening on the boat, happened somewhere outside his peripheral vision. Outside the zone, were the tall blond man walked, returning his wave with the sweep of a manicured hand. While his big familiar body, moved across the deck, in a slow, purposeful swagger. The way he always moved in the movies.

Jack really wanted to dislike this man. With his smart suit and face everyone recognised. But he couldn't. Men passed him every day, on their way to work. Some he could put a name to, others were familiar strangers. And the same face would be replicated in The Ship; slaking a thirst worked up during the day. Again there were those who would nod in his direction, or pass him on the way to the bar. They would stand in Lang's on a Saturday, while their wives ordered ham and pease pudding. The same faces handed him a collection box on a Sunday morning. They sold him the Chronicle and the Pink. Cut his hair; short back and sides. And when he was too exhausted for anything, they would flicker before his eyes, fuzzy and grey, boxed in by his rented TV. But none of these were anything like this tall blond, otherworldly man. Who was way too flash for Willington, and a hundred levels above him.

"Hope you don't mind us stealing your boy," he said while pushing a large, hand in Jack's direction. He's friendly, maybe the friendliest man the old skipper had met. But with him came an edge, a determination, that was not about to let time remain still for a second. And close up he could make out the imperfections, hidden by makeup and expensive lenses. Close up he was no different to any other man, with acne scars making tiny indentations into hollow cheeks. But unlike an ordinary man, he wore makeup, with eyeliner and the rivers spray had created rivulets, where paler skin pushed through.

"You must think we're a right bunch of pricks, taking over your boat, with not even a thank you," he said, flashing that white teeth smile,

Jack recognised from films at the Ritz. Then it had been fifteen foot wide, in Cinemascope or VistaVision.

"Can't say I noticed," he said in a voice that sounded small and hollow and full of lies. Not even the wood and glass of the cabin partition protected him from squirming embarrassment, burning inside like an acetylene torch. So like a love-struck boy, he stared at the man. He hoped silence would send him back in the direction of his pals. But where his mute stare fended off anything more than a nod and hello in Willington. It only encouraged the smiling celebrity, who hardly paused for breath before gushing out another apology.

"Sir it's an honour for us to be on your boat. A real honour for a working class lad like me. What you see are just trappings, emperor's new clothes. Down below beats a heart the same as yours, my dad

worked the dock's. He dodged those doodlebugs
during the war. He's dead now, but you know what, I
can see a little of him in you. There was no messing
with my old man, just like you."

Jack held the boat steady, reducing her speed down
to a slow paddle. Nodding his head when the man had
finished.

"I can see your busy mate, and with all this
distraction I'm not surprised you've missed our stop,"
said the man, pointing his hand
in the direction of South Quays receding ferry landing. And
from behind the man came shouts, calling his film star name.

"Come on, back to work you skiving bastard."
Now it was the film stars turn to look embarrassed:
"Think I'm wanted mate. See even people like me
have bosses, and their just as bad as any boss"

Jack watched this blond Viking make slow progress
towards the corduroy cap. He watched as the man was once
again called a skiving bastard, while the other suites nudged
themselves and laughed. Only the boy looked on, bewildered.
And it was like someone had depressed a giant lever, turning
off the day's light. Inside, he felt the sinking feeling in the pit
of his stomach. He felt the man's humiliation penetrate, like
a rusty cut throat razor. He felt the wood of his ships wheel,
pass through the palms of his hands, and the pain as it burnt
through a layer of skin. He watched as a seabird dived, then

just as it was about to collide with the blue grey water, it rose-up and flew skywards.

It was only later, when they had all left, and the great heaving mass of passengers had disembarked, that he found a chink of light to illuminate the gloom. And as he made his way, up the steep incline, away from Willington ferry landing, Jack found himself singing *Fare thee well*. Minutes before, the boy while threading his rope for the last time that day, said something, which not only made Jack laugh out loud, but caused them both to whoop and cry out. It was nothing profound, or satirical, or clever. And unlike the visit from their film star, it was forgotten the next day.

A WEEKEND IN JUNE

I

A warm breeze buffets the girl's dresses. And like a flotilla of clippers, their thin cotton garments follow the wind. They pass the shops of High Street West, filling the pavement with yellows, pinks and greens. Sparks fly from steel stiletto heels, and it feels like the first day of summer: where Hawthorne bushes are infused with white blossom; when drabness is no longer in ascendance. An eighteen-year-old Judith Pemberton is gazing into a mannequins fixed plaster eyes. Mairi stands next to her, admiring the dress. She can hear, a lovely burr: "mmmmm," as her friend's approval is about to be voiced.

"There's no word to describe this dress, Judy. Its reminds me of sex in a summer field, at the High Farm, when the bales are rolled and ready to be taken away. "

When she's not talking about it, she's doing it. But out in the grownup world she's the innocent who dutifully visits relatives and sings in the choir at mass. She talks transubstantiation with Father Flannery; boys with the humdrum crowd, and everything that comes into her head with Judy. And she's always ahead of the game, the first to get, what everyone gets later. There's nothing better than being with Mairi, nothing.

The red dress will be there tomorrow and the next day, unless someone frivolous or rich comes along and snaps it up. Otherwise the dress will be taken down and another put in its place. And like a rare butterfly in-reverse its life-cycle follows the path from fashion item, to sale item, to dead-stock; imago, pupa and caterpillar.

"Let's go and get a float, "she shouts to Mairi.

Her tone is an inch away from an order. An injection of reality into their daydreams. But Mairi doesn't mind, she's done with staring at things a working week and wage packet out of reach.

"Marchetti's or Mark Tony's?"

"Do you really fancy a trip to town, do you Miss Rose Mairi."

"It's Marchetti's and nothing else then pettle."

As she turned, Judith caught the smell of her own body odour. A pungent, dark, smell, that conjured up an image of her friend emerging from a hay bale with dishevelled hair and laddered stockings. She let the sensations and sounds of the day take over; the feel of an arm brushing hers, then linking, and carrying her along. Her weightless body, floating like an astronaut, an inch from the clean corporation pavement.

Coke float in her hand, Judith Pemberton was

momentarily a child. Her friend slurped a Knickerbocker Glory; levelling dark brown eyes coquettishly just above the cream and fixing them on old Giovanni. The café owner distractedly returned her gaze. He's the type of man used to a thousand stares a day; a specialist in the receipt of torture from young women who grow younger every year.

"They say he ran with the Partisans during the war, went over to Italy for a holiday, and gets called-up. "

The owner busied himself about the bar. He rolled-up his sleeves and began to work; occasionally lifting a glass or plate for inspection. There was no telling whether he was in or out of earshot; but that hardly concerned Mairi who had shifted her gaze, from the man to his reflection on the café's mirrored wall. There stood the clipped Flash-Harry moustache and wavy hair, replicated twenty times over.

"Then the Italians decided to invade some place or other. But he doesn't want to fight or join the fascists. Gio, as he's known then, goes into hiding. "

Judith Pemberton begins to feel a pulse of excitement. She catches a whiff again of that odour, it's animal pull. Mairi pauses and slurps loud and inelegantly, but not without a certain charm. Nobody sees the owner smiling to himself, nobody except Mairi. She catches her breath and begins anew.

"A story is circulated that he's returned to England, via Switzerland. And like Ann Frank he lives in an attic," Giovanni scowled at his empty café; two tables, four teenagers, and the rest glued to their television sets he supposed.

"Poor little Gio, eats, sleeps and defecates in his tiny hidey-hole..... UGGH."

Mairi slurps again; a picture of the youthful Giovanni hangs there in the café's sweet smelling air.

"Fancy a suck," she says, shooting Judith a ridiculously wide grin.

"No, ok your loss baby.....

One day Gio's mamma hears about the Partisans hiding in the mountains. She rushes to tell her son. And as luck would have it, catches him *pantaloni giu*."

"Fzzzzzz," went Judith Pemberton pushing a mixture of saliva and coke-float through her teeth.

"So what do you fancy doing tonight Judy?"

There was a flutter of sound as the jukebox switched singles.

"Take good care," warbled Bobby Vee.

"my bay-bee," sang the girls to each other, with arms outstretched and faces contorted like a pair of sorrowful crooners.

Through the town there is a murmur in the air; seamy stuff, the mud and glue that makes most lives. An unadulterated weirdness of social conformity; with no room for the misshapen and miss-formed. But behind closed doors, or out in the open, perversions of all varieties are practised.

"Testing.....one, two three," rumbles out from the dancehalls empty stage. A cleaner her hair in hairnet and curlers, polishes the sprung floor. Stilettos and cigarettes play havoc with it's surface; but the money he made from Teenage Hops, was more than he'd ever earn from the Military Twostep.

Kane moved away from the microphone and dipped his head, as if an audience were present. The gesture made him look more than a little ashamed. Like a man who lived for Friday nights when a hundred or so teenage girls crammed into his palace of fun. He's the thing they have to endure, in exchange for the latest tunes, driven down from London. And in the crush, his hands did as they pleased.

"How was that Mrs Marshall," he said; addressing his audience without amplification.

"Grand Mr Kane, grand."

She reminds him of someone he knows; the same mean little eyes, the hairnet and rollers and hand clutching a half of Milk-Stout. She reminds him that an observer, not the participant, owns the experience. He takes a snapshot of her, and twists it in his mind. Delicious, delicious.

Between six and seven thirty, his life flipped back to tea with Marion and the boys. Five boys, and not one of them an Astaire, Kelly or Lionel Blair, that was a piece of bad luck.

"Lock up when you're done." And the nimble feet of James Kane, twinkle-toes Jimmy, was out the door.

Five knock-kneed boys, at play in the adjacent front room. The humming of the hum-drum; a chair beside the TV, and a chalice of an ashtray, at its side. He sits smoking.

"Boys," he shouted from his tobacco throne. When their noise intruded into his space.

"Boys, boy's boys, boys – quiet please," he said, in a forlorn sort of way. And their noise automatically diminished. There was no room for cheek or answering back; just obedience or the back of his hand.

"A man needs his pleasures." He moved his hand rhythmically; squeezing his glands from time to time. On the screen, she is shot side-on, racquet in hand. The camera picks up the outline of her upper-thigh and the shape of her underwear. Tennis in Willington Park with Flannery and McMenemy was nothing like this. The girl bends forward. He's throbbing now, old twinkle toes.

"My goodness, my goodness," he mutters. And suddenly she's off the screen, they've gone into adverts. Barry Bucknell demonstrates a workbench; then washing powder, then cigarettes, then the refreshing taste of ....

There are freedoms that can only be expressed at home. Depravity begins at the hearth. The tennis girl parries, she struts; and he cums with his eyes closed. He cries silently because there's no love; no love for wife, for his children, or for anything much about his life; except for the sex he has with himself.

Before Kane's sock-hop altered the weekend forever. There were The Sea Cadets, The Boys Brigade, The Girl Guides, The Boy Scouts, and numerous youth clubs; designed with middle-aged pleasures in mind. Boxing, football and more football were catered for. And for the Mavericks, the Hop-Along-Cassidy's, the Laurel and The Hardy's; the Greta Garbo's, the Grace Kelly's, the Marylyn Monroe's. There were the remains of Willington's twelve cinemas, two to be exact: showing a mixture of old-time classics, cartoons and foreign films. And secreted about there flea-ridden seats, with cigarette stained armrests, were bored teenagers. Escaping from the organized fun, and organizing some fun for themselves.

Back before Mairi stays with Judith. Because it's too much trouble getting back across the river; because suddenly there's something to do in 1962. Something other than kissing, groping, and doing everything bar the big thing: There were Friday nights in the dark corners of The Ritz and The Electric. Mairi sits next to a shadow; the person is a shapeless unknowable thing in the darkness. His name is never given. He expects knee-tremblers before, after and during the intermission. They're sitting there as the girl comes round selling choc-bars and pop; his hand furtively holding hers. He smelt older than the sixteen he'd pretended to be. He smelt like someone who shaves regularly, who works hard during the day. Who washes before he goes out at night. From time to time he sucks on an ice-pop; making a squelching sound. A man used to have a bad taste in his mouth, modifying the flavour left by coal dust, with the taste of synthetic orange.

She felt older at the end of Jazz on a summers day. Like she'd lived out a life time with this sixteen-year-old boy/man. To relive her discomfort, she concentrated on the minutiae: the name of a novel, the scowl of an older woman. There was a girl, she supposed they were all American girls, sitting on a deckchair in the Newport sun. She looks like a young Grace Kelly; with her natural blond hair and light tanned face. She wears pink angora and a beautiful mustard headscarf. She's reading the Novel Camille. Why would you go to a Jazz concert to read a book? Unless of course there were other reasons for her being there

Sitting next to Grace is an ordinary looking, dark-pale girl, with badly cut hair. Her eyes are disguised by oval, white-framed, sunglasses. The makeup on her face is too obvious, as if it's been applied by someone unfamiliar with Max Factor's arts.

Mairi recognises something of herself, but not the fairisle jumper. That spoke of barn dances and ceilidhs. And that stunning blond to her right is the double of Judy. Anita O'Day is singing dressed like she's going to a Buckingham Palace garden party. Sometime during the films eighty-five minutes, Mairi decided that learning to ballroom dance would take her one step closer to a deckchair at Newport.

"My bay-bee," sang Mairi and Judith as they walk the short distance to Cedar Grove. The evenings unusual warmth raising their spirits to terrific heights. Quickening their pace, so they run rather than walk.

II

"It's tyranny on the radio; all they've got to give us is a bunch of shiny suited, grinning idiots, stepping in formation. And nobody knows if that girl Giving It Foiv, is for real. The kids like her because she's a bit dim; they listen to what's she's got to say, and they buy the records she tells them to like."

Judith envied Mairi's certainty, the way she saw everything through a pair of x-ray specs. Like she knew the ins and outs of ATV studios. And when she decided something, she rarely changed her mind. The girl on Thank Your Lucky Stars was never to be trusted, and men in shiny suits were nothing but clowns. Mairi's certainty protected her from the strangeness that settles-in after childhood. It was the armour that kept the badness out.

They pass the motor scooter man: leather helmet, goggles and brown suede gloves. He leers, but lets them pass without a word. Words are for those with nipples not ready for lactation, for those lacking a teenager's surface-gloss.

"Tutti Frutti on rooty," sings Mairi. She's going through a Little Richard phase; playing to death a 78 she'd bought second-hand. And some of his Tooty Fruity has passed into her.

Judith watches as Mairi jives down the street. Dancing lessons have added a little deportment to her body. But those suede gloves linger in the mind. Sometimes armour can buckle under the strain.

"Its Saturday night all you Willington kids. You Pop Pickers par excellence. You out there with the snake hips and silver toes; you with the garland in your hair. You the Judge, Jury and Executioner of everything that is Trad dad. You sailor off to Oslo and Bergen. You school kid pretending to be sixteen. You pair of sixteen inch bottoms; you pink sweater and sunglasses after dark. You've come here for one thing; one thing only: Rock and Roll, stuff-it in your pipe and smoke it!"

The needle hitting the record crashes in with a blast of pure noise; a whiplash fissure through the ballrooms fetid air. The moment life begins. Mairi looks at Judith and Judith at her. Their bodies are poised for motion. Bottles of coca-cola, dangle in hands, ready to be ditched.

The first record is never new; it's a crowd pleaser.

Something to get them going fast and furious. A song they know note-for note, bar for bar: mistake, bum note, and singer wandering an octave out of range. It has to be a song that stirs the darkness inside. Taking the listener on a journey back through a million generations, back home, that's where the music takes them.

The crack of the needle begets a G Sharp, an F Minor, a C Sharp and then a D Sharp. And back to G Sharp. Bodies hurtle towards the dance-floor; diving for a space. Hands grab arms, grab other hands. Motion both kinetic and graceful happens. Smiles stretch faces and heads are held back in joy. The two girls swivel left, then right. The dark one is a better dancer, but all the boy's eyes are on number two: the blond with a suntan; Judith Pemberton, Judith or Judy.

And there's no place for the music to go but up; up to the stratosphere where super-fortresses cruise and Sputniks orbit. Where gravity is weak and the airs so thin it's impossible to breath.

Her body is moist to the touch; it's a wonderful thing in motion, spinning a geocentric path. Moving close, then pulling-out. They collide from time-to-time with others; following the pattern:

One, two, three-a-four, five and a six. Left foot step back, right foot in place. Then Chasse - three-a-four, five and a six. A boy tries to cut in, but Mairi sends her spinning away leaving him stranded. At stage-right stands Kane, resplendent in shawl-collard dinner suit and dicky-bow. He

89

has a sheen the daytime man lacks. A way of standing that comes from years of close observation; old Twinkle Toes and his mirrored-walls are the best of friends.

Michael, or was his name Robert, comes in for another try. He's persistent, but too slow for Mairi; who sends her off spinning again. She crashes into a couple of dancers, who take her arms and hold her steady. Their grip is solid and strong; both capable of holding her alone, but neither willing to relinquish their trophy.

"Ok boys, flip a coin for her," calls Mairi. But the music's too loud and the joke evaporates.

"One dance each," says Judith in a breathless Monroe impersonation. And like the fool's men are; they release her.

You're getting better Judy; one day you'll be rivalling that minx Mairi. Kane felt that shifting in his groin and that light-headed, empty-headed desire.

"Tonight we're dedicating the evening to Peggy Gallagher, sweet sixteen and never been kissed. So let's hear it for Peggy Gallagher and for our very own Hank Marvin, who will serenade her in his own inimitable style."

A reckless, and inappropriately loud cheer, passes through the ballroom. Some of the crowd looked towards the stage; scanning every inch of its dreary construction for the horn-rimmed guitarist. Whilst others watch the entry door. The rest, rooted in Willington, groan as the distinctive Shadows twang fills the hall.

Peggy tries to fashion a hole for herself; she looks downward in embarrassment. Her boyfriend wears a curious look, a mixture of sadness and befuddlement. He too longs to be someplace else; somewhere safe from the vagaries of human behaviour. Kane, Kane felt sad for the pair of them. Too nice for this world, and too young for the next, and a whole lot of unhappiness happening in-between.

His eye roamed over the sea of teenage anguish; heads, arms and thighs, perpetually in motion. Judith and Mairi twisting to FBI. Even at fifty feet he could smell a whiff of experience, smell a situation arising.

III

Willington Park:
Trees and bright sunlight. Outcrops of people sitting in semi-circle: shooting the soft North Eastern breeze and eating al-fresco. A Victorian bandstand painted white and blue. Dappled music, drifting. A Colliery band resplendent in red uniforms play favourites; the songs of Joe Wilson give way to the Lambton Worm, to Cushie Butterfield, and to Abide With Me.

An atmosphere as light as cinder toffee descends on picnics laid out neatly. Faces glow with sunshine and sweat. God, in the form of a seagull, flies above the heads of enthusiastic eaters, tennis players, children swinging, bowlers leaning forward into the throw, and tennis players gently sipping lemonade.

It calls out a warning: you down below it says, you in pink, you in white and Panama, eating dainty little sandwiches. Stop for a moment and look down into the precipice. But no one does. Father Flannery resists the urge to visit the gents; instead he turns his gaze to a cyclist with thick sturdy legs, strong enough to break a mans back and to a boy decked out like Fred Perry, raising his racquet to the air.

Judith Pemberton eyes a small group of spectators, casually leaning against the tennis courts netting. The red dress appears ordinary on an animated figure; an everyday thing, as common place as the hats everyone wears. And her long white gloves; there're too High Society, too Princess Margaret. Timothy O'Donahue's hand encircles the woman's waist, he smiles like Frank Sinatra, and takes a toke from his pipe.

"So how's life treating you two," says the priest after a lull in conversation.

"Just wonderful father, wonderful, couldn't be better." says Mairi squashing a marshmallow into her mouth.

"And you Judith; you were missed on our tour of the Yorkshire Abbeys. Fountains was a treat, well worth the journeys discomfort. "

And after another embarrassing pause, and a

sideways glance from Mairi she lied half-heartedly.

"Works piling-on the work's Father…"

And she wanted to make it sound convincing, and add in a moan about the way she cried at night after one too many long days, but that was too far from the truth, so she turned her gaze to her friend, who chewed and gave the impassive eyes.

"Now is that the time, I have to dash, good talking to you girls," and he was off; padding through al-frescoers, a jacket draped on his arm.

Before Kane's Hop, a Sunday in June was very much like the previous years Sunday. The pattern of Mass, dinner, park and Benediction rarely faltered. There are memories, maybe real or imagined of her Mother sitting on the very same grass, eating sandwiches, watching her at play. There's a bottle of pop by her side that she's not allowed to drink. That's mam's pop Judy, and this one's for you. Mam's pop was sour, and tasted awful; it was decanted from a bottle hidden in the Kitchen. It travelled in her pram, tucked under a cream crochet blanket.

"He's got a nerve, "says Mairi. "A fucking nerve."

"Please Mairi,"

"Stop worrying about appearances for one second. Do you really think anyone really cares"?

And it would have been easy to see things from her point of view, see that swearing like a shipyard worker was the next step on from school and dull, dull conformity. But, and there was always a big but, while Mairi could take her Ferry home, she had to live in Willington seven days a week.

"It matters to me Mairi, so it should matter to you."

"Drivel, drivel, and I won't say it for your sake. Oh what the fuck. Fucking drivel. Now if you're a friend, you'll walk me to the ferry landing." Mairi stood up, lingering by her side. Some of the picnickers threw disapproving glances in their direction. Tennis play and children's play continued. Before the dances at Kane's, Sundays were filled with boredom. Now the boredom and listlessness was laced with fatigue. Judith Pemberton crumbled; she gathered her full-skirt and rose.

"Sorry Judy," Mairi said quietly, and all Judith could feel in her heart was love and lightness impossible to describe.

Benediction:

The chalice rises, theatrically; its gold edges catching the light. A rumble passes underneath St Vincent's fine marble floor: the six O'five on its way to the coast. There are two Priests at the altar. The young Priest could be Gregory Peck in Keys to The Kingdom. Father Flannery's movements are slow and lumpen in comparison; his broad shoulders, enveloped by a humeral veil. Altar boys, follow in procession.

Judith Pemberton, her grandmother and uncle stand in-line singing the Tantum Ergo. The Blessed Sacrament glows from within the monstrance; a smell of incense and candle wax pervades.

Flannery raises his arms; he makes the sign of the cross with the monstrance. O'Salutaris, her favourite of hymns, comes out clear and true.

"O'Salutaris......................"

She's soothed by the canticle; connected to the continuum. At one with god; at the place where troubles are washed away; down by the river side. There's no beginning, middle or end.

IV

Sunlight gives way to rain: sounding a brittle tattoo on the rooftops and windows of Willington. It beats furiously against the shipyards corrugated iron and steel; against the exposed skin of her face, arms and legs. The summer's brief incursion abruptly ends, and her headscarf wilts.

She stands inside the torrent and thinks of the cuddle Mairi gave, deep beneath the eiderdown; the Sunday dinner with pulverised vegetables; the living room table laid-out for three.

The radio's on:

"The time in Britain is twelve noon, in Germany it's one o'clock, but home and away its time for Two-Way family favourites."

Andre Kostelanetz and His Orchestra strike up With

a Song in my Heart; Grandma relaxes into her Parker Knoll, the one close to the telly. The electric fire bars are silver and dull. The smell and tastes of dinner, taken three hours earlier than any other household, lingers.

Jean Metcalfe begins:

"Miss Marie Wilkes of 20 Lowerside Estate Plymouth."

The girls exchange glances, sly smiles, and telepathic joy.

"Is shortly to be married, and immediately after that happy event, will be flying with her new husband Ray, to Cyprus."

Cyprus, so far away, and so exotic. Sunglasses and wine, and sunny cloudless skies. Cyprus, shame she has to take Ray. A Dirk, or a twitching Monty Clift would be better. A brooding Brando in greasy tee-shirt and rolled-up biceps; a Tyrone Power, soaked in alcohol and Spanish sun – frittering away his days in Pamplona. All would better than boring old Ray.

The joy curdles, as the prospect of forty years with a Ray, Brian or Kevin comes hurtling into view:

"A million good wishes coming from your cousins Gloria and Bride Wilkes in Gutteslow; they want us to include love from mum and dad, and the three Arabs at number eighteen. Plus, all friends and relatives in Plymouth, Swindon and Ilfracombe"

96

There's a laugh nestling in the back of the announcer's voice, it's supposed to convey the fun that the poor girl is going to have with Ray, and the tinge of envy in the words of those relatives, consigned to far flung parts of England. Ilfracombe, Swindon and Plymouth; Willington, Bamburgh and Tynemouth. They're all interchangeable, all a thousand miles from Cyprus. And Judith Pemberton thinks of her friend's doppelganger, mouthing a big fuck you, to all those in Swindon, Plymouth and Ilfracombe.

Silence entered the living room as the effortlessly happy Jean Metcalfe continued to pour honey over dreadfully ordinary lives:

"Marie, I suspect Gloria chose this record as it comes with a very special message for the ladies, especially the married ones. And because of this I took the liberty of including a request from the Roberts family, who are strangely enough in Gutteslow. They have a niece named Judith, known to the family as Judy, who's getting married to a nice fellah who answers to the name of Peter."

She shivered once again at the thought of her other self, drowning in married bliss; her clothes cling like an over-eager boyfriend. And she thought of Peter and Judy Roberts, as the rain, rained. And when the cold began to penetrate her skin, she moved to the shelter of a passage beneath the railway line. A mouldy green old place, frequented by

97

shipyard men and flashers, and sheltering girls. The stench of male urine exuded from every brick. The rain continued to pelt. She thought of that other Marie, sitting on a veranda, overlooking the Mediterranean; sipping cocktails she supposed. Ray, sunburned and happy, would be supping pints of whatever passed for ale in such places. And she wondered if men marked their territory, like cats and dogs; distinguishing another's scent with a sniff; opening a portal to an exclusively male club.

"I don't need sunny skies," she bellowed, praying that it wouldn't rain again until September; that the darkness would lift, and her way to the Ferry would be clear. Lights pulsated in the distance; great arcs of flame and flickering bulbs made love in the heavens. The heartbeat continued, at a steady pace, all night long. Engine Shed's taller than St Vincent's hummed. Men whose word for us was wor, who wore themselves out on perpetual nightshifts. And over on the other side, separated by a black-tide of river, was Mairi. Oblivious to her, Judith Pemberton.

It was all because of repulsive Kane and his repulsive interest in her. And it was more repulsive, because he'd started with Mairi. Strong, brave Mairi, who shook as she left the back room they'd named the seduction station. And when his wandering hands moved to her; it was sudden and unexpected. It was hateful and horrible. A little bit of her soul, remained alive while it was happening. While those bony fingers made quick incursions into her clothes,

98

underwear, and body. The rest of her shrivelled up and died. And she acted like a marionette, a hollowed-out version of the person she once was.

Late afternoon, down at the Ferry Landing, she watched Mairi leave. Her skirt billowing in a hot summer breeze, and Mairi looking down at the white-foam wash: looking, maybe, for words that never came; for a gesture of atonement; for the reason why all the men in Willington were bastards. Not once raising her head, and as the boat turned towards the south side, she disappeared from view.

Now Judith Pemberton watched the rain wash down the pathway that led to the Ferry landing; flowing to the river. She had no thoughts about the shipyard men being soaked; or of the grubby times being had out on the river. Or of anything else but her friend Mairi. She constructed a tunnel, thorough the wind and rain and river. A tunnel that slithered down back lanes and backyards, that entered via a keyhole, into Mairi's house. A house she'd never visited, never been invited or had the courage to invite herself.

The house of Mairi the mystery girl, who sailed effortlessly through life, while she struggled. The girl who in another life married a soldier named Ray: putting herself out of men like Kane's grope. Safe, and warm, and loved.

Mairi was right about Flannery, he did have a nerve. Like all men, he acted like it was his god-given right to take what he wanted, to smash and grab. Flannery just worked his magic on the same sex. He had a nerve because he was after all the Parish Priest, and supposed to be celibate; just like Kane was supposed to be happily married. He did have a nerve, but Flannery for all his faults was not a bad man; he was just not meant be a priest. The way girls like them were not meant for Willington.

The torrent, eased. Pockets of light extruded through rain-fat clouds. A wind blew in from the coast and the ground twinkled. On her way to the ferry landing she passes a man lighting a cigarette outside The Ship. She feels his eyes follow her. Not cold hard stares; appraising like a butcher would a joint. No there was none of that, there something approaching concern. McMenemy shook his match and then he was gone.

She boarded the Ferry with men from the late shift; sitting herself between oil smelling overalls and tool laden haversacks. They barley acknowledged her presence; save for an occasional glance in her direction. Tiredness had made them mute; and when they did make an utterance, it was a slow cowboy drawl, directed at some close companion. Oil, grease and the smell of damp tobacco filled the passenger cabin, and that other smell, that only working men had, made her think of how her dad would have smelled; coming in from work. Jack in his cabin, turned the wheel. He negotiated the river through a curtain of darkness. Following his nose and the smell of bones. A sour smell when dampened by the rain.

And when their brief journey was over, the men

sloped down the gangplank. Night swallowed them-up. Swallowed all that remained of their weekend. She asked the Ferry Man for the time of the last boat; shivering as she spoke to him.

"You shouldn't be out without a coat girl," said Jack, and she suddenly felt cold and exposed. Her sodden shoes, squelched as she walked from the landing. Her arms, wrapped tightly about her chest, squeezed and squeezed, but produced no warmth. There was little time for regret or reflection. The last ferry was in an hour and after that she'd be stranded or forced to walk ten miles or so to the nearest bridge.

She tried to remember Mairi's descriptions of her neighbourhood. But one street looked very like another: the same small, red-brick, terraced houses and narrow back lanes; a mirror-image of Willington's shipyard houses that rolled down to the river. And the uniformity of street names is the same; each street was a tree or shrub. Beach Grove gave way to Hawthorn Road, and Mairi lived on Laburnum, close to Holly Avenue and Ivy Street she supposed.

"So what's your street like Mairi," she'd asked once. "Well it's very much like yours Judy, the same trees and privet hedges. The same boring nameplates or names etched in glass. You know Lindisfarne and The Grange. Like they're lord of the manor, not a lathe Operator at Victor Products. There's a little garden at the front, but nobody does much with it except cut

101

the hedge; and a garage out back. Some of the neighbours have cars, but most haven't."

She lived on a pleasant avenue that led to the local park.

"It's got none of Willington's amenities though; just a couple of swings and a battered patch of green where old men exercise their whippets."

That was all she had to go on.

At the end of the imaginatively named Ferry Road, ran a small high street. All the shops were closed. There were no cinemas, or ice-cream parlours, or café's equipped with gleaming silver espresso machines. A dress shop displayed "Gowns fit for a lady on a budget." A greengrocer, butchers and ironmonger: offering no credit. And a small electrical shop displayed the latest disk from Cliff and the Shadows – squares-ville.

The walk had warmed her up a little, but she had no time to linger. A little way down the road were two pubs facing each other. Beer light diffused from opaque glass windows; they looked warm and inviting. The sound of a piano and an off-key sing-along became audible as she drew near. She could see customers acting out a shadow play through frosted glass. A sign directed her round the back to off-sales.

"Sorry we don't serve kids here," said a sullen faced girl as she approached the window. Her hair is formed into a beehive, dyed a fearsome blond and it moved independently of her head. She was barely out of childhood herself; but already well versed in the art of ejecting underage drinkers.

Judith hesitated, not sure of what to say. It was pointless arguing with the girl, because she wasn't after a drink anyway.

"Scoot, or I'll call the polis."

And then the words came, a little rushed, a little mixed-up.

"Can you...where Laburnum is. Its near the park Mairi says."

The off-sales girl looked quizzical, as if trying to work out a trick question.

"Laburnum, a park. Sorry I think you've got the wrong place. The nearest park is a good way down the road, at the coast. Or over in Willington, you can take the ferry. "

She made a backwards gesture, while beehive moved in the opposite direction.

"Yes that's where I'm from," she replied; and without knowing why, the anger rose inside.

"But you must know Laburnum; you have to know Laburnum."

Her voice sounded like someone else's; someone slightly deranged, and it sounded so loud.

"Alf, Alf, there's a kid out here going mad."

Alf's head popped in the window frame. His cheerful face, is a florid red. And instead of shouting or telling her to

bugger-off, he smiled. At that tears welled and she cried for
the first time that day.

"Look love, don't get upset, we can't serve you, you're
too young."
The sullen girl chipped in:
She doesn't want a drink, she's looking for a park,
and I told her we don't have one. Then she got
angry."
Alf smiled again, she could see he was a sweet man.
"It's a bit dark for going to the park," he said.
She resisted the temptation to shout, and repeated
the name of Mairi's
road.
"Ahh, Laburnum, that's near the coast. Down in
Laygate"
She thanked the man and shrugged her shoulders.
Laygate, where the black sailors lived, and even if the man
was mistaken or her mind was playing trick, there was no
time left to find out. The last ferry would be gone in half an
hour, leaving her stranded.

V

A cold wind blows in from the North Sea, sending shivers
through her still-damp clothing. The Ferry Man's boy lurks
outside the passenger cabin, and when he thinks she's not

looking, he casts a furtive gaze at her exposed legs. For him, she's as rare as a fish swimming through the polluted river, a vision of something from another world. His presence distracts her from thoughts of Mairi. Good friends are entitled to secrets. Hers are buried deep inside, and Mairi's; Mairi's are also hidden. She decides never to mention her ferry trip, never to ask why Mairi chose to lie and locate her family five miles west. Sometimes lies were better than the truth, more comfortable to bear.

The imprint of Kane's fingers, remains with her: like the coldness of her dead mother's skin. Like the front room sofa, converted into a bed, and the women reciting the rosary. And the white stuff, blocking her nose. And her lifeless face, as yellow as parchment; translucent in death.

"It's time to get off miss, Willington's the last stop, "says the boy, catching another peek at her lily-white legs.

The first weekend of summer ends with heavy rain-filled clouds pouring tears over the small town of Willington. It ends with Judith Pemberton, catching up with sleep. And as she goes to bed, tucked beneath a winter eiderdown, she thinks of Cyprus and its warm sun, and the smell of lemon trees and the sea.

The water rolls out from the rivers mouth and meets the sea. Violent and angry waves as high as houses rock against and over the twin piers. Somewhere south of Germany there's a Marie sipping drinks with her husband Ray.

MCMENEMYS AFTERNOON

McMenemy pulled out the choke, and turned the ignition key. His vehicle had the smell of new leather; with insides, barely marked by human ownership. Only the faintest smell of tobacco, tainted its rarefied interior. The Hillman started first time, always a surprise. Mirror, signal, then manoeuvre, and onto the open road. He felt a little cheated by its reliability, by its precisioned response. So he wore calf skin driving gloves, and a car coat in all weathers, and he wondered if there would ever be a need for the breakdown truck again.

He stopped first at the races where sleek thoroughbreds, ran. Eyes bulging in anticipation, nostrils flared and spitting moisture. Across the lush green of Gosforth Park, a white fence, snaked round the track. The smell of manure, cigars and alcohol pervaded. Jockeys in bright theatrical clothes, strode. A carnival of leather whips, ruddy-faced trainers and horses, magnificently tall.

He was in the middle of a great performance; orchestrated by men in fedora hats and white coats. They stood on crates, conducting. Spectators milled about, watching old-odds wiped out, and new-odds chalked-up. He in turn watched the semaphore pass across the course; in seconds one man's gestures are replicated ten, then twenty times.

And he recalled his dad taking him to the Pitmen's Derby for the first time. The crush of people, had him holding-on for dear life. His small body surrounded by giants. Women looked impossibly glamorous; like Northern Ginger Rodgers. And men wore dark sunglasses, Hollywood sunglasses. And the horses a hundred feet tall shone in the afternoon sunlight. But it was the men in wide-brimmed hats, waving their arms about, shouting in some strange language who filled him with terror. And his father, in a rare moment of compassion, held his shaking body close.

The men, "are tic-tac men passing on the odds," he said. Then he was raised a little higher, above the heads of the tallest of the tallest. His dad pointed to a man with two hands on his head; the gesture, as before, moved across the park at lightning speed.

"That's 9-4 odds son."

Another tic-tac man crossed his arms and laid his hands flat to the chest.

"And that's 33-1, much better odds."

He remembered the smell of beer on the old mans breath, and his spiky stubble, pin-pointed the moment. In a month or so his Dad would be gone, and there would be no more visits to the races. And now here he was drinking Champagne from the back of a silver Bentley. Sharing sandwiches with the type of people who viewed his community as barely civilized peasants. They toasted his return from the bookies, whooping like children at a magic show, when he produced their betting slips.

"And now for my next trick," he said, tipping the brim of his hat, and slapping the nearest man on his back. Jobson, their driver, choked on his champagne bubbles. The Alderman and his underling Cook; along with Sullivan, a Morning Suited bank manager, all shouted their disorderly approval. They laughed, at Jobson who continued to retch. And McMenemy, joined in, prodding the poor man with his fist. It was a cheap joke, at the expense of someone with no redress. But the urge to please, and his own insecurity drove on the cruelty:

"Here, drink some of this, "he said, taking a glass of Champagne and waving it in Jobson's face. The laughter was goading, malevolent, vicious; it begged him to continue the humiliation. But Jobson was finding it hard to be all yes-sir no-sir three bags full sir; he was finding it was hard to hide the resentment, the itch below the skin. It passed across his eyes. Eventually when he could take no more, the man cried "stop." McMenemy saw the driver for what he was. A fellow parishioner, who'd probably, saw him as a brother under the skin. A fellow left-footer, who'd succeeded in a world sewn up by Masons and people who were members of the right kind of club. A Conservative club.

McMenemy withdrew the glass. There was no possibility of apologising to this man. He saw his face amongst the congregation; amongst the heads who watched his as he read one of Paul's letters to the Corinthians. An apology, at this moment, would be a humiliation. And the jackals, who were still laughing, shouting and cajoling, would turn on him. They would devour him as they'd devoured poor old Jobson.

Make money McMenemy, but make it with your values intact, said a voice in his head.

"Let's hear it for Mac's Master Plan." He waved the glass in the Alderman's direction. The laughter petered out. His change in tack just hung there in the air. A joke at the expense of Macmillan and his slaughtered Cabinet, may just be too close to the bone for these dyed in the wool, true-blues. The Night of the Long Knives was not something traditional Tories were proud of. The silence before Sullivan spoke dragged on for what felt like an age.

"Yes let's hear it for Supermac!" said Sullivan. His red face glowing with delight.

Then the Alderman chipped-in:

"And hears to Selwyn Lloyd, may he have a long night of retirement." That had them all laughing, all except Jobson who just looked bewildered. McMenemy sighed, inwardly. He'd managed to sound Tory, without actually being Tory. He handed out betting slips to each of the men. The Alderman got the 33-1 outsider, because he was the secret favourite. Cook got a Bismarck, because of his obsequious smile, and uselessness in his eyes. And Sullivan, he got an odds-on favourite, to keep him sweet. Cook appeared foolishly happy with his favourite (expected to sink), and proposed another toast. But this time the mention of another sacked Tory minister's name, had the Alderman scowling.

"I think it's time for a change of subject boy's, McMenemy has something with him that concerns us all."

Jobson, as expected, retreated to the car. The real business of the day had no need for witnesses. It would happen in sunlight; in plain sight, but under the protective shroud of Gosforth Park noise. And by the last race, alcohol had done its work and reduced the day's business to a pile of spent betting slips. McMenemy entertained himself with thoughts of espionage, and secret rendezvous; a Harry Lime running through the sewers of Vienna. He left, just as the driver opened another magnum. His own car parked further away was waiting. He'd drank enough, any more and he would have to leave it overnight or risk another accident. Ahead lay a short drive to Willington. He decided to drive via town; take a longer run to clear his head.

Girls in summer dresses strolled into Exhibition Park; exact replicas of the one worn by the girl he'd spotted at mass. He saw the same peach skin, the same back-combed hair. Their concerns would match hers, their tastes would be hers. The windscreen was his window on the world; his television screen, displaying the untouchables. Clicking along in court shoes and pastel cardigans. Money can put older men and young girls together; grease the cogs of attraction, until they are running like a Rolls Royce Engine. Of course he knew the girls name. It was easy to run an enquiry past Flannery. To make it sound innocent. He was on the lookout for a good Catholic girl, that's how the story went. Someone for his new office. The Priest knew about The Piazza, his name for the shopping mall in Willington Square. He'd given up Judith Pemberton's name and carried on their conversation, without so much as a flicker of concern.

The Oxford Dance Hall advertised, free admission to girls before eight. Nothings free he though, and he thought again of a girl he'd seen at Gosforth Park. His fingers stroked the steering wheel, following patterns in its grain. If wood were skin and her skin as close as this.

At the Byker Odeon they were still showing Swiss Family Robinson. Children, very much like his own, were leaving the afternoon matinee. On Shields Road, the great workshops of Parsons, hummed with activity; turbines rolled, a small part of a larger whole. One of the greatest concentrations of skilled men, the world had ever seen. An engine that would never stop.

Shop's along the High Street were beginning to close up. Wooden poles pushed shut canopies. Greengrocers removed crates of fruit and vegetables from their pavements. Willington Square, bulldozed and flat, faced Woolworth's and Boots. The old, and the new, squaring-up to each other like gunfighters.

He was at the office long enough to lock the filing cabinets and see his secretary off with a cheery goodbye; to call his wife and make excuses for the evening. He could hear his children making noise in some distant room, and he sensed the resignation in his wife's voice. It was not the first, and certainly wouldn't be the last time she ate tea alone. And he thought she'd get used to it after a while, and learn to enjoy the material benefits. But always she answered the phone brightly, and always she signed off with that mournful tone. And always he had to stop himself from thinking of her as ungrateful, as a hindrance rather than a help.

As he entered St Vincent's bar, Father Flannery was singing I'm a rambler and a gambler and a long way from home. He was joined, in the chorus, by a small group of men. The hard-liners, who played snooker in the afternoons, and dominos as the evening players arrived. Men who, except for a barmaid or two, avoided contact with women. At Magic hour St Vincent's began to fill. The bar was bathed in a dull orange light. Ugly people took on a new attractiveness. Drinks glistened; the gentle burr of conversation became a little more raucous.

Thick tobacco smoke hung in the air, and the deep rumble of maleness pervaded everything. The click of snooker balls chimed with the dull thump of darts hitting a board. Heavy trophies decorated the bar and a one-arm-bandit provided entertainment for the lonely. A man, dressed in paint-splattered bib and brace, belched. He articulated the word pardon as the escape of his stomach gas reached a crescendo. Another took his hand, and made eye contact. He said "Hello," then moved on to the next.

Not a pint had passed his lips since entering the bar. Yet he felt the warm fuzziness that precedes extreme drunkenness. Those champagne bubbles on an empty stomach were doing their work. He felt safe from the undertow. From the girls in summer dresses. From the Tory Prime minister and his Cabinet sackings. From the home comforts that make people soft. He needed to make a confession of sorts; some reassurance. Flannery would be the one to make the approach. Give their meeting a veneer on innocence. She looked older than eighteen, old enough.

THE YARDS

I

He sits studying Willington's official guide. All the company names are as familiar as people's names; each a fixture on the landscape – rising above the towns small squat houses. And in most cases he could make a reasonable estimation as to their function. But somehow the translation of these names into hard cold facts, made his decision more difficult. There were too many choices, and after the fifteenth description of a companies rise from workbench to world domination his eyes glazed-over.

Mairi would be round later; drinking tea, delicately nibbling on fondant fancies and marzipan slices. Pursing her lips and making his heart swell. Would she be impressed if he took a job in the Yards, or would she prefer a job with romance. A Merchant Seaman. Away for six months of the year, then back with a kitbag full of gifts. The only problem with a life at sea, was the sea itself. Anything more than a ferry across the river turned his stomach. And anyway Mairi was too attractive to be left twiddling her thumbs for half the year. She needed romancing; nights out at St Vincent's and walks in the park.

She needed the sort of attention a delicate flower needs, constant attention; watering with cups of tea and a steady supply of tinned salmon sandwiches. She needed dedication, a fat wallet, and a feverish desire to keep her happy.

Mairi in a Public Library, no. She was suited to other things. He put away serious things in her presence; none of it mattered.

"Keith, can I have a moment alone," he imagined her saying. Yet all he got was:

"Keithie can I have another piece of cake." And he felt ten years' old

when she called him that childish name. Only his mother chipping-in with her:

"Go on Keith..ee, go fetch Mairi a cake," was more humiliating. And Mairi saying:

"So how've you been keeping Keith," always managed to surprise him.

Forcing his eyes away from her anatomy, and into embarrassing contact with hers. Whatever had been occupying his week was permanently erased by her pretty brown eyes; along with any stored up witticisms or casual banter. Instead the mumbling spirit of James Dean and Monty Clift surfaced; talking control of his tongue-tied mouth with something inane like:

"I'm doing fine."

But her visits had whittled down to nothing and her

interest in anything Keith Henderson, never materialized. She'd seen right through him; he was the invisible man. And there were those sad fantasies that accompanied his new found powers: sneaking into her bedroom while she undressed, following her into the ladies changing room at Fenwick's. All with the same outcome; a feeling of elation then self pity.

Down by the waterline, he could take a ferry across, and survey the ships lined-up, looking magnificent. He could watch a launch, when the slipway gave birth to another steel-child, and a hundred tons of water was displaced in its wake. Where a fanfare of screaming chains and the smashing of wooden supports, was joined by the roar of relief from men who had slaved for half the year to see such a moment.

From his perspective, some way from the river bank, he could see the stern of the ship slowly disappear from view as it descended to the water. And then there was that day in June, when he had just turned thirteen. When somehow he and a bunch of short-arsed boys, had gained entry into the Yards. Escorted by somebody's dad; a foreman who held enough sway to conduct an unofficial tour. The man wore a fitted blue boiler suit and a jacket with a badge clipped to its lapel. Steward it said in bold capitals. Launch day was the only time outsiders were let in the man said, while pointing-out visiting dignitaries and women dressed up like the ladies at Ascot. Everyone was caught up with the atmosphere of expectation.

On launch day tools were downed, the riveters silenced. Boys from the drawing office wore their Sunday best; welders took off their masks and painters brushes soaked in turpentine. Crowds gathered on the South Side of the river, where they would see the ship glide into the water, watch as the ferry landing was buffeted by the large displacement of water. The foreman explained the ship being launched was merely a shell, with an engine. It would be fitted-out following the launch, and then sent down the river for sea-trials. But first it needed to be born.

"Bless the baby born today," tripped spontaneously from the foreman's lips as a champagne bottle broke on the ships stern. And despite being drowned out by the launch, it persisted in Keith Henderson's head. Growing and accumulating, until it resembled the great roar of working men. This is what you should do it said; this is where you will work.

The Yards dominated the Willington Guidebook – its cover depicted a ship under construction, and a two-page advertisement showed SS. Sir Winston Churchill, 90,000 tons DW – an oil tanker built for Mr Hilmar Rekston of Bergen. Its broad hull cut a white foam swathe through a grey-blue sea. Romance with Mairi, if there were any chance of that, would have to accommodate a shipyard worker.

II

There were times when he would hear Geordies voice, as if he was present in the room; not just a stuttering of his subconscious.

"I've got a message for you Mr Revell," he said to the back of the welder's head. Sparks flew out and over the mans shoulder, dancing around his metal mask like a halo.

He kept his distance, shielding his eyes from the intense light. A brown paper envelope wilting from moisture in his palm. But there was no reaction, no indication the man was aware of another's presence. So Keith stepped a little closer.

"Back off son before you get burned," rumbled out from the mask. A deep thunderous growl, low and threatening like a subterranean monster.

"Hold your horses, I've got one more seam then I'm done."

Stepping back, he waited for the man to finish. He watched as the space between two solid bocks of steel was filled with molten metal. Each joint a piece of precision engineering, forming an unbroken scar down a solid sheet.

And when he was done the man turned off his lance, and disengaged his front visor. He removed the straps that held his metal breastplate in place, and raised himself to full height. His knees were covered with heavy metal armour and his face blackened by the mask, dripped with sweat. Red welts ran across his cheeks where something had repeatedly rubbed. He wiped these with what appeared to be an oily rag; then discarded the cloth along with his gloves.

"So you've got a message for me son," he said after taking a long draft from a lemonade bottle. Liquid dripped from the sides of his mouth and down over his chin. But he let it remain, glistening among the stalks of his stubble. Despite his fearsome appearance, there was something welcoming about the mans eyes and the flash of his gold toothed smile. The smell of the bone yard wafted through the air, its pungent ammonia odour causing both of them to cough.

"Another stinker, looks like we're in for a lovely summer," continued the welder, producing another rag from his pocket. He wiped away the spittle and for a moment Keith thought the man was going to offer him a go with the cloth.

"Here's your note Mr Revell."

An inspection of the rope would have revealed a hundred or so discrete tears; some no larger than a thumbnail. But there was a problem, the damaged section hung a hundred feet above ground. As the rope was lowered and raised, tension snipped through weaker threads. But the rope held, supporting one corner of a wooden platform – suspended on the ships side. As the vessel grew, so did the height of the platform. Welders and riveters were replaced by painters when the hull was completed. Two seasons and a thousand or more steel-capped work boots pulled and stretched the damaged rope. But it held; bending with the wind blowing in from the North Sea.

And the frailty of the human eye, meant it passed inspections week by week. Missed opportunities for sure. But in a Yard crammed with a million and one components, the odds that one may break or have some in-built flaw were high. The betting men knew their lives depended on quality engineering and quality control. On a gang-plank a hundred feet up, holding. On the welder's mask and leather gloves protecting them from burns and splashes of molten metal.

Geordie liked Keith Henderson on that first meeting. He liked him enough to talk openly about the bosses who patrolled the Yards in bowler hats. People in the Yards had their own sign language. Warning signals that could be seen above the constant din of construction. So he set about teaching the boy.

"There's a circular motion above the head; a drawing of a halo. It says oncoming bowler."

And when that sign was made, conversation changed to something less controversial. Another sign of a boss was his three-piece and pocket chain. Geordie forgave Keith for his tie-pin and the neat creases in his trousers, and always called him Keith no matter what his nickname happened to be. The man had his own set of rules.

"Most people are like you Keith. It's the rest of us who are strange. Someone said that back in the old days, god gave Northumberland a good shake and all the nuts fell down to Shields. Now sit down son and tell me about Miles Davis."

Geordie, come rain or shine, spouted random thoughts and proclamations; he cackled and shot them out like a welding lance flame. He could turn from mad to bad on a threepenny bit. And Keith's first reaction was fear; his second caution; then finally acceptance and enjoyment. Geordie entertained the way television did not.

"There's a trick to fooling the bosses. Make it look easy. Most of them will end up believing they can do it themselves, or hire someone cheaper. It means they sleep at night knowing how everything works and how they can handle everything. And one of these days they'll wake up and sack one of those men who make it look easy. And for a while they'll feel good about themselves, vindicated. But when the new lad just can't get the hang of the job, they end up hiring another. Then they'll have two men's wages to pay for a one-man job. Deep down the boss will know it's costing the firm dear; filling the sacked man's boots. But he's got his face to save and a job to hold onto. Who's he going to tell, the snoring hag in the hairnet who sleeps beside him?"

Grey greys give way to an orange morning glow. Hunched figures collecting rag worm; digging into hard Tynemouth sand with trowels. Buckets swinging and fishing tackle stacked up against the pier. Geordies arm draped over Keith Henderson's shoulder. The fishing fleet returning to Shields. Rod and line hung loosely over the harbour wall. Early morning sea fishing, eyes stuck together with sleep. The green slime of seaweed and algae, floating in rock pools below. Afterwards they ate a breakfast of Craster Kippers and headed home just as everyone was waking up.

"You'll never forget the first sight of your bairn's eyes. The way they stare out of the cot; drilling holes into you like they hold all the experience in the world. I'll trust those eyes above any politician or boss or smarmy TV host. What do they know – blather mouths the lot of them. "

Geordie rarely expected a reply; his dialogue was with the wind. It happened when they sat fishing or sharing bait at dinner time. During quiet moments when the conversation flowed. Geordie questioned everything. From the way Macmillan and his Etonian cronies ran the country; to the way the Yards were ran. He expected Keith to do likewise.

"There's no shame in being young and naïve Keith, but it's a bloody shame when these beggars hoodwink grown men; old enough to know better."

First there were the fishing trips to the coast, then the visits to Geordies home. Where his wife would sit with Keith while Geordie prepared tea. His daughter played out in the back lane, a ten-year-old, oblivious to anything but jacks and

123

bays. To the swing of a skipping rope and the rubber bounce of a ball against backyard walls. She would look in to say hello, but mostly she inhabited the world of children. A world Keith Henderson felt was close by also quite distant.

And one of those simple hellos from his daughter would transform Geordie. His face becoming brighter, infused with light. Like the face of a saint who'd just conjured-up the Virgin Mary.

"I learned how to do this in the army. Found it relaxing; doing the prep was my speciality. Although most of the time it was peeling buckets and buckets of spuds. I got to watch the chefs prepare food for a battalion of men, they would be dripping, melting in the humid heat of Hong Kong. And there's times when it's hot in this kitchen, and the steam rises from everything, when I imagine I'm back in that place halfway across the world."

When he got home, his dad seemed lost to the TV world. Adsorbed with trivia and useless facts, framed in BBC English. He worked, went home, ate his tea, and then watched TV. On Saturday nights there was the Go as You Please at St Vincent's; the lowlight of a monotonous week. He could hardly ignore the contrast between the life in Geordies home, and that of his own.

"There are invisible hierarchies everywhere. Take the band you've just seen at your Club A Go Go or whatever you like to call it."

"It's the Flamenco Geordie"

"Aye all frilly sleeves and castanets."

Sometimes his friend could be as infuriating as his parents when it came to popular music. There was nothing wrong with it, he would insist, but there was nothing right with it too:

"A bunch of vacuous sentiments strung together with syrupy violins,

I'll take Blind Lemon Jefferson over that shiny suited guff any-day," he liked to say:

"Blind Lemon Jefferson froze to death in the winter of twenty-nine. Yet all these buggers do is wear matching bum freezers. Give me the blues not a bunch of pimply headed..."

Fragments of conversations, recalled, not at will – but as an act of remembrance. A celebration.

"He that burns brightly will live a hundred or more lives than those who watch shadows."

Mad flashes of insight; interspersed with conversations of a working life.

"Compare your fingernails with those of your dads. See how cracked and broken his are. Look into his eyes as he watches TV night after night. No matter how hard you look, you will never catch the light that was once there. All you'll see is a reflection of that bloody cathode ray, dancing on those dead-dull eyes. There's no dignity in labour, that's the lie they tell to babies like you Keith. It puts another generation on the road to nowhere. Live life and don't look over your shoulder. Keep your eyes away from the TV screen; it's got half the population hypnotised. And don't believe the man who says that by doing nowt you are doing something. Use your vote Keith, join the union, refuse to watch things flow past you. The river will still run when we are all gone. Rain, water, sea, evaporation, cycling round till the end of the universe. Now hurry up son, or I'll eat your bait for you."

In The Yards the mornings are a mix of grey and black. Monochrome colours mingle with the orange of arc light and the sullen-white flesh of shipyard workers. Keith Henderson's pasty face is among them. Moving soundlessly between stacks of wooden supports and idle machinery. Men stream hither and thither, flowing like human tributaries to their workplace.

He catches flashes of his face, reflected in glass and steel-silver. A wraith passing through the Yards subterranea. His humanity sucked out by alcohol. His gimlet-eyed stare and the small flecks of vomit on the underside of his shoes, were just window dressing. And there was that look; half disapproving, half taken-aback, that accompanied his entry into the office. He could almost feel the presence of other hangovers, being nurtured about the Yards. All young heads thumping, and just about capable of work.

"What you need bonny lad is another soak down The
Ship, that will see you right," Geordie had said. With
his eyebrow raised slightly, he looked inscrutable;
almost Fu Manchu. But he said nothing else, the
matter was finished for him.

During the day pieces of the night came to him as
jagged fragments. The sort of dream that follows you out of
bed and on to work. That changes with the progress of time,
till eventually it's distilled down to a single image. First there
he was standing at The Ship's bar, soaking up the end of the
working day. He looked up from time to time. Taking in the
movement of men from the door, across to the bar; and on to
their places. The men he saw, week-in week-out. A mirror
above the long bar, gave him a panoramic view of the pub.
He could see into corners, where familiar faces were huddled,
conspiratorially. Where men who kept their own counsel,
drank gloomily, alone. And some would be in transit, saying
goodbye to one group, before joining another. There were
the gamblers like Bob Forrest and Frank Marshall, occupying
small round tables, where money was already changing
hands. Where someone would be short of housekeeping
money before the night's end. The same men who had played
pitch and toss against the school wall; who forever cycled
between boom, bust and the pawn shop.

That was the first fragment, an innocuous panorama of The Ship, a spit and sawdust bar popular with workingmen. The vision arrived as he awoke. A dishevelled lump; still clothed in a shirt and tie twisted at the collar. After the deafening sound of the buzzer stopped reverberating in his ears. After Geordie had inspected his ragged presence with a raised eyebrow, he'd retreated to the post room and the slow sorting of letters. The mind numbing tedium of such a job fooled his brain a little. It provided a distraction from the beer-sweats and the fog that descended like a North Sea mist.

But there was no escape from the night before. Inside bar-staff rushed back and forth behind the long bar. Men strained to catch their eye. And like an elusive woman, they would always be looking elsewhere. Tending to a favourite, smiling at someone else.

"Let me get you a pint, I can see that thirsty look in your eyes," he heard himself saying. The recipient of his generosity was lost in the translation of night to day. His eye focused on the barmaid, who'd already moved her body forwards, to meet his. She's mouthing "same again", so he puckers up his lips, and mouths back "two." Broken fragments that revealed little of the night's shenanigans.

There was a chance he would be asked to deliver a message to some distant part of the Yards, where he could hide away for a while. Nurse his hangover in peace.

"Can I have two whisky chasers to go with that love", had come to him reflexively. His unseen and unremembered companion was already away from the bar and heading towards an empty round table. A pint glass for company. A spirit on the way. Close up the barmaid was pretty. Her hair is dyed a raven black. It's furiously back-combed into a style that suggested, fifty degrees north of Hollywood. And she was warm as toast, like a two bar electric fire, glowing red across the bar.

Her makeup was on the heavy side. But on a Thursday night after four beers and a whisky chaser; she reminded him of Mairi. Their conversation, whatever it amounted to, had happened off camera. All he could be certain of was the noise and a bar heaving with men.

"Henderson. Yes, I'm speaking to you son. Time for you to stop skiving in the post room. I've got a message that needs delivering pronto."

Caught up in last night's reverie he had ignored one of Geordies pieces

of advice:

"Always make sure you have eyes in the back of your head. The bosses have a habit of sneaking up behind the unsuspecting. Work-shy detectives that's what they are. "

He left the office with last night still happening in his head. Somehow his brain had to play catch-up. Even as he left the office, note in hand, those shards of second-hand reality cut into his working day. A man had to drag him out the path of a swinging steel girder. "Your lucky not to be

dead son," he shouted after him; but already the reality of
steel and rope had been replaced with smoke and mirrors.
The reflection of the bar heaving with men intent on a good
night out.

He couldn't remember his side of the conversation;
but the barmaids reply had fixed itself in his brain.

"You were just about to ask me out, tomorrow night;
and I was just about to say, come back in ten years'
sonny." And that should have
been that. Except he was already drunk, and not likely to
pause for thought. He was a little in love with this facsimile
of Mairi.

A second round of seduction was more successful.
She accepted his offer of a drink; pouring out a generous
Port and Brandy. The darkness of the drink matched her hair.
It reflected the dark outline of her eyes.

"Want a taste," she said, offering him the lipstick
rimmed glass. And he drank, not because he was curious
about the taste. It was the intimacy that attracted him; the
shared smell of her perfume, and the imprint of her mouth
against his lips.

Keith Henderson's first foray into this new world of
sex happened an hour after the bell for last orders rang. It
happened in what had once been a coal-house, at the back of
The Ship. A cold empty place, with blackened walls, and
broken beer barrels. And it lasted no more than ten minutes,
the time taken to undo his fly, and kiss her, full on the mouth.

She tasted of the fifteen cigarettes, smoked during her evenings work, and the Port and Brandy they had shared. She tasted wonderful, and warm, and said very little. And the silence felt better than a hundred halting conversations, dribbled over bar stools. She sounded like no girl he'd heard before. She was a new sound, he wanted to hear again and again; and into the wee small hours.

The Yards buzzer sounded, waking him from his coal-shed reverie. Reality dug in hard, and the sound of men jubilant because of the break, filled the air. He'd find himself a little space to hide his dishevelled body. A place to sleep amongst the noise. He allowed himself another minute or so of relaxation, before making his way back to the office. Everything was as it should be; men had already left their places of work and were forming gangs. Some rushed, some ambled, and other's dropped to their haunches and rested for a while.

It was easy to see later. The commotion was happening over by Geordies ship. But on the periphery, he only saw men running, which was not unusual at dinner time. The buzzer neutralised all sound, so the action played out like a silent film.

He'd carried on walking; head down, hangover rendering the faces of men blurred and indistinct. His internal compass, pointing to the offices close by the Yards main entrance. But fate had not finished with him yet. With his eyes set low he missed the sprinting man about to cross his path.

His profile was blue black. Straight dark hair, blue stubble forcing its way through his cheeks and chin. His face an inch away from his. Mild halitosis, cigarettes and sweat. Then the pain of the collision, hitting his sides and back. The contents of a first aid bag, spilled across the ground. Bandages and ointments; morphine and a spray for damaged eyes.

Small droplets of crimson flowed from one of the man's nostrils; they flared as he disentangled himself. Then he was gone, sprinting in the direction of Geordies ship. The remnants of a first aid kit, bundled-up in his arms.

The buzzer stopped and his eyes continued to follow the running man. They picked out others. Some with arms raised, waving frantically. Some pumping like athletes. Ten, maybe twenty or more, heading for the same spot.

"Holy Moses," is what he was supposed to have said. But with him so high up, it was difficult to make out what he was saying. There's a shadow that falls on a man as he is about to die; a shape that moves over him. That's what people said about Geordie; the shadow was there just as the rope gave way.

Keith Henderson stood at the back of a crowd, two or three deep. He peered between the elbows, and legs of those blocking his view. A crumpled form jittered and shook on the ground. He could make out a boot, twisted round so it faced backwards like a cartoon characters' foot. A large patch of red, circulated out from the mans head. Someone held a jacket, between the ground and his cheek. Another man, crouched down, maybe he was offering comfort. From their dress, and the way they held themselves, Keith could see all those present were fellow shipyard workers.

There is a song that's played when the Yards are working to full capacity. Even as the crowd continued to grow, others were making music about them. Over in Dry Dock number 3, the pneumatic sound of a drill, combined with the screech of sheet metal being cut. But there was a sweeter tune being played that day. Men old and young were crying. It felt more shocking than the sight of the prone man, twisting in silent agony.

"People take an old song and if they're any good they'll make it their own. Do that with your life and you'll be a lucky man Keith."

He remembered those words as he clocked off that day. There'd been little work done. Foolishly he had pushed through the crowd and come face to face with Geordie. Except there were no more mad proclamations coming out of his mouth; only blood and what some would later describe as his insides.

THE BIG CHILL

The sea at its wildest makes me think of him. It reminds me of the Island.

The Girl:
She took a coach from the Haymarket station, alone, with a cardboard suitcase and Jean Plaidy novel for company. And the snow started as she crossed the causeway to the island, and it continued as the child moved inside her. It snowed more that winter, than any she remembered. And the snow kept her in, cutting off the mainland, keeping out non-islanders. The coldness meant people sat in groups, indoors, hugging fires and oil heaters. And underneath heavy, shapeless jumpers, her body expanded.

1962 is drawing to a close and she, just turned eighteen, was lodged by the Society of Vincent de Paul. The Moriarty's, devout as St Cuthbert, took her in. They cleared out a room and gave her a bed. They made excuses for her that sounded like lies to her less than holy ears.

Her hermitage is a small fisherman's cottage close to the harbour, close to the Castle and Priory. Everything was close except for a Catholic Church, that's situated on the mainland. Each Sunday they cross the causeway; taking a bus to Bamburgh. Because she was young and knew no better, she accepted this situation. Her life reduced down to a journey to the mainland once a week.

And no one asked questions, or demanded anything but a *hello how are you Peggy*; she was accepted without condition. And before she became too big, there were dances. Where girls like herself passed from partner to partner - young farm boys and fishermen. And the music was a heady mix of reels and slow laments, played on Northumbrian pipes. While fiddles played under kerosene lights, raised the tempo, until men, boys, young girls and mature women spun round the hall. Piles of oilskins were left at the door, and a smell of fish rose with the evaporating moisture - greeting late comers with its pungent odour.

Peggy would sit in the corner, next to the Moriarty's, joining in like a daughter, deferring to their decision to leave, before she had finished enjoying herself. And she lost herself in the life of the Island, where the daily routine kept her busy.

When December came she worked in the Moriarty's souvenir shop, where St Cuthbert biographies vied with Lindisfarne Mead for attention. Where her day began at One O'clock and finished at six.

And her head was full of imagined visitors and their stories; tales of travel across Europe. The Americans wore loud sports coats and necklaces of heavy cameras. They attacked en-masse, with open apertures and bright magnesium flashes. Ask a hundred and one questions; and

135

marvel at the sheer oldness of her tiny island. They would take her accent to be Scottish, and get her to repeat huge chunks of speech for their delectation. At six the imaginary tourists would leave her to turn the open sign to closed.

The shop was no bigger than a modest front room; and like many buildings in the small village, it was once a fisherman's dwelling. Quaint was a word she heard uttered, when the wide head of her only customer passed through its narrow door. The man had smiled at her, like she was an exhibit in a museum; then left empty handed and silent.

At night while the Moriarty's slept, the shadows of her former life crept back. Shapes danced on her wall, taking the form of oh-so familiar faces. And sometimes the shapes would coalesce, playing out scenes from the summer just gone.

The shapes stretched out like Tynemouth Long Sands. The Shuggy Boats rocked back and forth. The shape of the small St Johns Ambulance Station, delineated by its pointed roof. A boy sat lazily at its entrance, his uniform sleeves rolled up. And he had a simple, ordinary name. But everything else about that August Bank Holiday Weekend was far from ordinary.

"What's happened to all your friends," he said.

"They're walking to the station and I'm supposed to be catching up. But I fancied a go on the Shuggy Boats."

"There just for kids," he said.

And she felt flattered and insulted all at the same time. She wanted to say something funny back, but her mind was running away with his rolled-up sleeves.

"If you wait until my shifts over I can take you to the Spanish City. We can go on a real ride."

The shadows on her wall shifted and there she was devouring a pink stalk of candyfloss. Her hair was dishevelled from the waltzer, and she still spun from its motion. She reeled in the fairgrounds gaudy artificial light. An accident waiting to happen had been her mother's words as she was chased up the stairs later that evening. And that's all it had been, until things became serious a month or so later.

The St Johns volunteer was nothing like the Lindisfarne boys, who rode towering North Sea waves, risking their lives every week, for a ton of fish. And like holidays of the past, there was a special boy. A boy who caught her eye, who she thought of at night, when the shadows receded. When all that was left were lights out in the harbour; swaying as trawler men put to sea.

He was a fisherman who wore a heavy woollen jumper, with thick corduroys, tucked into boots worn down by work. He kept his hair long and natural, and it curled over his ears like a girls. And in her night-time dream, she would stroke his damp hair, while he rested after a week on the boats. Outside the snow would be falling, and they would be close to the fire; as warm as toast.

At the beginning of her eighteenth week and over halfway through the second trimester, Peggy began to think of herself as normal. The sickness abated, and she experienced an unusual surge of energy. There was a dance scheduled for Thursday night that gave her four whole days to prepare. And although she knew it would be another rough and ready affaire; she felt the need for new clothes. She had a feeling about Thursdays dance. After a month on the Island Peggy put all the names to all the faces. Decided who she liked and who she disliked. There were few she could find fault with, but out of boredom or sheer bloody mindedness, she'd single out an unfortunate couple for her distain. The intrigue kept her mind live in the cold deadness of the shop. It saw her through the second trimester.

Dressmaking:
Jean Moriarty helped her with a dress pattern. A Doris Day number, more suited to a slimmer girl. She assisted in the cutting of a tracing paper pattern, while Jean expertly manipulated the unwieldy dressmaking shears. Peggy pinned the pieces to a roll of fabric, reserved for unmade curtains. Her fingers, holding tailors chalk, were guided round the pieces. And the pieces snipped-out, by the nimble fingers of Mrs Moriarty, who tacked together a rough version of her dress. Peggy's body served as tailors dummy and model.

"Does that feel tight Peggy."

"Just a little tight."

And slowly a seam would open up, allocating a little more space for her latest growth spurt. Making do and mending is how Jean Moriarty had grown up. But Peggy, despite her cheap clothes, had grander designs. The shop windows of Fenwick's and Binns were where she liked to go; her face pressed against the plate glass, trying hard to make-out how such creations were made. When there was no bus fare for town, there was Bon Marches on Willington High Street; with its dark wooden counters and pressurised tubes firing orders about the store. A stiff and unchanging place.

"I think it looks a picture now Peggy, see for yourself."

The real sewing would happen on the day, to allow for further growth, or shrinkage as Jean Moriarty put it.

"I've left you half an inch at either side; any more movement and you're going in your birthday suit my girl."

What must it be like to have all your clothes made thought Peggy, as she circulated in front of the mirror. Her arms splayed out, fingers enclosed in imaginary gloves. What must it be like to afford more than one pair of shoes, to wear silk underwear and sheer stockings. Such women stepped out of heavy-weight Humber's, negotiating the dirty pavement for a matter of seconds. Brushing past hand-me-down little girls in a cloud of perfume and crisply pressed clothes.

"Do you have any perfume," she asked.

"Now, now Peggy, we are going to a dance at Lindisfarne Hall, not the Palais de Dance. I've some toilet water you can dab behind the ear, lavender. Lavender's blue, dilly dilly, lavender's green, When I am king, dilly, dilly, you shall be queen. Who told you so, dilly, dilly, who told you so? 'Twas my own heart, dilly, dilly, that told me so. "

The song took Peggy back to Willington, to washing being hung out in back-lanes. To women singing as they hung out grey-stained sheets. Flakes of soot would land on the drying clothes, and the smell of drains would be as high as that from the bone-yard. Women the same as Jean Moriarty, would stand at back doors chatting. Some wore scarves to hide undone hair, others hairnets to keep their perms in. It was this picture that saw her to sleep that night, and the song Lavender's Blue, playing as a sad lullaby.

The dress came together in a morning, it's blue and yellow pattern, lighting up the scullery. She watched as Jean's foot worked the Singers peddle, as she threaded the bobbin by hand. There was no yellow thread, so they made do with white. She felt no desire to sew herself, or learn the rudiments of good housekeeping. The picture of women, hanging out clean washing, and a dirt filled Willington sky kept such sentiments at bay. To become an unloved washerwoman, a seamstress, a wife. It was better to become one of those women, clicking their tipped stilettos on

Northumberland Street, creating sparks as metal made contact with pavement.

 She felt a little queasy come Thursday, but the feeling passed, and she was zip-fastened into her dress and walking arm-in-arm with the Moriarty's by the evening. The kerosene lamps rocked a little harder that evening. With the fiddle and pipe players in Alnwick, Tam the emcee came laden with a collection of disks shipped from America. He produced a jerk of surprise about the hall, as each new tune stuttered from his turntable.

Poetry in Motion followed a slow Elvis tune; that's when he sidled up to her. And at some point during the song, he was singing the lyrics to her. She felt so high, he could actually sing, and there was a lilt to his voice, like an Irishman had inhabited his body. Danny Savage smelt of the sea. The skin of his neck tasted like a week old barnacle and his long unruly hair felt like it was full of whale blubber.

"Poetry in motion," he said after their bodies parted. And three thousand or more hours ago, she would have dismissed him with a laugh in the face. But on Lindisfarne people were less conscious of themselves, and his quoting of song lyrics felt impossibly romantic.

She made Smalltalk with adults on the far side of Lindisfarne Hall. The hard wooden seat felt like it had velvet cushions. She floated above its surface. And the lamps hanging from wooden beams resembled chandeliers. Danny

Savage huddled in a group of fisher-boys, trying hard to look like Tony Curtis.

Peggy was kept awake, the following night, by indigestion. She thought of him out in the harbour, working, collecting nets and lobster pots. And she felt a bit of that recklessness creep back. Like she was standing with a pink stalk of candyfloss, contemplating her next move.

Danny Savage had said goodbye with a nod of his head as they left the dance. Protocol meant there would be no holding hands walking home, or kisses stolen behind Lindisfarne Hall. Protocol and pregnancy meant the chance of another dance with him was as likely as her parent's forgiveness.

Her mother's Christmas card made no mention of her predicament. Instead she talked about her sister who was now working at the Ministry. She lingered about the favoured one's life a little too long. And there were no crumbs of forgiveness; just the scent of a dried rose petal she had secreted in the envelope.

Danny Savage (Things always change):
A shadow on the blind shaped like the back of a man's head. He wears a narrow brimmed hat and a piece of braided hair hangs from it. Time spent on land is merely an interlude. Like a drunk negotiating nighttime pavements, stumbling his

way through life on dry land. There is a sure-footed certainty about the sea that disappears once anchor is dropped. Skipper, George Ford, David Stuart, Martin Stark, Kevin McArdle and he, Danny James Savage. A small six-person universe; floating freely upon the sea.

Love is a word only uttered in song. My love is like a red red rose that sweetly blooms. A drunken lament echoing down backstreets and through their kitchen door; the clattering of a man unsteady on his feet. A face carved from granite, broken veins and weather-beaten skin. Animated by alcohol, still and emotionless when sober. Silent sea fishing from the harbour wall, digging out rag worm for bait. His first voyage at fourteen. Rope burns and stinging salt corroded eyes.

All of the six has a fisherman for a father. A mother, who worries when they are away at sea; some have wives who do the same. Grace Darling the Bamburgh girl who rescued a boat load of men in wicked seas, is their patron saint. She guides them through a stormy North Sea; whispers sweet nothings in their ears, while wave's crash and ships-rope screeches.

He feels restless; too much time on the land is making him itch for a roll underfoot. On Lindisfarne there are too many eyes watching from windows, following a lone fisher-boy down to the harbour. The snow has subsided and the causeway is clear.

Where the snow has melted, small holes in the sand

reveal the rag worm's work. A memory of his father bent over, digging with a small trowel into wet sand. The granite face, broken by a smile.

"The slippery buggers are hiding today lad; we need to charm them out of the sand."

With hands almost blue from the cold, old man Savage continued to dig; while he shivered and watched.

"There's a legend, Greek I think, about a fisherman who could charm the fishes alive. Glaucus was his name, and he became a merman by eating a magic herb from the gods. Turned his skin blue and his hair copper-green, and he grew a fish-tail instead of legs. Now look at me, I'm becoming one too, look, "he had said, waving his frozen hands about like a swimmer. There was a lot of superstition and myth that went with the sea. And from time-to-time the old man passed it on.

"Mermen work your magic," he muttered to the frozen ground. On a clear day, with a wind behind him, he could make Bamburgh in an hour or so.

It was on the way to Bamburgh that he caught sight of Peggy and the Moriarty's. They were heading by bus across the causeway, dressed-up like a Victorian Sunday. He was sure she looked back; sure she had given him a discreet wave. Bamburgh was bustling, a fair spilled out of St Aidan's Parish Hall. Attracting visitors from the Island and nearby villages. When he strolled into the Castle public house, there was a nagging feeling. The sort you get when something's pulling you out of your life. He drank under a canopy of smoke, adding to the pollution with an un-tipped Woodbine. The Bass poured down like lemonade; two became three. His extremities tingled with a fuzzy edged drunkenness.

After an hour the bar began to fill. A coach party, dressed-up in dinner jackets and fancy silk scarves took all the seats. The remainder formed small groups about the bar. Some were already steaming, their faces ruddy from the cold and alcohol. They were big, young and overdressed. Talking loudly, drowning out the local brogue with a well-spoken drone. A short bald headed man appeared to be their skipper.

Awash with glasses of whisky and pints of varying hues; the bald man's table was constantly replenished. His companions downed each of their drinks in rapid succession, but a glass rarely touched the skipper's lips. Instead he talked intently and puffed from time-to-time on a pipe. He had the look of an Alderman, a politician. Prosperous, but with and ordinary man's tastes. In contrast his young followers exuded the self-important arrogance of boys born with money.

Days of wine and roses was belted-out with the subtlety of a rugby song. One of the revellers beating out the rhythm with his fist. At six he was joined by Kevin McArdle who slipped through the swaying toffs like a fresh-water eel. Somehow he managed to procure a couple of drinks from the bar, crowded with dickey bows and starched wing collars.

"When does the pantomime start, "he said in a loud voice.

"I've been waiting an hour for the conjurers to do a disappearing act. But all they've done is made fools of themselves and bloody great racket to boot," said Danny.

"And I suppose the landlords done nothing?"

"He's kissed each and every one of their fat arses; look at him squirming," said Danny. His voice shifting from melodious to a rasp.

"I think it's about time we moved on," said Kevin.

"One more to strengthen our legs for the walk."

Kevin McArdle would later regret his hesitation; he could have been
more persuasive, but the prospect of another pint before a cold walk along the coast had been the clincher. At half past seven a good-natured scuffle broke out between two of the dinner suits. A punch was aimed, but made no connection. Men huddled together like footballers before a game. Hands slapped backs; a spirit drink was forced on the protagonist and a cigar lit.

The bald headed man, puffed away at his pipe; watching the melee with a studied casualness.

"In twenty years' time places like this will be an anachronism. People will be getting pissed on pills, lying on comfortable sofas, without a care in the world," he said. Keeping his eyes trained on the jostling suits.

"So all the excitement would be removed Alderman."

"Harry please, it's our Christmas do, let's drop the formalities."

"Harry," he repeated uncomfortably.

"Twenty years ago only the rich could afford a refrigerator, a car and a TV set. Now they are in the grasp of working men. In the future we may look on the pub, like we do the hand-mangle or the horse-drawn cart. All things must pass."

Songs circulated the bar, and the hush of conflict was replaced with a noisy bonhomie. Danny Savage slurping down his fifth pint missed the subtleties of the situation. He saw a stranger throwing his weight about, and felt a frisson of anger. He watched as the pugilist took leave of his friends and made for the outside toilet. The man, had a roll to his walk, but his shoulders were straight, unbent and powerful. And before the beer was settled in his belly, he was outside pissing together with the man.

There was a nod of acknowledgement between fellow pisseurs. Up close the dinner suit was only a few inches taller. His extra height consisting of an over-large forehead and bouffant of blond hair. He imagined his head connecting with the bridge of the man's nose, then let the thought disappear along with his bodily waste. It was Bamburgh fair after all, and his legs were feeling unsteady.

The Alderman took another hit from his pipe. He watched the two locals, dressed in oversized fisherman's jumpers; the dark haired boy was drunker, and his movements had a jerky uncoordinated quality. He was too drunk to fight, but he may start one by accident. Falling into someone, or taking an innocuous remark the wrong way. Over at the bar, the pugilist had an arm round his former enemy; they stared glassily into each other's eyes, like a pair of punch-drunk lovers.

"I would hazard a guess those two nincompoops will be sleeping all the way to Gallowgate. Can you see they don't get into any more trouble."

He emptied the spent tobacco from his pipe and refilled it from a silver tin.

"And keep an eye on that dark haired local lad. He's also giving me cause for concern. But no manhandling; just watch he doesn't come in contact with our boys."

He lit the pipe, gently moving a match over moist tobacco fibres.

The polished tip of manicured fingernails, and his mother of pearl cufflinks, glistened in the bars half-light.

The bald headed-man reminded Danny of a variety performer, cracking the whip at his bunch of performing dogs. Each gesture magnified to please those in the cheap seats.

"Can you send over two pints of Bass to the local lads, but don't buy the landlord another, he's had enough."

Again a request was translated into a theatrical gesture. Two foaming pints were placed in front of Danny Savage and Kevin McArdle, The Alderman raised his small glass. The boys countered with a toast.

"To the gentleman in the corner," they said. The Alderman raised his glass a second time, but returned it to the table un-drank. He stuffed and lit another pipe, and deftly moved the conversation back to Willington.

"Take a bus from the Quay to Willington, by way of the river. Is there anything in that shoddy stretch of land which would persuade a sane man to live among the gritty houses and patches of waste-ground."

He rapped his pipe against the table, like a judge in court.

"Their houses lack the basic amenities: indoor toilets, bathrooms, hot and cold running water. If they go to the lavatory, a neighbour may greet them in the shared yard. If they want to make love, they may need to wait for the snores of that neighbour. Damp, cold and decrepitude are not natural; but they are the unwelcome guests thousands of families suffer."

Kevin McArdle wondered aloud about the consequences of Danny Savage mingling with cold Bamburgh air.

"I can't see us getting out of this pub alive," he slurred.

His friend's eyes rolled haphazardly round their sockets, and he let out a barely intelligible

"What."

"I said I can't see us getting out of here alive."

"What."

"Oh forget it Danny."

Watchful eyes followed Danny Savage as he swayed about the bar. Groups of dinner-suited drunks, politely moved aside, as he made violent changes in direction. The ever watchful Alderman puffed on his pipe. It was quarter past nine when he came level with the adjacent exit and toilet doors, and only a second later he was outside, flies undone. A familiar voice shouted his name, so he shook away the last drips and buttoned himself-up. As he turned, the urinal wall appeared to evaporate, and before him stood a group dressed in Victorian Costume.

"Danny, what do you think you're up to," was followed by screams when the group were sprayed by warm vomit fresh from a fisher-boys mouth. He was too far gone to recognise Peggy and the Moriarty's; or the helping hands that bundled him away.

"I told you to keep an eye on that lad. Wait until the local press find out I paid for his drinks," said The

Alderman. He took another hit from his pipe and cracked a wicked grin.

"Now what do you think about fourteen storeys, made from prefabricated concrete."

Peggy itched all the way home. Her Victorian costume was made with nylon petticoats that chafed against her skin. She quietly thanked Danny Savage for rescuing her from Bamburgh fair. But she also looked back at the Castle pub, with a feeling of regret. The fool had scuppered any chances of a future dance; the Moriarty's would see to that. As the shadows from Willington moved across her wall, she listened to the front-room clock chime midnight. A heavy gust of North Sea wind buffeted her window. Underneath a thick eiderdown and blanket, Peggy stroked her belly. She caressed her unborn child and wished it a better, more loved life than hers.

A bus full of rowdy dinner-suited men, wound its way south along the coast road. In the front sat a bald-headed man.

"You know I recognise that young girl from somewhere, the pretty little Victorian, with the green eyes.... So where were we."

"A new Pompeii, built from the rubble of a Victorian slum."

Christmas Future:

Lindisfarne in winter possessed a strange and unearthly light.
And if she screwed-up her eyes really tight, the effect was
like looking through a muted kaleidoscope. Reds washed out
blues, the grey of rocks, stone yellow sand and speckles of
green; a landscape she had never witnessed. She thought of
Willington and a Christmas morning. Instinctively she
stroked her stomach.

"Happy Christmas little one," Peggy whispered
quietly to her belly,

"this coming year will be your first."

The beauty of Lindisfarne had caught her unawares again. It
left her yearning for an end to isolation, and for life to begin
again. A bird flying out to sea reminded her of Danny Savage.
With his saltwater smell and uncomplicated ways, he was as
free as any wild animal. She imagined he wanted for nothing;
his body fitting into the space between island and sea like a
gull drifting on a current of air.

Yet she was still too young to see that he would
drown in a place like Willington. Suffocate under the layers
of modern-life; until he became a tobacco store Indian; a
curiosity from another age. She thought of his perplexed face,
as it recognised hers; and his body crumpling like a
concertina.

A girl's mind enclosed by a woman's body. The girl
wanting everything to be just so; to fit into her little

Christmas Day fantasy. The woman thinking of her unborn child and how it's life would be.

"Your breakfasts ready, "called Jean Moriarty; as the kaleidoscope sky shifted to monochrome. She negotiated breakfast and mass like a dutiful daughter. Singing heartily along to Faith of our Fathers. She took the communion wafer on her tongue, and said amen in all the right places.

At the end of mass, she lit a candle, and dipped her fingers in holy water. There was nothing of her old innocence left. But the good-girl charade felt comfortable, like a worn-in pair of shoes. And she even allowed Good-Peggy to feel a faint nostalgia for ghosts of the past.

In the afternoon Miss Boyd, a spinster friend of Jean Moriarty joined them for dinner. She arrived with Will and Matty, two awkward cousins. The women drank sweet sherry, the men pale ale. Peggy had a snowball and enjoyed herself despite the company.

They watched TV on a tiny television screen. Reception was bad on Lindisfarne; a series of lines crossed the presenters face periodically. A faint mist also appeared to develop between his image and the cameras lens. Peggy felt like getting up and wiping the screen, but Jim Moriarty was in there first. He whacked the wooden framed box with his fist. The picture adjusted, displaying a clear-faced man, who looked younger now, less distorted. But this was merely an interlude, the mist and interference returned.

"Bugger," cursed Jim Moriarty.

"I'll have none of that swearing in front of .... Now be quiet, I'm missing what he's saying about little Prince Andrew," replied his wife.

Her face morphing from a picture of mild irritation to acute concentration, as she hung on the mans every word. Whatever was said about Prince Andrew was lost in the general hubbub of the room. Matty moved his chair, making a scraping sound. Will lit a pipe that burned with a furious flame; filling Peggy's lungs with an acrid smoke. Her cough was loud and brief, but it managed to drown-out all other noise.

Abruptly the newsreader shifts gears, he moves on from Royal children to the Queens wayward sister. Princess Margaret had previously threatened to cause a constitutional crisis by attempting to marry a divorced man. But that was all behind her now. Anthony Armstrong Jones – Lord Snowdon, her husband, had no skeletons rattling in his cupboard. But there was something in the expression of the newsreader that suggested trouble was buried in a very shallow grave.

News shifted from the Royal Family to a massacre. Jean and Jim Moriarty, Will, Matty and Mrs Boyd maintained poker faces during this serious interlude. Words like massacre, explosion and shot, floated about the living room; independent of meaning and context. A metallic buzz weaved its way into silent space. Her head felt heavy, weighed down by the world's troubles.

The muzzle of a gun, in the hands of an expert shot. Pointed, aimed; bang goes another. Bang bang your dead fifty bullets in your head. The hot movement of air as it expelled from a hotel kitchen. His body pressing against hers. The Park Hotel Whitley Bay, full of August wedding guests. Glimpsed briefly through the window, a small child dressed in white shirt, black trews and patent leather shoes. A hand roughly pulling down her knickers, another over her mouth.

Massacre, explosion, injured, dying, dead.

"Peggy would you like a glass of sherry?"

She accepted the drink with a raised hand, her eyes lingering on a spot somewhere in the recent past.

"God save the Queen," circulated the room like a choral round. Punctuated by the chink of glass and the slurp of pale ale.

"God save the Queen, god save her," they all carried on saying; until glasses were drained and stomach's rumbled. Sometime later the mist lifted, and Peggy quietly slipped into her ordinary skin.

Jean Moriarty (God is everywhere by the sea):
Later as evening approached they walked the shoreline. Snow had abated, but the searing wind cut through wool and

sheepskin. They walked vigorously to counteract the cold. Jean spoke, Peggy listened.

"When I was a girl, the de Stein's would come every summer. Their big old fashioned car, laden with fishing rods, picnic baskets and people. The old gentleman always drove; he wore a Norfolk jacket, the type country squires wear.

I must have witnessed this spectacle only twice, but it's stayed with me. They gave up the castle in 31, and rarely came back after that.

Some say he is still alive; old Milburn, who looks after the Castle, claims to have met Sir Edward, as he likes to call him. But I think the nearest he has come to Sir Edward is that big old portrait hanging in the great hall.

In the old day's children wandered the Island unaccompanied by adults. There were few visitors, and fewer strangers. Life was simpler. It was before TV, people looked no further than the causeway, and the adventurous no further than Morpeth. I remember the first radio, it was installed in Lindisfarne Hall, and the whole island would cram in to listen. Later, when the de Stein's left Lindisfarne, people started installing radios in their front parlours, and for a while dances at the hall were poorly attended.

But the War changed all of that; people came from

the mainland. The army set up a small barracks and a listening station. People needed someplace to go at night, so the hall got busy again.

I worked in a munitions factory on the mainland, plugging my ears with cotton wool and wax. The noise was terrific. I was a different person then, wild as the North Sea wind.

Some Yanks were stationed close to the factory; they would chat to us while we ate our bait. Hair tied up with a scarf, and a lumpy boiler suit; I must have looked a sight. But those soldiers were extra polite and insisted on calling me mame; which made me feel like I was in a film. I suppose all their attention must have gone to my head. I was a godless eighteen. Men is what interested me; men, men and more men. Just before D-Day, the Yanks shipped out. Soldier's stationed on the island thinned down to a skeleton force. We were put on piece-work on account of all the bullets and shells that were being used-up over in Europe.

Social life was put on hold, and we worked flat-out right up to Christmas. The war was supposed to be over by then, but it wasn't. The orders kept rolling in, and we kept on working like slaves.

I would day-dream on the lathe, thinking about my favourite subject. At night I would be so tired, that once my head made contact with a pillow that would be it until morning. And it's not like it was in the films, that's all propaganda. People moaned and complained, but were told to shut-up. There was none of that whistle while you work. More grumble while you fight to keep your fingers from being cut off.

People were no different then than they are now, and don't let anyone persuade you things were much better back then. It was a blessing when rationing ended and we started to get things like TVs and washing machines. I know it's difficult to imagine, but I was very much like you.

When Christmas came around, the factory kept on working. But we were given Christmas day and Boxing Day as holiday. New Year's Eve fell on a Sunday, so we had that off too.

Monday January 1st 1945. The devil was in me that New Year's day. But when I looked in the mirror, all I saw was the same little girl. A face as pure and innocent as yours.

The last New Year's Eve party of the war. The last one of my childhood. Oh I was all grown up on the outside. I borrowed a dress for the dance, it fitted well. We were all thin as rakes, starved by five years of war. Underneath all this fat, a thin girl once lived. Now I hold it in with panty girdles and elastic.

My thin-self had no steady fellah; there were too few to go round once the soldiers had left. I remember we had visitors from the mainland; a small party of Norwegians. They were rumoured to be spies, but seemed quite happy mixing out in the open. They were tall and blond, great Norway Spruces; whose shoulders hunched as they walked through our small doorways. And I was taken with the younger of the group. He looked no older than eighteen, with a thin wispy beard.

But it all felt impossible, the spies were instantly surrounded by girls. Girls from the Island and the Mainland, girls I'd never seen before. I suppose the rumour of available men crossed the causeway. They may have even been some from the listening station, but seeing as that was hush-hush, I had no idea who they were out of uniform.

So I danced with a fisher-boy or two; danced with single girls like me. And I could see the anticipation in their eyes. Like me they were waiting for that tap on the shoulder. The Millburn's had made rum punch, so by halfway through the night us single girls were tipsy as well as lovesick. The band played songs of the day and folk tunes; local music with a little Irish, American and Scottish thrown in. Halfway through the dance, there was an air raid warning and everything stopped. People sat chatting in the darkness; their voices and the chink of glasses filling the hall. I remember spilling a drink on my borrowed dress, and dabbing the stain with water from the tap outside.

It was past eleven, a clear night sky, with a big moon. The mainland was clearly visible across the causeway. While I cleaned, the warning ended and music started up. It was then I became aware of another's presence. There was the rustle of his matchbox, and the sound of a flame being ignited. And when he spoke, he spoke to my back, bent over the tap.

Do you want a smoke, he said. His voice was heavily accented, but the words came to me, clear as a bell. And I said "I don't mind if I do," even though I'd never smoked. Or at that point, turned around to see which of the Norwegians he was.

He was a little smaller than I had imagined, but still taller than most Englishmen I knew. And underneath that blond fuzz, his face was smooth as a girls. He said his name was Ole and I gave him mine.

Like Jean Harlow, he said. And I laughed so much, the cigarette smoke made me cough. And he held me, while my chest heaved. He held on so long I forgot where I was and held him right back.

It was a bitterly cold night and my coat was inside. But I had the rum-punch for warmth, and Ole wrapped me around his fur lined coat. I took him to the Priory, where he produced a bottle of something that tasted strong and warm. It ripped down my throat like hot turpentine, burned me through and through. Inside the cocoon of his big fur coat, I rubbed my body against his. And soon we were moving rhythmically.

Tuesday 8th May 1945, VE Day; the factory was running. Churchill's speech pumped through the public address system, followed by the King. But I wasn't there. The sickness that had started a week before, had me under the bedclothes, wrapped in heavy blankets. I listened as the radio relayed the good news to all and sundry. Daddy and Mam cheered, and if they'd been drinking people, I would have expected a chink of glass to follow.

Later in the afternoon I took a turn for the worst and the doctor was called. I remember the remnants of bunting clinging to his jacket, and the smell of whisky on his breath. But he examined and prodded in the usual way; took out his stethoscope and listened to my chest. Then he left to call for an ambulance.

Because of the celebrations I was made to wait a full four hours. The ambulance had been attending a car accident, where a drunken man had driven into a tree; killing himself in the ecstasy of victory the ambulance driver had said.

In the waiting time Doctor Cooper persuaded Mam that it was he who would accompany me to the infirmary. He assured them the trip was only precautionary, and as my personal physician he would be best placed to pass on my medical history. I still say a prayer for dear old Cooper. Still thank god he was tolerant and good, a true Christian if there ever was one.

He kept quiet in the ambulance; until events took a violent course. Between Bamburgh and Morpeth I miscarried. Evacuating my five month old child, onto his jacket sleeve. And in the mass of blood, limbs, placenta and skin; I made out his tiny dead hands. They were reaching out to me for help. So I held his tiny body close, while the blood seeped through my dress. I held him to Morpeth, where he was taken away and never given back.

Doctor Cooper told me the child was a Mongol and had passed on to a better place. And because I was a young girl like you, I accepted without question. I recovered physically, from my brief bout of illness; explained away as flu. But inside, a part of me remained incomplete; ragged and broken. I took long walks by the sea, looking to the tides rise and fall for explanation. I saw god in those waves, and saw him in my dead child's eyes.

God is everywhere by the sea, and he was in me when Ole was conceived. I christened him Ole, after his father. And during these walks, I imagined him and how he would have been if he'd survived. "

They paused at a rock-pool, filled with fetid water. It contained a jumble of dismembered crab limbs, and soft shell mutations. There was nothing but deadness there.

"Don't spend your life not living Peggy. Seize every opportunity."

"Does that mean I keep my baby?"

"No Peggy it means you give your baby a life and you have a life too."

"But I thought..."

"God never gave a choice to me. But my silly eighteen-year-old self would surely have made the wrong choice. Sent me packing to the mainland and a pauper's existence. Your home is Willington, not here. Have your baby, give it away, go home. Go to that Dance at Lindisfarne Hall. Dance with that drunken fisher-boy you like. And don't make it your last."

Pan Haggerty:

The temperature dropped down the thermometer on the day before the dance. The harbour froze over and people stayed indoors. Peggy had no new dress for the party, so she improvised. Fashioned a scarf with material borrowed from Jean Moriarty. In the afternoon they cooked Pan Haggerty together.

Through the kitchen window a desiccated garden was visible. Trees bent by the North East wind moved to the side. Bowing in respect of a superior power.

"Lessons in life part two."

The suggestion that they make some dinner had been Jean's. Peggy, used to hot cooked meals, emerging fully formed from the Moriarty's kitchen, just assumed she was there to keep the older woman company.

"I can hear the cogs of your brain working overtime Peggy. Crunch, crunch, crunch."

"But..."

"Ah, but you don't know how to cook."

Peggy nodded vigorously, as if her ignorance needed emphasis.

"So how do you suppose that child of yours is going to eat once it's off the breast?"

"I thought..."

"You were giving your child away. That's still true. But just supposing you have another, sometime down the line. Or supposing you get married, end up falling in love with a big hunk. Then what happens?"

"I don't know Mrs Moriarty."

"I know you don't know. You're a girl in her teens. Your husband and child would starve to death. That's why it's time we give you some cooking lessons. So tell me child, what type of husband would you be looking for. "

"Tony Curtis or Rock. I went off Dirk after Song Without End."

"So it's an American you want, with a huge appetite." She felt a little of her courage return.

"Tony's quite slim Mrs Moriarty, he must hardly eat."

"And he's not much choice with a girl like you. It will be fish and chips every night."

Peggy laughed along with Jean Moriarty. But inside there was a dread of the whole adult world. A dread that god had something much worse in store for her than a cooking lesson.

"I'm going to make things easy for you Peggy. The potatoes, while not peeled or sliced, have been washed. There over in that large sliver pot on the stove."

The simple act of peeling, slicing, then placing in a frying pan followed. Jean Moriarty took care of the onions and cheese. She sliced rapidly through both, with razor sharp skill. Peggy worked slowly, peeling each spud like a Faberge egg. And when she was done, her fingers ached from the effort.

"Choose wisely Peggy. Choose your man wisely. Think of doing this day-in day-out with not so much as a thank you. Choose the him that cares about you, not filling his belly."

166

With the potatoes, onions and cheese cooked. She, with a little help from her teacher, placed the mass under the grill. Then once dark brown, she cut the crispy Pan Haggerty into slices. While she worked at her snails-pace, Jean Moriarty cooked black pudding and Cumbrian sausages, fried a dozen eggs and prepared some greasy fried bread.

"Now it's your turn to put it all together. Husband is waiting in the parlour. He expects it all on a plate – piping hot. "

Jim Moriarty accepted his plate with a silent nod. He was sitting at the dinner table, his face fixed in concentration. The radio turned up a little too loud, spewed out a frantic football commentary.

"Don't let her fool you into thinking this is a weekly occurrence. It's me that usually does the cooking. This is her special treat, "he said as she turned to leave.

Oh the Shark babe........

In her dream Bobby Darin dripped like honey from the windows of Lindisfarne Hall. It was the night of the dance. Peggy peeked through the hall windows, trying to imagine the scene back when Jean Moriarty was a girl. An emcee dressed in sombre black; his hair slicked down with pomade. Music that swung, and paper decorations spiralling through the rafters. Good cheer and bonhomie in abundance.

The rusty remains of a small tap went unnoticed. So did the absence of oilskins at the halls entrance. One of those freakish coincidences had her think of Glenn Miller, then the emcee segued into Pennsylvania Six Five Thousand. And she imagined a slim Jean Moriarty, Jitterbugging below the magic lanterns, while servicemen hugged the wall and savoured another day on this earth. A feeling of nostalgia for a time she had never known passed slowly through her, like a premonition of what it would be like to be old and full of memories.

A small animal or bird scuttled on the ground, and her gaze moved down. It was then she spotted the forlorn little tap, broken and rusted brown. Inside the nostalgia gave way to sadness. Tears came from nowhere; her body shook with the cold. She caressed the growing mound under her dress, and whispered "go to sleep little one."

Something of the melancholy was with her when she woke. Melancholy tinged with foreboding, and a feeling that she'd missed something important. But she put aside these feelings; washed them away with the lack of sleep and night-sweats.

Night Fishing:
At the beginning of the day a small drifter sets sail on a night fishing expedition. One of its crew Danny Savage combs his

hair into a large sculpted quiff as they leave the harbour. The Stella is small and unsuitable for a storm; but the sea is calm, and the coastguards forecast, good. And the five fisher-boys are in high spirits. As the skipper steers, they sing. They twirl their razor tooth knives, and strike poses, much to the annoyance of their old skipper.

"Get on with your work lads," he shouts. For him the old superstition of not whistling at sea extends to singing. But the boats engine drowns out his voice. So he lets them carry on. Soon they will hit open water; attention will turn to the nets and preparation.

The five boys spread the net ready for casting off to the right; another superstition even they adhere to. At night the location of fish has to be guessed. No surface oil of whitebait and mackerel to follow. Just the head of a seal, or a notion there may be a school of fish below.

All are too young to remember the great herring fleets, following fish from Fraserburgh to Great Yarmouth. Where girlfriends and wives trailed the great fleet south, gutting, salting and packing at every port. Like an armies' camp followers, pitching themselves in rooming houses along the way. But these modern boys catch what they can, whitebait, mackerel and herring in the winter. Crabs and shellfish during the summer months - subsistence fishing.

The herring would go to the smoke houses of Seahouses; or dinner tables in Alnwick, Bamburgh and Lindisfarne. Like their catch today, this would feed many festivities to come, and provide much needed sustenance for themselves.

Danny Savage threaded the net through his hands. Like all the boys, he worked without gloves, despite the cold. His fingers needed to work quickly and nimbly, grabbing, gutting, boxing. He sensed the boat slowing, getting ready for the drift net to be cast. From his cabin, skipper gave the signal, and the boys worked in unison, so the net flew as a single object overboard.

Gulls were already circulating; following the stale smell of last week's catch, following fish smells from a thousand other voyages. Keeping close, watching for the bat of a tailfin, or guts discarded to the deck.

Danny's mind moved on to the evening, where he would dress proper for the dance. His new suit, bought in Alnwick the previous month; his winkelpickers, tight and uncomfortable from a shoe shop in Bamburgh; topped off with a white shirt and dark green skinny tie.

"Do you fancy a dance," he would say to her, and she impressed by his getup, would oblige.

"So which one will it be tonight Danny. The posh one from the mainland," asked one of the fisher boys.
Flashing a wide grin to the
others.

"You never know, got my pick of a bad bunch. And if you're lucky, I'll throw you some scraps," he said. He curled his lip like Cliff, and that sure enough shut them up.

He hoped none of them were mind readers, because the mention of a certain mainland girl had reminded him of his lacklustre performance at Bamburgh fair. Of her look when she crossed the causeway, and of the Moriarty's glaring at him.

A fisher boy after all was an acquired taste. Not much of a catch for a young girl from the mainland. And he was sure the boys were well aware of this, but like him they understood the sea had its complications. It clung to your body like a possessive lover; or if you had a wife, it was the mistress who always talked of marriage. So they chose to overlook his failure; they were loyal like that.

The Dance:
Lindisfarne is such a magical place, cut off from the mainland. It's kept its holiness. I expected to see the ghosts of long dead monks, walking the shoreline with St Cuthbert's bones. I expected Pilgrims like Lourdes and a host of other holy things. But all I have is a cross on my bedroom wall and a sacred heart picture in the hall. There's not even many Catholics on the Island. But Jean and Jim make up for it with their devotion.

The mass in Bamburgh is as boring as home. Sundays are as boring as home. But the people are nicer to me, and I like that. I'm worried about what they will say when I start to show.

Jean and Jim have been very kind. Just wish mam and sis were the same. Before I took the bus from Haymarket station I thought myself grown up. Then the engine started and I blubbered like a baby for a good twenty miles. It wasn't that I was alone, or in-trouble. It's because nobody came to see me off. Seeing as only mam, sis, and Father McVeigh knew, I shouldn't have been bothered. But I was. It was the start of the loneliness.

Nobody's up in the house yet, and between me and you dear diary I'm a little excited about the dance tonight.

Peggy prepared her breakfast and ate alone. She watched as the kitchen clock ticked round to seven thirty. She savoured the moment looking out into the darkness of Lindisfarne, emptying her mind of everything but the sensation of peace and quiet. The previous day's bitter chill had subsided. Buffeting North East wind caused windowpanes to rattle. And the smell of yesterday's Pan Haggerty hung about the room. A breakfast of porridge with jam sat uncomfortably in her stomach; weighing down like a trawler-man's anchor. She drank her tea slowly; it was cold by the time Jean began her journey, outside to the netty.

Later in the morning Jim Moriarty asked her if she would like to see a film.

"It's an old favourite of mine," he said.

172

In her mind a picture formed, of a prairies wide expanse, covered wagons, roundups and a plethora of ten gallon hats. A Saturday morning children's show revisited. This time there would be no cartoons for light relief; or games of hopscotch and bays, outside during the interval. Or mouths full of pop and fizzing sherbet, re-enacting the last peril of Pauline.

"And don't go expecting a war film or a cowboy. Even Mrs Moriarty finds my taste soppy. So will I have the pleasure of your company Peggy?"

She knew that turning him down would cause no upset. He was trying to be kind; there was anticipation in his face, of the good natured sort. An affable air, only possible with the absence of sex. Unaware that he was the first man to ask such a question of her; Jim Moriarty simply saw things from his perspective. To step into the shoes of Gregory Peck and feel the Roman suns warmth against his skin; that's what he wanted. He was, as Jean would put it later, being selfish. But that was later, when everything began to unravel.

Overnight the Stella ploughed through an empty sea. Each time the net went over, each time it came back empty. A few silver sprats wriggled under the harsh deck light. Dead and live crabs landed pincers down, and jellyfish slid out like a disembowelled man's insides.

"You know our job is a hundred times more dangerous than any other, "said one of the fisher-boys. All the rest exhaled loudly, widening their eyes in exaggerated surprise.

"I can't see any of us holding down a landlubber's job. The sea always claims you back," shouted Danny.

A chorus of laughter rose above the sound of boat engine and sea. Above the slap of fish as they were thrown dead into boxes. Only a large wave, breaking over the deck; extinguished their laughter and lit cigarettes. Soaking what had remained dry, and shifting the meagre catch across deck.

Just before daybreak, the crew wedged into their tiny sleeping cots. An unlucky soul took the watch. Sleep does not come easy on such a rough-and-ready sea; but they manage a fitful rest. For a few precious moments Danny glides across the dance floor of Lindisfarne Hall. The Everly Brothers sing Cathy's Clown; he is at ease floating like a light-footed Lionel Blair.

He takes a girl in his arms, but she recoils. Her dress is sodden, covered with seaweed and dead fish. And he looks down to see himself clothed in dripping oilskins and heavy fisher-boots.

Everybody might be somebody else (if their luck was different):
The princess has a boring life, bed early with a glass of milk and biscuits. She is read to by a condescending secretary. And instead of something interesting, the woman just reads

a list of dull meetings that seems to go on forever. The dullness is relentless; so dull in-fact Peggy begins to feel detached. Her gaze wanders about the hall, left then right.

Everyone looks content on their wooden fold-up chairs; the same chairs stacked to the side at dances. The shiny surface of a bald man's scalp is illuminated by the projectors beam. A wisp of a cigarette sends smoke rings to the ceiling. She's the youngest person in Lindisfarne Hall, by a good decade. But the sexes are equally represented. Young men and old sit with their respective partners; single people are scattered about. All stare at the flickering black and white picture, mesmerised. Suddenly the girl on screen starts screaming. Pulling at her hair, and finally retreating into the pillow. At last some action Peggy thinks. The secretary calls a doctor, who injects the princess with a drug, he claims, is perfectly harmless. He tells the girl to do what she wishes for a while.

If wishing were that simple, then I would be with Danny Savage. If wishing were that simple. Peggy wanted to like the film, if only to please Jim Moriarty. But the whimsical tale of a drugged princess, escaping her palace, and wandering the streets of Rome began to grate. The chaste exchange with the newspaper man and womanising sidekick felt like a fairy-tale. The sidekick's beard and the implausibility that such a famous person would not be recognised, had her attention drifting.

Instead she focused on the pattern of a dress here,

and a horrendous headscarf there. It was like mass, but without the incense and singing. She time travelled forwards to the evening; when their chairs would once again sit on the wall. A Ceilidh band plays and girls, boys, women, men swing together. And there she is, in the thick of it. Her skirt swirling, face glowing, eyes glistening; under the kerosene light.

Jim Moriarty smiled at her, just as a vision of Danny Savage and her body made sweaty contact. She smiled back at Jim, the barnacle smell fresh in her mind.

Bossa nova music pumps out of the halls PA. A slow lazy chug, miles away from the Ceilidhs jagged fiddles and stomping feet. The languid movement of dancers under an open sky, draws her back to the film. Gregory Peck is dancing with Audrey Hepburn. His hands, circle her waist, and there is a moist look of romance on his face.

There are comic-book villains, dressed in black with twirling moustaches, circulating the dance floor. Like men who habitually tie Pauline to the train-track, then creep about with exaggerated stealth. They're supposed to bring the princess back to the palace, but an almighty fight breaks out. Jim Moriarty laughs out loud when a villain is banjaxed by the princess wielding a guitar. And he, along with everyone else, gives out a little sigh when Peck kisses a dripping wet Hepburn.

They recovered four bodies from the Stella. Burnt beyond recognition. There was no sign of the fifth man, and it was presumed he had jumped overboard to escape the inferno.

A mass of charred oilskins was all that remained of their clothing. Everything else was carbon. Skipper had died in the first explosion; the top of his head was all that remained of him.

A second explosion, of greater intensity, happened when the fuel tanks blew. Engulfing the tiny sleeping berths in a fireball; incinerating the sleeping fisher-boys. It was presumed the missing man had been on watch, he possibly surviving the explosion, but blown out to sea by its force. Another theory speculated he may have jumped overboard, rather than burn alive. The North Sea at that time of year was cold enough to kill a man quick.

The four fisher-boys were identified by possessions, welded to their bodies. George Ford had the remains of a St Christopher's pendant, identified by his mother. David Stuart a gold wedding band, inscribed with his wife's name. Martin Starke's Russian watch, with its metal strap, was fused to his wrist. And Danny Savage had a Ronson lighter in his pocket. A souvenir from a trip to Germany.

Kevin McArdle was unaccounted for and listed as lost at sea. The search for him was cursory; due to the storm that extinguished the flames. The storm that presumably drowned him. By the time the sea calmed, he would have spent a day and night in the freezing water. Too long for a man, unable to swim.

But at four o'clock in the afternoon, none of this was known. Film goers filed out of Lindisfarne Hall, with their hunger for romance sated. Although the storm had abated, heavy gusts blew in from the harbour. Creating a wind tunnel down Lewins Lane. She held on to Jim Moriarty, who pushed forward, sheltering her with his body. And she was glad there was little opportunity for conversation, a post-mortem of Roman Holiday, would have been embarrassing for both of them.

Halfway home they sheltered in a doorway, and Peggy collected herself as best she could. Her neat hair, meticulously brushed and lacquered in the morning, now resembled a banshee wig. She examined her reflection in the window glass, a windblown, dishevelled mess stared back.

"I think we'd better push on Peg. Jean will be wondering what's become of us," said Jim. And she caught a glimpse, of a different man, the henpecked husband who was a little afraid of his wife. His body was tensed, like a boxer before a fight. A month on the Island and she had hardly noticed this husband and wife dynamic. Not even a peep out of Jim Moriarty was heard. No raised voices, or curses, except when the television misbehaved. And then he had been shot down, by a cross word from his wife. In another month, she may learn something more about Jean and Jim

Moriarty's marriage, but for now she was quite certain the wife wore the trousers.

They stopped for a moment outside The Northumberland Arms, which Jim referred to as The Tavern. It was deathly quiet. A favourite of fisher-boys, the pub had a raucous reputation. But on this windy evening, only a glum faced landlord stood at its bar.

Between five and seven thirty, Peggy repaired her hair. From the bedroom window she watched a donkey and cart, making slow progress from the harbour. The cart was used to carry fish; a tarpaulin strapped down with rope covered its load. She was far enough away to miss the activity on the harbours side.

If Peggy had stood at the harbour, she would have seen the burned out Stella, listing to one side. Its innards obscenely exposed. She would have recognised the faces of mothers, wives and sisters; their faces distorted by grief. Nobody speaking; lifeboat men securing the stricken boat; grown men staring in wonder at the blackened galley. A penny for each of their thoughts would have revealed an uncomprehending horror. A scream so loud it would have carried itself across the causeway to Bamburgh.

The bodies were gone; in transit to a makeshift morgue at Lindisfarne Hall. Each former fisher-boy labelled like a GPO parcel. Down at the harbour, their smell lingered. The smell of burning human fat, and of fuel ignited by the accident.

A Protestant Priest stood at the water's edge, praying. Trying to make sense of young lives extinguished. He thought of Lindisfarne Hall, where the boys would lie; waiting for the mainland authorities to arrive. Where he would be expected to offer spiritual guidance to those overwhelmed with grief. He thought of his wife and children, alive and whole. And the fact those brittle twigs of black had once been animated human beings; with families of their own.

From her window Peggy only saw a beautiful evening sky, the clearest she had seen. And she wished her knowledge extended to the names of stars and constellations. But all she saw was a mass of twinkling light.

Somewhere out there Danny Savage may be looking at the same sky. She pictured him lying on a deck, his face pointed to the heavens, his arms outstretched. In the dressing table mirror she assembled and reassembled her homemade scarf. She copied a one worn by Audrey Hepburn in the film, and said a silent prayer for Danny as she tied and untied the garment: *Please god make him look at the night sky and think of me.*

No one thought of dismantling the Film Projector, or to take down the cinema screen. Seats were left in rows, and peoples detritus, remained where it had fallen. The projectors artificial eye witnessed four fisher-boys and their Skipper, placed delicately on tarpaulin. Their crispy flesh

180

covered with winter blankets. At six thirty members of the Ceilidh band arrived, an hour later, the Islanders. They were all turned away by a policeman guarding the Halls entrance. Some headed for the Northumberland Arms, others congregated close by. Some were crying, others in the throes of heated speculations. There was wild talk about a Russian submarine; but mostly people talked about the missing man. A story was doing the rounds concerning a fisher-boy who went overboard during a storm. A ship, a year later, fished up a skull in their nets. The skulls two front teeth were missing, like the fisher-boy lost the previous year.

By the time Peggy, Jean and Jim Moriarty arrived; the small crowd had grown to a throng. From a distance, the situation looked normal; a group of people waiting for the dance. But as they approach, an atmosphere of sorrow and mourning became apparent. It took seconds for her to hear the name of Danny Savage, mentioned among the dead. Her eyes followed the horizon to the clear night sky; the same collection of stars blinked back at her. And the picture she had made of a young fisher-boy marvelling at the multitude of stars, crumbled.

She felt the heaviness of her womb, and a pressure from her distended belly against the party dress. As if the garment had suddenly grown too small. Reaching all the way from Willington, a cold hand took hold and moved its fingers about her cranium. The crowd's faces distorted, like people in a hall of mirrors. She heard the words Spanish City; pass

181

from her lips, just before the darkness descended.

His cold dead hands:
Willington had come back to claim one of its daughters. Just as she hovered on the edge of consciousness, Peggy saw her mothers and sisters face; both wore pained masks of concern, both recited the rosary along with Jean and Jim Moriarty.

In her lucid moments Peggy asked the faces assembled:

"Where have all these flowers come from."

But nobody answered. It was winter after all, and natural blooms were scarce; so where had all the flowers come from. Peggy tried to raise her head, but there was no strength to move. A part of her was still outside Lindisfarne Hall, hearing the crowd speculate about the horror visited upon those unfortunate fisher-boys.

"Is it true they all burned to death," she said. But nobody replied. The faces in her room continued reciting the rosary:

"I believe in God, the Father Almighty,
Creator of heaven and earth;
And in Jesus Christ, His only son, Our Lord;
Who was conceived by the Holy Spirit,
Born of the Virgin Mary,
Suffered under Pontius Pilate,

Was crucified, died and was buried. "

A person's life summarised in such few words. As her strength returned, she considered Danny Savage. Had he been a figment of her imagination; a sprite, a merman returned to the sea. During her lucid moments, she kept his name hidden; but when the blackness returned, words would come spontaneously. And Danny Savage, was one of many names babbled when she embraced incoherence.

The Stella rocked back and forth like a Shuggy Boat; tipping it's bow then stern into the sea. Its mast and cabin, aflame. Poetry in motion. The Virgin Mary kept coming and so did the suffering under Pontius Pilate, the familiarity of those phrases, illuminating the dark.

From time to time a spoon would enter her mouth, and then withdraw. Its contents, sometimes sweet, sometimes savoury, melted on her tongue. Water followed, cool as the Cheviot Hills; cleansing her dry mouth and throat.

Minuscule events became magnified. She observed a spider build its web; each day the structure grew. Soon there were decaying insects attached to the web. The spider moved horizontally and vertically. His presence, invisible to the rosary reciting adults.

On a day when her eyes became fully open, she noticed the web had gone. It was night and she forced her body, upright, and looked outside at the stars. It was like the night of the dance revisited, except the position of the twinkling lights had shifted.

"I believe in God, the Father Almighty, "she recited.

Peggy waited until sunrise before rising from the bed. Her legs were weak from inactivity, so she stumbled a little on the small journey between bedpost and dressing table. And she almost forgot what had brought her to Lindisfarne; all she could see was a flaming ship, and the faces of those reciting the rosary. In the red diary, there was a single entry; but this gave no clue.

But the child inside was an insistent presence, it weighed down on her bladder; forcing her to pass water. And as she squatted over the potty, her altered body shape became more apparent. The bulbous hump of a gestating child, announced its alien presence. And as she evacuated, the steady stream told the story, from candyfloss stalk to St Vincent de Paul.

A fresh fall of snow had covered Lindisfarne; the sky was a pure blue, and she shaded her eyes from the sunlight. Out in the harbour, fishing vessels bobbed on a gentle tide; the stricken Stella had been removed. Her baby gave a kick, and she felt a new connection begin.

Bless the baby born today (Third Trimester):

Her body, heavy with the excess weight of pregnancy, felt cumbersome. She found it difficult to sleep and suffered from successive bouts of indigestion. The doctor prescribed a sedative, to ease her into sleep. But she preferred to see the night through with open eyes.

The time just before dawn could last for an eternity; it was then she thought about Willington, and how her return would be greeted. How she would behave once her baby was born.

But sleep deprivation, and the never changing image of Danny Savage combing his hair in the mirror, got to her. She took the sedative instead, finding darkness preferable to the pre-dawn blues.

It was while she was sedated, that Peggy found a new self. Sitting in mass between Jim and Jean Moriarty, her distended belly occupying the full depth of the pew; she caught sight of the new priest, watching from the wings. He was dressed in the uniform black jacket and pants, but his hair was cut in a modern style. He was like President Kennedy, a blue eyed, blond haired Ivy Leaguer. Barely a priest in profile.

February 26th
The only time I'm out is to go to mass. The rest of the time I watch TV and listen to Radio Luxemburg. Horace Batchelor, Department One, Keynsham (spelt K-E-Y-N-S-H-A-M) Keynsham, Bristol; his famous Infra-Draw Method. Elvis

Presley singing Wooden Heart. The German bit reminds me of Danny Savage; all that was left of him was a Ronson lighter, that's what the rumour mill has to say.

I don't see anyone else now. Just Jim and Jean, and the doctor. Jean keeps me in most of the time; she's afraid those North East winds will blow me over. Makes things easy, not going out, seeing I've only one dress that fits.

They have a new priest in Bamburgh; he looks a bit like President Kennedy. Jean worships John Fitzgerald, as she likes to call him. He's replaced Kirk Douglas as her new Saint. And I can see why girls prefer the strong dependable types; solid, reliable, and always good in a crisis.

I watched the sky tonight, when it was really dark. I saw a couple of grey clouds move towards the moon. They were oblong and wavy, and a little see through, like blinds in a harem. They moved slowly over the moon, slicing it in pieces. A shuttered moon is what I call it. In the end the cloud covered the moon, then everything became black.

The priest who looks Like President Kennedy. He made me think about the man I should marry. He made me think I should forget the Danny Savage's of this world.

And it would be handy if I had somebody who could hold my hand in the hospital, any sex will do. I'm terrified. Scared to death of giving birth, and all the stuff that will happen afterwards. Jean's been kind and I know she will see my baby finds a good home. But I just can't stop myself thinking about what he or she will be like.

Syncom 1 circulates in an elliptical low Earth orbit, a thousand miles or so above the planet's surface. It passes, unobserved, over Willington, then the Holy Island of Lindisfarne.

Jim Moriarty sits watching Grandstand, a cup of tea by his side and a cigarette on the go. Peggy sits at the kitchen table. April sun bounces off silver cooking pots and flagged stone flooring. The sound of sports commentary diffuses through living room, hallway and enters the kitchen as a muted drone. Jean is busy preparing food.

"Don't have any more, Misses Moore, Misses Moore, please don't have any more.
The more you have, the more you'll want, they say.
But enough is as good as a feast any day.
If you have any more, Misses Moore, you'll have to rent the house next door...
Oh! They're all right when they're here, but take my advice, old dear – Don't have any more, Misses Moore."

Jean raised her voice on the final "Don't have any more," she was lost in the reverie of cooking, slicing and chopping; boiling a pan of water; intermittently checking something in the oven. Seemingly unaware of the pregnant teenager sitting at her table, and of the insensitivity of her song. Peggy pretended she wasn't feeling awful inside; she turned the pages of her book without having finished the page. Then she turned back and started again. But it was no good. Mrs Moore was planted like a seed in her brain, and the vision of an old Irish washerwoman became insistent. Begging her to say something to Jean Moriarty.

But this was not the time to start a fight. Her body, drained of its usual vigour, agreed. The kindness of her hostess was tempered with a callousness particular to those with a rigorous religious conviction. Jean had acknowledged the hole left by her missing baby, but had never said why she and Jim had not tried for a child. Or maybe she had; Ole being the only child she would ever have.

And Peggy, with her mind too full of pregnancy and emotional turmoil, had failed to notice the dip in Jean Moriarty's mood. The lessons in life, ended just after her collapse; instead there was bed rest and isolation. And an awkwardness when they were alone together.

Jean told her stories from her past. She returned to wartime, a period of endless summers and happiness. She retold the same story on different occasions, embellishing or changing details. The RAF man, became the American, the Lindy Hop, became a Jitterbug. Life during wartime, felt more real, than her life now. A dull meandering existence, revolving round an old souvenir shop; a trip to Bamburgh once a week, and dances where she sat ridged like her husband.

"I fibbed to you about the war," she said. Her voice a conspiratorial whisper; hands in the sink scrubbing dishes.

"I pretended it was miserable and that we moaned. Oh we moaned, wouldn't be human beings if we didn't. I wanted to disguise my disappointment. I was changed by VE day. Not because my child died, or because of the circumstances, and the intolerable embarrassment. It was the end of the war that ruined things for me."

As Peggy listened to the babble of Jean Moriarty. An intermittent pain shot through her abdomen; like a period cramp but subtly different. The kitchen filled with a smell of boiled turnip and cabbage greens, of a steak and kidney pie cooking in the oven.

She pictured Jim Moriarty at his dinner plate, slurping the orange mass; impervious to the foods heat or the spectacle he was creating.

"And don't go thinking I want another war. An H bomb war will.... well you know what it will mean."

Peggy felt obliged to nod in agreement, although she was far too preoccupied with the pain in her abdomen to worry about a Third World War. The kitchen and all its activity, melted away. She stared at the tables wood grain, then looked into Jean's eyes. There was no need for further conversation; Jean Moriarty extinguished the stove and quickly removed the pie. She arranged turnip and greens on a plate, and disappeared from the kitchen. Momentarily the sports commentary became louder, an announcer emitted a torturous scream. Peggy's waters broke as she sat alone, soaking her clothes and forming a puddle at her feet.

An image of a ship rocking on the ocean settled in her mind, it's motion mirroring the rhythmic shots of abdominal pain.

"Jean," she called out.

Without transport or a local clinic, the birthplace of her child became a tiny box room on Lindisfarne. As Jean led her upstairs, the TV announcers voice interrupted her train of thought.

"Hamilton Academicals one, Hearts Nil.

Cowdenbeath two, Kilmarnock five"

The midwife would be thirty minutes, the doctor was on his way; announced Jean Moriarty from behind a pile of towels and a washing bowel.

"Just try to breath steadily and keep on pushing," she advised. Tears were running freely down Peggy's face. And each wave of pain, filled her with a burning terror.

"Wolverhampton Wanderers nil, Leeds United nil."

The sensation of another life moving out of her body; felt strange and otherworldly. The doctor's stethoscope felt cold against her naked belly.

"Your child has a strong heart," he said, before

moving round to face her. His less than gentle hands prized her legs further open.

"Keep on pushing girl, I can see the head."

Her hand moved out, hoping someone would take it. But Jean Moriarty had retreated when the doctor arrived and there was no sign of a midwife.

" Keep on pushing, I'll be back in a minute," he repeated, before leaving her room. Outside the murmur of voices was interrupted by the sports announcers voice.

"Newcastle United Two, Arsenal Nil."

A loud cheer from downstairs was joined by the doctors crying: "Jean come quick." It drowned out her screams, and the sound of a baby being born. Peggy would remember little of what followed. A blur of hands and the cries of a baby. Blood seeping from her torn vagina, a sensation of emptiness.

"I want to sleep for a hundred years," spilled out of her along with the afterbirth. The doctor passing her child to Jean Moriarty; the touch of a hand against hers, unidentified but reassuring.

Finally, she held a wriggling figure in her arms, and purred in his ear. Closed eyes opened and connected with hers. His skin still red and swollen had a slippery quality - a merman with beautiful eyes.

NOLLAIG NA MBAN

The song of Wandering Aengus accompanied him on the
train into Willington. It's mellow rhythm contrasting with
the vehicles stop-start motion. It's setting, a thousand miles
from this Northern industrial town. Snow was the theme of
his Christmas, snow and a relentless changing landscape.
From Dun Laoghaire, were he joined men, steadying
themselves for the journey with alcohol. To Holyhead, where
some careered down the gangplank, tragically drunk, unable
to forget the awful loneliness of leaving home.

Through hollow lands and hilly lands, went the poem.
But all he could see was a flat expanse of white, shot through
with smoke stacks belching out grey pollution. England
reeled before him like an ancient tobacco fiend, bent double
with emphysema. And he travelled incognito, as plain old
Jim Flannery, his dog collar rattling around in a borrowed
cardboard suitcase.

The big freeze had taken the sensation from his
extremities, replacing fingers and toes with blocks of ice.
Twenty foot drifts and temperatures twenty degrees below
crossed the Irish Sea with him, covering cars and telephone
poles in its wake. But it was the cold and not the snow that

felt unusual. The freezing air cutting through his Ulster coat as if it was made from Chinese silk. Wrapping itself round his legs and privates, his torso and arms. He imagined his intestines, frozen like the pipes of Limerick; storing up the meagre sandwich that was supposed to sustain him.

Frozen upturned cattle legs, protruded from virgin fields; people huddled round braziers, running gloveless hands above the flames. Boys in short trousers, their knees red raw, waiting at stations for a train. A relentless shunt of the steam trains engine; railwaymen melting iced machinery with blowtorches. The petrol flame of his lighter flickering in a darkened carriage. Hot cigarette smoke infusing his lungs.

Christy, one of his drunken shipmates had said entering England was like passing through the gates of hell. Their destination in his words:

"A godless place, where no one, except for a few solitary parishes, celebrated the Epiphany. Just like no one celebrated Nollaig na mBan outside Cork."

And with that thought, the great brute of a man had grown misty eyed, pondering the women in their shawls, sipping porter in snugs all over town. Eating corned beef sandwiches, while their men folk, floundered about in abandoned kitchens. Nollaig na mBan or Women's Christmas where men did housework and women were allowed to act like men was happening while they sat on the twelve thirty mail boat to Holyhead.

"Of course, through hells gate, the sight of women

193

downing beer is a daily occurrence, but in the land of Harold Macmillan it's just a bad habit, without significance or ceremony."

The man drew him close, like a father would a son. Embracing him with a beery intimacy:

"I've developed quite a taste for all the bad things she has to offer. Mother London is a bitch. There's things I could tell yer, that will never pass through a confessional grill. Put hairs on the chest of a young lad like you."

A moment longer and he would be part of some exquisite secret. A voyeur at the big fellahs orgy of depravity. Already he was steadying himself for the shock; trying not to recoil from the man's foul breath. An image of the big man stripped naked, his great hairy thighs pounding against soft flesh. A dribble of saliva, and a fist connecting with tissue and bone. Pummelled senseless by the buckle of a leather belt. An opening and closing of a cameras aperture, the flash of a flash-bulb. The man's lumbering gait, staggering; framed in his mind.

The anticipation caused his heart to race, and he hoped Christy couldn't sense this. But still there was that urge to jump, like a man standing at a cliffs edge. It welled up inside him, building and building, anticipating the great wave massing a mile away. Everyone could feel its energy, feeding on everything that got in its way. God help us, thought Jim Flannery; god help me. Is this his punishment, his retribution? Sex may be natural, but not the sex he craved.

Time froze, a pause before the wave hit MV Cambria, causing her to lurch violently left. He caught a puzzled look in the big mans eyes, and then he along with everyone else shifted violently with the ship. People were thrown about its insides; drinks passed out of stomachs and joined the swill below deck. Projectile vomit landed on backs and shoulders. It clung to people's hair like brylcream. Glass littered, cutting on contact, those who crossed its path. A group of pilgrims sang:

Ave, Maris Stella.
Hail, star of the sea.

God help us had been his brief prayer, before the ships motion had him in a stranger's arms. And afterwards, when jackets were dusted down, and flecks of vomit brushed from shoulders, a creeping silence spread about the ship. The man selling rosary beads and holy trinkets moved among passengers who were suddenly interested in his wares. Spontaneous acts of worship followed a tannoy announcement that the stabilizers were coming up. A pair of first class stewards knelt and prayed in their white jackets and shiny black bow ties. Drunks, miraculously sober, sought out members of the clergy to make a final act of contrition. Jim Flannery, a priest on the way to his parish, resisted the temptation to reveal his vocation. He prayed silently; just another anonymous sinner.

In the end, the angry sea abated and Jim Flannery was not required to atone for his sins. Drunken tears broke out at Holyhead, and men like Christy held on to each other for dear life. From the deck looking across Anglesey to Snowdonia all he could see was a beautiful covering of snow. And the cadence of WB Yeats burned brighter in his mind than any cigarette smoked or candle burned. It became his companion for the remainder of his journey, shivering next to him on that British Rail Sleeper. Whispering as sleep dragged him close; dragged him down to Summerhill.

Big John McCormack I wish you well, Father Edward J Flanagan I wish you well, came the shout of fifty boy's voices as they entered Summerhill College. Officially the College of the Immaculate Conception, it's grey stone set against blue skies, it's windows tall and Georgian. Boarders with short cropped hair, smelling of carbolic soap. They are naked together, skinny, lily white frames, knock kneed, limbs chattering with the cold. And then come the abrasive towels, a minute a piece and a second inspection for head lice. Later in the evening, boys masturbate, their muffled orgasms pour out below coarse woollen sheets. Father Garvey sleeps near by, in cotton and eiderdowns; soft like a mammy's breast.

It's Father Garvey who has him by the ear, taking him for a cold shower at two in the morning. *Giving his vocation a kick up the arse.* In the cold bathroom his penis feels like it will fall off, a shrivelled acorn, shrunk into retracted testicles.

"God's punishment will be far worse than this, "says the Priest as he batters his thighs with a thin wooden bat. In between showers and beatings, Father Garvey recited the Song of Wandering Aengus. His beautiful speaking voice, echoing about the bathrooms. Summerhill College, an echo from the past faded as a railway man rapped hard on his sleeping berth. They were in Newcastle Central Station, and the temperature was four below zero.

On the morning train into Willington, a boy's transistor diffused music about the carriage, the incessant drum of British Beat music. He looked no different from Irish youths of his age. The same pimples, the same neatly cut hair. A thick Arran sweater and duffel coat combination. A nice clean boy. Posters on hoardings advertise familiar products. DAZ, OMO and McLean's. A good-looking man smokes a cigarette, his head held back in ecstasy. *God had granted him another shake of the dice. God had made it all available to him.* He rummages inside his empty suitcase and takes out the dog collar. *Time to put away such thoughts for the time being; they'll be plenty of opportunities when the thaw sets in.*

Tunnels thick with black smoke, shabby worn out livery from the Great Northern Railways. Jet age Britain, with it's That Was the Week That Was. With David Frost and James Bond, nowhere to be seen. On his train into

Willington Father Jim Flannery caught a glimpse of row upon row of terraced soot stained housing, stretching down to the waters edge. Cranes and the stern of a ship looming over the landscape like steel stegosauruses. A tidal wave of men moved through the snow filled streets, down towards the water. Striding, impervious to the cold. They laugh and smoke, carry tool bags by their sides and haversacks on their back. He felt like calling to these happy men, maybe one would throw him a crumb of their happiness, and warm him up properly. But the train was slowing and he there was that stiff lock to negotiate. Extinguish cigarette, put on hat, pull-up suitcase, fit dog collar and make for the door.

The station master had retreated to the comfort of his office, where a coal fire burned. He left the trailing note of his shrill whistle, and Jim Flannery alone, shivering. His clothing inadequate for the ice wind blowing in from the coast.

By the sixties, in Britain, a modern style of housing was established. Flat roofs were often used, although the main roof was more likely to be pitched. Garages, porches and dormer windows all had flat roofs covered with asphalt. Sixties semis were often bigger than those from preceding decades. They occupied more land. They were generous in size. A large drive, as well as a garage and a large garden came as standard. The through dining room/lounge became the norm; doing away with a separate dining room and lounge.

An estate built by the house builder Wimpey advertised the following features:

- Thermoplastic tiles to ground floor
- Fibreglass insulation to roof space and all pipes lagged
- Copper plumbing throughout
- Fireplace with back-boiler providing domestic hot water will be fitted, together with provision for gas ignition to grate

- Fire surround (choice of five types)
- Immersion heater, complete with cylinder jacket, and indicator switch in the kitchen
- Power points to all rooms, except bathroom and toilet
- 800W 'Dimplex' heater or similar to dining room
- Curtain rail battens will be provided to windows in all rooms, except kitchen, bathroom and WC
- Bathroom with 5'6" x 2'0" bath, together with wash-hand basin and low level toilet suite (white)
- White glazed tiling to bathroom and kitchen
- Kitchen with single drainer
- 'Supataps' to kitchen and bathroom
- Cooker control panel
- Gas points
- Plastic decorative finish to ceilings
- TV point in lounge

WILLINGTON

The slow fall of a branch, followed by another, then another.
Branches of great ferns, falling into mountainous piles.
Trunks the width of roads, cracking down the middle; jagged
stumps protruding to crimson skies. Like broken ramparts of
a once grand castle, they stand damaged and exposed.
Searing, bubbling, damp heat; infused with insects and
decomposition. Ten thousand or more years pass in the blink
of an eye. The giant ferns are no more. Instead below ground
there are thick black seams of coal; a hundred feet down.
Pockets of gas, trapped for an eternity – wait to be disturbed.

Through layers of coal and dark damp clay, is fresh
virgin soil. And lush green turf laid by McMenemy and Co.
Steel capped toes walk this way and that; they carry planks of
wood, ten feet long. They lay down masonry, drains and
paving slabs. Across the area which had once been pasture,
houses emerge.

On the edge of this place; commonly called High
Farm McMenemy has erected a large wooden billboard.
Designed by a firm of hot-shots. Ideas men, who think in
bold primary colours. A smiling young couple, with two
similar smiling children; jump out on unsuspecting passers-
by. Behind them the copy boys have imagined a completed

house, with a sold sign marking the end of its generous driveway. An impeccably waxed car stands on the gravel. Flowers already bloom in ordered beds. And if you were to look closely, the woman has a slightly rounded stomach that suggests the beginnings of a new baby. New home, new car, new child; a new life.

The price for a two-bedroom maisonette or three-bed semi is affordable. All for just ten percent down and a mortgage arranged by the builder. Half of these half built homes are already allocated to one buyer: The Corporation's Housing Department. Carefully separating these identical houses is Queens Drive; a generously curved road, cutting through private and council occupied bricks. A bus route runs through the estate. New shelters stand empty. New street lights illuminate new pedestrian crossings. Traffic lights blink off and on; filtering cement trucks and wagons. At night the streets of half built houses are still.

At night, wild animals chased by bulldozers scuttle back to their former homes. They hunt for food amongst the cement dust and asbestos. Small rodents find scraps discarded by men. But most leave starving and very disorientated. An ecosystem away from home.

A night watchman sits by a burning oil drum. Sides punched with holes. It's winter, one of the coldest on record. His breath freezes on contact with air. A balaclava covers his face. Thick woollen gloves afford him some protection against the ice-wind. He guards the entrance to High Farm

Estate; keeps watch on the bricks and wood that lay about the site. He goes by the name of Geordie, a common name in the area. A name that describes a population as it spreads north to Northumberland and west to Newcastle. An accent, a dialect. A way of meeting the cold north wind; with a pinched face and a quick determined drag on a smouldering cigarette. *Tab* as Geordie put it.

At midnight, round midnight, there's no room for toothpaste smiles and shiny bright tail finned cars parked on pristine driveways. No indoor lavs, no electric ovens with built in rotisseries. At midnight ghosts emerge from the shadows. Blinking, covered in coal dust. From head to toe, from eye to alveoli; with bent knees and worn elbows. They cough out the coal from their lungs. A hundred yards into their walk, bodies slowly adjust to standing erect. Some remove helmets and extinguish their Davey Lamps. Some wipe thick black from sweating foreheads. The temperature is well below freezing, it's winter, but they are hot from work.

The old A pit, pumping out coal well into the night, comes alive again as the man looks into the flames. Its Eighteen Thirty something. A hallucination of wagon ways take coal to riverside staiths. Wooden tracks with a gauge that fixed a hundred thousand railways around the world. The wagons travel; self propelled, following the lands slope. Men pour coal into great barges bound for Rotterdam and Southampton. Men sing and shout; they break down, crying with tiredness. Exhausted. Black as the ace of spades. Broken and bent double in a hospital bed. Breathing in oxygen from a mask; feeding lungs damaged beyond repair. Dead at forty-six.

Geordie looked away from the flame and into the empty night of High Farm. His eyes required correction, but he had no time for glasses. He misses the girl walking brazenly into number 15 Rothbury Way. And when morning comes; the show house, with its electric oven, appears undisturbed. Microscopic traces of semen on the nylon sheets are hidden by a plump quilt. Missing toilet paper goes unnoticed. A light left on in the back bedroom is switched off. A dripping tap is secured. Small drops of moisture inside the cupboard holding crockery and glass; droplets of water in upturned whisky tumblers, are all overlooked.

There's no sign of infidelity at 15 Rothbury Way. No sign of human interaction. Couples lingering over mod-cons are looking for clues to their future happiness. They test the electric shower and run fingers, festooned with engagement rings, over white storage heaters. Engaging with the house and its contents, like they would a lover. Men work outside. Completing the half built houses adjoining number 15 Rothbury Way. They carry hods, laden with red bricks. They work cement mixers and theodolites. They lay plumb lines to mark an outside wall. They whistle to give their works rhythm a melody. The smell of Judith Pemberton's cigarette, smoked after sex, has dissipated. There's no trace of the satisfaction it followed. No trace of her warm body filling the show-house bed. Stockings draped over the wooden arm of a chair. Clothes fastidiously folded.

Softly as I leave you, sang McMenemy as he left. Before dawn broke over High Farm Estate. He crooned like Matt Monro; the singing Shoreditch bus driver. And Judy, she was already gone. Making her way down the old wagon way towards Willington. And Geordie, he had entered that blissful state, just as dawn broke.

KEEP YOUR HEAD DOWN

Keep your head down, down, keep it down, said the voice in his head. A voice that sounded like old Willy, the trainer. A beaten up old voice, with fight, but no stamina. And like old Willy, his legs were buckling, so he let gravity do the rest, and hit the deck. He joined what remained of his Brigade, their faces pushed into wet sand, sucking in air through seaweed. All rumpled with sweat stained fatigues.

Some had fled half dressed, their uniforms mixed with civilian clothes, taken from washing lines and dark oak wardrobes. An astrakhan coat with army boots. A woman's coat stretched across broad shoulders, and pink scarf's covering dirty unshaven faces. If they looked ridiculous, no one laughed. Instead the formalities of rank were observed, and men saluted officers dressed up like pantomime dames. If anyone did laugh, or smile, it was because their dead faces were twisted in a rictus of phoney mirth. One of these clowns lay next to him: a blood soaked fat man, in a white and blue butchers apron. Some of the offal seeping through to the tunic below, may have been destined for the mess tent, but most was the corpses own, leeching out of a great gash in the poor man's side.

For a moment, when he rolled over, and into the dune; he'd taken the smile for a sign of life.

"A pound of your best ....," he started to say. But a cluster of flies, bathing in the poor sods eye socket's, put an end to that illusion. So here he was, keeping his head down, moving his short squat body from left to right. Ducking, weaving, avoiding the bullets. And he knew that if one had his name on it; no amount of moving about would save him. Because the small hard metal thing, moved so fast, it was not going to wait for anything. And he recalled a show at the Theatre Royal, where a man, dressed as Zorro, caught a bullet in his mouth. The showman bowed with great ceremony, throwing a wide brimmed black hat to the shooter. He'd believed it was real, until dad laughed; and he could see it was just another Pantomime.

Now his mind was stuck, fixed at a time before basic training, when he was the little battler, who'd never lost a bout. The short squat, bull of a boy, who knew no fear. Then he'd played on beaches like this, fashioning castles from wet sand. Now the same stuff filled his boots, and was moving its way through his clothes and underclothes. Like all soldiers he'd heard the stories of angel lust, where dead men developed stonkers, and bored desensitized soldiers placed bets on the size of a dead enemy's erection. Stories.

Fifteen-year-old Euan Spencer had been full of stories; ones which started with "I was..." and ended with "then he". They were always about boxing matches, which had happened a year before he'd come on the scene. Where the loser always thanked Spencer for his beating. He'd been way too light for an official fight with the older middleweight, but he knew how to pick a fight. Push the bigger boy to the top of crow bank: where lovers gathered at night, and children fought during the day.

Spencer's short fuse would have gotten him killed on the spot. No amount of muscle was going to stop a bullet. You could roar as much as you liked; use all the words that would make God blush. Look fierce and bare your teeth, just like Euan Spencer liked to do. But a couple of dunes away, was a man with a machine gun, who would cut you in half, with casual detachment.

On the day of the fight, after he had insulted the elasticity of Spencer's sister's knickers. All he had to do was nod when Spencer said "Crow Bank," everything else; including his bloody nose, was a certainty. On a day very much like the cold damp wet of the sand dunes, he'd met Euan Spencer. Five other boys, dressed in their older brother's hand-me-downs, climbed the steep slope of crow bank; and a newsreel ran, simultaneously, through each of their small unclean heads:

He lying, prone, with a busted lip, full of blood. A wide blue/black shiner forming nicely under his left eye. And Spencer taking him by the hand, raising him gently from the small gravel circle. The caption reads *"No hard feelings."*

Overhead seagulls circle; and above the cloud, planes circle. Like the birds below they watch small figures, crawling through the sand. Below the clouds, smoke rises from burning vehicles and people. A thick smell of kerosene mingles with cordite; and the damp smell of sand, soiled with human waste. And the fat man continues to smile, open-mouthed. Offering himself as an incubator, for the larva of flies. Somewhere close a man weeps; great heavy sobs of a strong, powerful man, reduced and humiliated. Like the sound of a defeated Euan Spencer on the small gravel path of Crow bank.

He looks down and around, as the other boys look on dumfounded. He remembers the shaking of hands. Euan squeezed, trying to crush every digit, but all that happened was a crack. So he puffed out his chest and strutted, like a bantam cock. Some of the boys sniggered, and a fierce middle weight crumbled, like an out manoeuvred army. He surprised him with a rabbit punch that knocked Spencer off kilter. The bigger boy then rallied with a sweeping right, that missed, and set him spiralling off balance. All that was left to do, was take him down: with a foot, and another punch, left side, just below the head. It was easy, the great Euan Spencer, was crawling through the gravel of Crow Bank.

But he knew this was not the end. The boys expected closing titles for this newsreel. So like one hundred other saps, he took Spencer's hand, and pulled.

He found himself rehearsing Spencer's tired old line, for the first man in a grey uniform to cross into his dune. Sometimes the man would be no more than a boy, with straw blond hair and a plump face; who stared in disbelief as the bayonet penetrated his insides. He would cry like Euan Spencer, then crumble with the same astounded look. But most of the time he imagined battle weary regulars; and it would be he whose eyes widened, while they moved relentlessly forward.

Outside, over the roll of the dunes, the man's sobs subsided. But the fat man's smile remained fixed, a reminder that for most, the choice was to die slowly or explode in a flash. To be the opposing end of a machine gun, spitting bullets and flame, in a rat-a-tat-tat rhythm. There was the cry when bullets connected with flesh, but mostly there was silence, and the sound of seabirds, cutting above the crossfire and exploding shells. And when one of the shells exploded a great volcano of sand would rise into the air, accompanied by small dark fragments. He like to think of these things as driftwood and seaweed, not pieces of a person ascending to the skies.

And he gave no though to the passage of time: measured by the tide rising, and encroaching darkness. If he thought about anything, it was about the time before basic training, when he was a boy. When time passed slowly, stretching out over summers in fields, where hay was gathered as circular wheels, and nothing else mattered, except for a Saturday afternoon at the Boys Club, boxing. Where he moved round a heavy leather punch bag, with knuckles bound in white cotton, like the boy king

Tutankhamen.

And he tried to resist the refrain of old Willy, "keep your head down boy, keep your head down". But the voice grew insistent, until he could feel the hot breath of its owner's voice against his ear. When a hand grabbed his tunic and pulled him down, he saw the voice belonged to a skinny man, with a medical orderly's cap.

"Don't be a bloody fool, what you trying to do. Commit suicide! . Keep your head down, do you hear me, keep your head down."

SATURDAY CLUB PLAYLIST

SATURDAY CLUB INTRO

EDDIE COCHRANE – C'MON EVERYBODY

KENNY BALL

PADDY LIGHTFOOT

JOE BROWN AND BRUVVERS – ROCK 'N' ROLL

JOE BROWN AND BRUVVERS – SPANISH GYPSY DANCE

BRIAN POOLE AND TREMELOES – DO YOU LOVE ME

TOMMY ROE

KATHY KIRBY – BIG MAN

KATHY KIRBY – STAY RIGHT HERE

EVERLY BROTHERS – WAKE UP LITTLE SUSIE

EVERLY BROTHERS – YOU GOT ME RUNNING

ROY ORBISON – INTERVIEW

ROY ORBISON – ONLY THE LONELY

KATHY KIRBY

TOMMY ROE – EVERYBODY

TOMMY ROE – INTERVIEW

TOMMY ROE – FOLK SINGER

ANDY WILLIAMS – THIS IS THE MOMENT

EVERLY BROTHERS – INTERVIEW

EVERLY BROTHERS – WALK RIGHT BACK

EVERLY BROTHERS – ALL I HAVE TO DO IS DREAM

FRANK IFIELD – WOLVERTON MOUNTAIN

BEATLES – I'LL GET YOU

BEATLES – SHE LOVES YOU

BRENDA LEE – MESSAGE

BRENDA LEE – DUM DUM DIDDY DUM

KENNY BALL – 1919 MARCH

TOMMY ROE – SHELIA

JOE BROWN AND BRUVVERS – PICTURE OF YOU

CLINTON FORD – FINNEGAN'S BALL

KATHY KIRBY – GOT A LOT OF LIVING TO DO

FRANK IFIELD – I REMEMBER YOU

EVERLY BROTHERS – BYE BYE LOVE

BEATLES – LUCILLE

CLIFF RICHARD – TELEPHONE INTERVIEW

THE END

CLUB A'GOGO

Cathy took Mairi's hand:

> "Don't be nervous Mairi, nothing bads going to
> happen to you. All the bad stuff happens in the Jazz
> Lounge, and you're going to the Young Set. Its going
> to be lemonade shandy's for you girl and nothing
> more."

Mairi sniggered. They'd shared coffees laced with
whisky in the Arimba. Enough to diffuse an alcoholic heat
throughout her body.

> "We are all successes in the beginning. Then as we
> age we become failures. Flotsam floating on the Tyne.
> Swimming frantically for a shore that's always just
> out of reach."

Tumbled out of her mouth after the tenth cup of
coffee.

> "I think we'd better go Mairi. Tommy on the door lets
> all types of girls in the A'GoGo. But he's not too keen
> on the drunk variety. Pace yourself. The night is
> young." A sober Cathy said.

Now here they were outside the club. Music filtered
through the buildings walls. Its bricks sweating out the
sound of guitars, singers and cymbals. Its tall red bricks

inhaling and exhaling. Directly ahead lay a small entrance corridor and staircase leading into darkness. A tall man's frame filled the doorway. He was deep in serious conversation with a group of lads. One of their number, swayed badly. She could see a couple of his friends were trying their best to steady him. The tall man was having none of this deception. His finger zeroed in on the drunk boy: pointing, jabbing and probing. Eventually the boys left without an argument, and the queue moved forward a step.

When the line was two people deep she could see further up the stair. The entrance of what looked like a busman's café jutted out from a small landing halfway up. Men in peaked caps and blue uniforms entered and left. They shared the stairway with kids and young adults, heading skyward to the Club A'GoGo.

"The busmen were here first, so nobody can shift em. And I don't think they want to move, with the just station over there."
Said Cathy pointing in the direction of the Haymarket Stations shelters.
"And every night the conductor of the 276 along with his driver and a hundred others gets to watch a parade of lovelies. All for the price of a mug of tea and wilting stotty."
Cathy moved her description up another flight:
"A bit further up and you come to a second landing. On the right is the Young Set, to the left is the Jazz

215

Lounge. Groups have to lug their equipment between both as they generally play a set in each room. The early set is us, and the late one is for the older crowd. "

"So how do they know we're not old enough?"
"They don't Mairi. But they do. Must be something that happens to men when they grow-up."
"Maybe they can smell you; maybe the older kids smell differently."
"Don't be horrible Mairi, I think we'd notice a different smell."
"Not if it's like a dog whistle. Invisible to a younger person's nose. Some primitive cave dweller thing."
Mairi felt pleased with her idea. The shame was that Cathy didn't pick up on her cave dwellers joke. Maybe she's not read Merseybeat thought Mairi. Maybe she prefers the Junco's or the Animals, groups without a record. Cathy her new friend from work, someone born outside of Willington, who lived in the wider world.

They inched a little forward. The man on the door stared quizzically into her face.

"I think we have a new girl here," he said after what felt like an age.
"It's her first time Tommy, go easy on her, she's led a sheltered life."
The bouncer laughed.
"Go on through, but keep her away from the Jazz

Lounge. I don't want..."

The ceiling of the Young Set room felt impossibly high. Its dimensions were that of a warehouse. A room designed for storage, not living. A perfect room for a club. At the far end is a small stage; barely a platform it rose a foot or so above the dance floor. And there was no showbiz mystique going on in the Club A'GoGo, punters mixed with musicians, everyone was one.

Right at the centre of the dance floor a pair of identical twin mod girls performed a hand-jive. Dancers fanned out around them. Groups stood against walls, smoking. She breathed in and felt the room spin. Then she, along with Cathy were spinning across the floor. Some American sounding group was singing a super fast version of Come On. She liked it so much she would have listened to it backwards.

A boy, another boy, a pair of boys all made attempts to muscle in. But it was Cathy who gave her permission to let go. Her friend disappeared quite quickly with a boy who looked more like a man than anyone else in the Young Set. So she too exchanged one partner for another when the fancy took her. She rode through a sea of hands and sweaty bodies.

"It's more casual in the Young Set. Jeans and jumpers. The Jazz Lounge is another matter. Bum freezer jackets and fashions from Italy. People who can afford to shop in Marcus Price, that's the type you get in there," said Cathy, making the Jazz Lounge sound like just the place Mairi wanted to be.

"In the Jazz Lounge they have a fluorescent mural of the New York Skyline. How about that." Cathy of course had been inside the Jazz Lounge many times, although if pressed she would always say: *a couple of times.* It sounded less boastful. And she knew the security in and out. The adult's only room marked each of its members with a fluorescent pen; that way they could easily be identified when returning. One way round this was to bump a hand that had been recently marked, scarping some of the fluorescence onto your hand.

"Promise you won't try that today Mairi, Tommy would kill me if he found out. Or worse he'd ban me for life."

Mairi agreed, although she had no intention of keeping any promises once midnight was gone.

The DJ spun another number; the Juncos were on next he'd said. Already the dance floor was reconfiguring, turning to face the stage. She too stopped dancing, but instead of facing the stage Mairi turned her attention to the hands of those now joining the dance floor. The older types who'd come to check out the Juncos, their hands a glowing in the dark. The possibility of bumping one of those hands and getting a glow herself was remote, but that hardly mattered, she gave it a go.

Her hands brushed against some unsuspecting glowers. The Young Set was heaving with a crowd for the band. She walked from one end of the room to the other. Carefully trailing her right arm. Twitching it outwards at the point of bumping. She dared not look down at her hand when she was done, but she did and it was now glowing, slightly. Already a story was brewing; she'd accidentally washed her right hand, forgetting about the marker.

But look, there's still some of it left. A simple enough tale of female stupidity. It would satisfy just about any cave doorman in any part of the world. Not that she'd seen much of the world; except for glimpses of France caught on the way to Lourdes. And nothing of Frenchmen appeared to be no different from Englishmen, Irishmen or Scotsmen. Only superficial stuff like clothes, smell and language was different. Mairi felt confident her ruse would work, but was still amazed when it actually did.

The Jazz Lounge was not so tightly packed. But it was early, and some of its crowd had transferred themselves next door. Stretching across its black walls were glowing skyscrapers. There were more tables and a smattering of sharply dressed Mods. She now had a second hurdle to negotiate. She had to order a drink confidently and without hesitation. Because of this her first drink was a coke with ice and no lemon. Nobody would pay attention to a sweet soft drinker she supposed.

There was less leaning against the walls in the Jazz

Lounge, so she sat at a table and took a sip of her drink. She was quickly joined by two men, who persuaded her to add some rum to her drink. Despite its name, the Jazz Lounge played very little Jazz. The name being a hangover from the Trad boom, which was now dead as a dodo. The owners of the venue had shifted their interests to blues and rhythm and blues. They played soul too, and Mersey. And she half expected to see Cathy explaining this subtle change to some sad sack, but her friend was nowhere to be seen.

Two men introduced themselves to her, but she couldn't for the life of her remember their names. She fluttered her eyelashes, cooed in all the right places, and that worked. She danced with Stan and Olly, as she'd decided to name them. One dance per man. That way she only had half the time with the boring one, Olly. Stan was funny and kept her supplied with cigarettes. He wasn't exactly clearing a path to her heart, but he was pleasant company.

Midway between a switch with Stan and Olly she noticed a group of people from Willington enter the room. She recognised one of their number from Mass - McMenemy, the local hotshot. The other men she'd seen about and in the paper. Behind the men was their entourage. Two older and one young woman. The youngster looked a lot like Judy. That was her thought before she realised the girl was actually Judy. And then Mairi was gone, before anyone in the Willington crowd noticed her.

KIND OF BLUE

London appeared on the horizon; a daguerreotype, tinted blue. Tips of spires and domes stood alongside tall square monoliths, out of focus and distant, they appeared to him as a man-made mirage. The languid opening of Miles Davis's Kind of Blue stretched out along the Great North Road. Buses, lorries and cars; motorbikes buzzing past. A cornucopia of shapes and hues. Slick and streamline Ford tail fins; squat and functional Land Rovers. Metal vibrating at speed, steam rising from radiators. Overheating engines pushing on into town. Hot air rushing in through open windows, filling the bus with fumes, and the houses of suburbia stretching-out to meet the city.

Keith Henderson was neither happy nor sad; rather he occupied a neutral ground – where light and shade are indistinguishable. *So what*, the music of the wheels and engine was telling him. So there were two hundred and fifty miles between him and Willington. So why couldn't he just mourn Geordie and let the man rest in peace. Let the flesh fall from those twisted bones, until they were white and pristine.

So what if London was going to swallow him whole, spit out his cheap suit and Brylcream with distaste; leave him alone and naked. People: jabbered and smoked; they stared out the window with eyes made docile by fatigue. They ignored his hunched figure squashed in at the back of the bus. In London he could hide; disappear on day long trips.

"Golders Green next stop," shouted the driver.

London was opening wide now, small milk teeth sprouting in the form of endless shops and restaurants. Roads felt wider; houses - bigger; pavements – crowded and dense. Tall mansion bocks on the Wellington Road, became Lords Cricket Ground, became Baker Street – home to Sherlock Holmes. People ohh'd and ahh'd as they drove down Park Lane.

"Look the Dorchester," someone said.

The moment passes; people sit silently as they negotiate the road round Hyde Park Corner, then on to Victoria. But the sound of those ohh's and ahh's play through his mind as he watches the faces of those on the outside, oblivious to the watcher inside.

Throat dry from smoking too much on the Journey; suit crumpled and lived-in. Let loose on a London pavement. Following the rest of St Vincent's as they blindly follow their uncertain Priest. Down at ground level with the tramps; cigarette butts and fish and chip papers. Bright neon signs outside cheap plastic café's. A beggar holds out a white enamel cup, while his mouth blows tunelessly on a harmonica.

"Someone give Larry Adler a penny, "she said absentmindedly to the stranger next to her. A tall sleepy-eyed man. Peggy had hardly been serious, but the stranger thought differently. There was a ping as coins entered the cup and just enough time for her to glimpse the tramp thanking his benefactor.

She felt embarrassed and a little ashamed that her sarcasm had precipitated some genuine generosity. So she let the stranger stride out ahead. His black mop of hair weaved in and out, between the St Vincent's party, until he reached the side of Father Flannery. Later she discovered his name, Keith Henderson. He came with the sad story of a shipyard accident. But she'd spotted something else; the simple kindness he'd shown to the beggar. That's what stayed with her for the remainder of their journey to Camden Town. Fate or just plain coincidence had him choose the room next to hers. Bodies separated by paper thin walls, two to a room, in a grimy hotel at Mornington Crescent.

Peggy chose to stay in her room and read, rather than sample the delights of North London. Before sleep took her, she thought once again of the Dark Haired man. Low male voices murmured through the hotels thin walls. Then came a knock on the room next door and a commotion in the corridor. The sound of heavy plodding feet slowly diminished, until she was left with silence and her book.

She slept for three hours or so, until the person in the next room decided to crash their body against the adjoining wall. As the vibrations moved through her headboard, pillow and head; she cursed the hoodlum, before rolling back into the land of nod. Somewhere between midnight and morning this first incursion of Keith Henderson's was forgotten. She woke to a greasy London sky, with her head filled with the simple thoughts of a tourist. A jumbled-up scrapbook of images from Picture Post and Television. There were no pavement café's like Paris, but there was the Lyons Corner House in Piccadilly; the shop windows of Oxford Street, and a plethora of other sights.

Peggy chose everything carefully. From her clothing, down to the day-trips she booked. Take the holy sights of London; she preferred to think of Denmark Street and the 2i's Coffee Bar; the London Palladium and Harrods as shrines to visit. But there was no time allotted for such frivolous trips in the five-day schedule. So her choice that morning was either a cricket match or a mix of churches and monuments.

She parted the curtains of the Mornington Hotel. Outside an assortment of cars and commercial lorries trudged by. Her roommate was already down at breakfast. Mairi was the type of girl with flair. She had drive and flamenco sketches on her wall. She could tell.

In the morning light London appeared shabbier; soot stained and a little careworn. The plasterwork was crumbling on some of the tall Victorian houses nearby, and railings, once shiny and new, were rusting at the tips. Decay was the first word to enter her mind. The second was noise – a relentless incursion, seeping out of houses and shops; trundling along the Hampstead Road. Roaring-up Camden High Street.

His first proper look at Peggy was through slit eyes; further irritated by the noxious grease rising from a plate of sausage, beans and egg. Anaemic toast sat between them, and a cuckoo clock chimed the hour. Dilapidated tableware and horse-brasses compete with threadbare furnishings for the diner's distain. While a surly waitress, barely out of school, threw plates down. She challenged those who dared to engage her, with a stone-cold stare.

"Cheer up love," Keith said. But the waitresses face remained Easter Island still. Peggy laughed, once the girl was out of earshot.

"I don't think you've made a friend there," she said in a mock stage whisper.

"You're probably right; but I expect they pay her washers…and feed her our leftovers. I'd say the girl is starving by the day's end."

And there was no hint of humour in his voice, just sympathy for the bedraggled girl and her awful job. Just like the ping of coins in that enamel cup, he'd set her off thinking again. The easiest thing to do in his situation would have been to complain, without thinking. But instead he'd tried to inject some humour into the poor waitress's day. And when she'd reacted with stony silence, he'd felt even more sympathy for her.

225

For a moment she had a window into the waitress's life. Aggressive guests at the Mornington Hotel, complaining about the food. Cheap commercial travellers with wandering hands. New faces, week in, week out; challenging her to give-up the job she so obviously needed. A lacklustre pay-packet, with tips deducted by the owner. Scraping off the detritus from willow patterned plates. Patting out the rhythm of the day's drudgery.

Her walk from the Tower of London to Tyburn Convent followed in the footsteps of martyrs. But whoever planned their journey had overlooked a pertinent fact: those condemned to death at Tyburn were transported by cart, and not underground. Peggy's first ride on a tube train was a one she hoped not to repeat. The delights of a Routemaster bus was more her style. But what most concerned her was not the dirt or the smoke, it was the way they were crammed-in. The carriage could barely accommodate their party. Many stood, holding on to straps hanging from its ceiling. It seemed crazy to smoke in such a confined space, but nerves had her lighting up. Somehow she managed to find a space to flick her ash and avoid setting light to the person next to her.

The woman opposite kept glancing at the line-map above her head, Tower Hill (Mark Lane), the woman nodded as she counted the four stops. Peggy had managed to avoid eye contact with this nervous stranger; instead she watched the other passengers and inspected the numerous cigarette buts and sweet wrappers littering the train-floor.

What troubled her most was not the prospect of a fire starting between the floors wooden slats. Or a stray cigarette smouldering beneath passenger's feet. And she was unconcerned when the train stopped in a tunnel. Rather it was the occasional arch-light and the screech of train wheels that troubled her. The sound she supposed could be a prelude to death; or worse her shattered body, trapped in a mangled carriage, listening to the calls for help and the moans of others. There was no beauty in this subterranean world. It was a place of horror and death. When she closed her eyes she could see the faces of the dead, crawling out from their spaces behind the tube wall. But when they finally emerged, blinking in the mid-day light, at Mark Lane; everyone just strode out, nonplussed. As if it were natural to travel underground at a ridiculous speed.

Father Flannery led the way, closely followed by a posse of St Vincent De Paul women. At the Tower they met their guide. He reminded her of a cheap Holiday Camp comedian, who hectored rather than entertained. During their slow circulation of the Crown Jewels, she found herself easing to the back of their group; so his voice became a low inaudible burr.

St Olave's Church had survived the Great Fire, by a whisker he said. They were shown the Pepys family vault, under a communion table. Then at St Margaret Patterns they were treated to a long description of St Margaret of Antioch's martyrdom. She, like Rasputin, had resisted death by poisoning and other means, but eventually a Roman Governor tired of the Saints iron-clad constitution and had her beheaded.

The guide quoted TS Elliot as he strode up King William Street, and he stopped briefly at St Paul's Churchyard to describe the death of Father Garnet, a Gunpowder plotter. But the method and circumstance of yet another horror story had Peggy retreating to the railings for a satisfying smoke. She was joined by others, who exchanged furtive smiles as the guides voice droned on.

Then Newgate Street, Ludgate Hill and on to Fleet Street. His commentary switching from Martyrs and Poets, to the Hot Metal of Newspaper production. Fleet Street: the rush of men as they cross the road, telegrams in-hand. Red London buses move slowly. Motorcyclists weave in and out of traffic. The pub they enter is a warren of small wood-lined rooms. Some are occupied by men in heated discussion, with loud beer-soaked voices. Journalists she supposes, concocting stories over a pint of Draft.

Despite his inability to entertain, their guide had cleverly chosen a pub lunch as an antidote to all the sackcloth and gore. In the dark musty rooms of the Ye Old Cheshire Cheese, where men outnumbered women by ten to one, she found herself longing for the company of one particular male. Keith Henderson, the man with those eyes.

228

For Keith the cricket proved to be dull. The sun bored into his head like a Martian death ray. He'd done the Daily Mirror and Daily Worker by the first wicket. Chomped through his sandwich by the second. Nothing was going to alleviate the boredom of the Gentleman versus Players match. After an Italian fruit seller had pursed change from his wallet, he slipped away to somewhere shady and cricket free.

He found a small park at the end of St John's Wood High Street, and a tree to rest underneath. Starched uniformed Nannies, pushed babies in large perambulators; while older children, swung, slid and chased. Young tinny voices whooped with joy, and dappled sunlight filtered through wide spreading leaf-cover. He took-in the gentle atmosphere of his surroundings, and allowed it to soothe his sun-burned head. On a sunny day such as this, scenes were being played out in thousands of parks across the country. The only difference was the people. Young and old, without exception, reeked of privilege; of comfortable lives, lived without pain.

Tiny feet, well shod, scampered about. Small dogs, groomed and clean, walked obediently. He could see these young children growing into adults, unencumbered by the trials of an ordinary life. Money might as well grow on trees as far as these people were concerned. And with the mundane necessity of earning a crust removed, they could be free to do as they wished. Freed of indentured slavery and the incredibly dull existence lived elsewhere.

Be careful what you wish for Geordie had said. But Keith Henderson found himself wishing he'd be reborn as one of those St John's Wood children. To leave every single shred of his life behind. When he left the park, dusk had put a chill in the air. The sound of cheers drifted over the tall walls of Lords Cricket Ground. Somehow the world outside had changed, gently shifted on its axis.

Keith Henderson satisfied her requirements in size, temperament and occupation. Apparently he was handy with his fists, and he had swagger. But there was also something imperceptible that made him stand out; like a jigsaw piece in the wrong puzzle. She couldn't picture him in a Willington High Street bar or running up that shipyard slope. But she could see him behind a desk, or stalking office corridors – slide-rule in hand. Standing with a group of suits shaking hands. Riding in the back of a Bentley or Jaguar. Smoking filter tipped cigarettes and cigars dipped in Napoleon Brandy. Whether that picture was her fantasy for him, rather than the destiny fate had mapped out, hardly troubled her. Keith Henderson at this moment in time felt little more than a figment of her overactive imagination. Like a Kirk Douglas or Tony Curtis, smouldering in the recesses of her mind.

Once again the sullen waitress dropped a plate of bacon and eggs at her table. But this time Peggy felt a certain kinship with the bedraggled waif. Rather than blame the poor girl for the greasy mess; she found herself wondering how the girl managed to get through the summer months – when the hotel heaved with guests.

Before, London had felt impossibly glamorous. But close-up, its façade was as cracked as the stucco of Mornington Crescent. People like the waitress and the beggar were hardly the stuff of tourist brochures or newsreels. Nor were the navvies who waited, on the streets of Camden Town for the chance of a job. They were the life that happened beneath the surface – the living-breathing life of London. Everything else, from Beefeaters to Buckingham Palace was just window dressing. And no matter how pretty she found the dresses on display in Oxford Street, Peggy knew that her meagre spending money would barely stretch to anything more than handkerchief, wishing was all she could do.

"Mind if I join you for Breakfast," he said. Startling her for a moment. His eyes looked clearer this second morning and his appearance reminded her of Summer Holiday. He wore a cream short sleeved shirt, with the sleeves rolling over solid biceps. And his narrow-cut Italian trousers tapered down to shiny black loafers. A seersucker jacket was draped over his arm. All that was missing was a pair of Persol Sunglasses and a Vesper.

She let him stand there in anticipation, longer than was necessary. And if she was ever asked to conjure up a picture of happiness it would stand before her holding a seersucker jacket.

"Yes.... yes. Breakfast, join me," she said, trying to sound casual. He asked her about her day and she found herself lost for words – the memory of all those churches had seeped away overnight. At the corner of Oxford Circus, she'd been ushered away from the windows of Peter Robinson. And by the time they reached Selfridges, she was seriously envious of shoppers sauntering in through those grand glass doors. She described the warren of rooms in the old Fleet Street pub, and the smell of age oozing from its wooden interior. Then she skipped on to Oxford Street and Regent Street, where she found it impossible to disguise the disappointment and regret in her voice. He in turn nodded sympathetically.

"Sounds like we both could have done with a little excitement," he said, emphasising the point with a mock-yawn.

The waitress arrived with a plate of eggs and beans.

"The bacons finished for today," she announced. There was a hint of apology in her voice and gesture, as she sat his plate down delicately.

"That's fine...just save me a piece tomorrow and I'll be a happy man." The girl blushed slightly and moved rapidly to another table. Peggy could see he'd melted another bit of her icy exterior; she felt a small fissure of jealousy pass through her. He'd transformed the poor creature with some

232

kind words, and she wanted some of that too. Even though his eyes remained level with hers, she felt some of his energy move about the dining room with the girl.

"It's much nicer when you're around...I mean she's much nicer to you," Peggy said. Immediately wishing the floor would swallow her up. But her slip appeared to pass unnoticed, all he said was:

"Treat people with civility and they'll act civil, a friend of mine used to say.... I'm Keith by the way," he said without skipping a beat.

It was nine fifteen when they left the breakfast room. She to Westminster Abbey and Cathedral; he to the Royal Observatory at Greenwich. And somewhere in between their exchange of names and talk of day trips, a night out in Camden was mooted. He mentioned a visit to the old Music Hall on Camden High Street and maybe a walk along the canal to London Zoo. Before darkness fell, they could return to Chalk Farm Road and maybe take in a folk group. He warned her the pubs would be heaving with sweaty Irish workmen, but she'd replied that seeing her family were as green as The Clancy Brothers, she would fit right in.

"Then it's settled," he said with a nod of his head.

On the boat trip to Greenwich Keith Henderson found the river-sights muddy and out of focus. From the Dome of St Paul's to Wapping Docks all that filled his mind was the girl at breakfast. With her blond hair and correct way of speaking. She'd sharpened his mind. Forced him to slow down his thoughts so they became measured and precise. And he'd just known Peggy would like an Irish Bar; the way others may prefer the glitter of a Top Rank Ballroom.

I'm troubled by your lack of spontaneity kidder,
loosen-up and you'll have a happier life, rumbled
through his head in the gravely
tone Geordie liked to use. He looked round half expecting to see that big dark face, streaked with grease and oil, smiling back at him. But all there was, was a pockmarked City of London receding.

At Geordie's wake they'd sung Oh Danny Boy, and his wife who'd remained stoically calm throughout the day, disintegrated. Her very being shattered into a million little pieces. And here it was again issuing from an open pub door in Camden Town, sending a bolt through his heart: *Oh Danny Boy.*

"You've gone quiet Keith," she said after their silent stroll along the High Street. I expect he's a little tired from the river she thought; quietly hoping that nothing said had spoilt his mood. Music Halls whether derelict or intact, were just not her thing. So their excursion into The Old Bedford Music Hall, had left her with nothing to say. She'd just let him ramble on about the artist Walter Sickert and stars such as Marie Lloyd.

"Trying to find my bearings Peggy. I've been given
directions to a pub called the Stags Head, but for the
life of me I can't remember if we take the second or
third right after Camden Lock. "

Her tension subsided. We're just a little lost she
thought, but that's good the man's human after all.

"Underneath the railway bridge he said and make
sure you're on the right hand side of the road. We
should see large walls to our left and the street will be
to our right. "

He pointed left then right, making a humming sound
– like she supposed a water diviner would make. Groups of
men, their faces flushed with alcohol passed them by. Some
wore clothes soiled by work, others sported shirts and ties.
Every few yards there was a pub; some were empty, while
others teamed with life. And in-between there were bakeries
and dress shops, everyday ironmongers. Ordinary run of the
mill places.

"I remember walking in the park with my dad as a
boy; one of those rare moments when we were
together outside the house or mass. He wasn't saying
very much, that's his way. So I decide to pipe-up with
something that would please him. I was no more than
seven, so what came next shook me through. There's
a low wall that runs close to the bowling green; I was
balancing on this wall, fancying myself as older and

taller than I was. Dad seemed impossibly big then, a giant to my small eyes. He strides along beside me; smouldering cigarette in one hand, his hair glistening in the summer sun.

He's in a sports coat and grey flannel trousers. The trousers have turn-ups and they flap. Dad's old-fashioned, its Oxford Bags all the way for him - anything narrower is a sign of degeneracy. Anyway he's striding along, barely conscious of me tottering along beside, when I say: *I want to be just like you when I grow up dad.*

And the funny thing is, I don't really mean it. Even then my little mind had worked out that dad's life was not the life for me. But like all little boys I wanted to please dad, wanted him to pat me on the head and ruffle my hair. Maybe he'd lift me up onto his shoulders; or punch my arm affectionately. The way Spencer Tracy and Mickey Rooney were together in Boys Town.

The last thing I expected was the whack across the back of my head. I remember his voice barking: *you don't want my life boy, wish for something better.* He stunned me into silence, and in an instant the skip had left my step. We've hardly exchanged two words since."

Keith took a large draught from his pint glass and wiped the residue from his mouth. There was a melancholy in his eyes that matched those of the men about the bar. A longing for things do be different. She could hardly remember the starting point of their conversation, or how it had led to this wistful moment. But it appeared to echo the mood about the bar. A haunting version of My Lagan Love played on uilleann pipes had the attention of even the most raucous.

"Now Peggy let me hear a sad tale from you," he said, with just the barest glimpse of a smile. But she knew that no matter how sympathetic and Kind Keith Henderson appeared; her saddest story would always remain under lock and key. Instead she proffered her version of Great Expectations, the way a child sneaks in a few fictitious sins to beef up their confession.

"When I was young."

"Just last year."

"No Keith don't be daft, I'm as serious as you." Peggy surprised herself with the bluntness of her reply. She had, if she was very honest only half listened to Keith Henderson's little anecdote. Instead her mind had danced around a whole set of scenarios. One involved a little innocent romance, she preferred not to see his melancholy side, sadness did not suit him.

"When I was growing up, dad collected books. He bought them from that second hand stall in the Grainger Market. Great hulking volumes that were an effort to hold, never mind read. Often when he tired of one he would take it to the stall and exchange it for another. Or he would give it away to a cousin or an aunt. One Christmas he wrapped one up for me, somehow my sister was overlooked. I remember feeling special – so special when the present was passed around to me. As I opened the packaging I could feel his eyes on me. His anticipation filled the room. So like you, I gave him what he wanted, a big beaming smile. I remember saying thank you daddy far too much, only stopping when he tapped me gently on the shoulder. I would change nothing about that day except for the book. "

She paused to sip her half-pint; the Guinness tasted of nutmeg. It lined her throat with its richness; coating it ready for the big lie. In the context of lies this one was a mere tiddler, a one so small it would be washed away in the stream of conversation.

"And I would change nothing about that day except for the book. He'd wrapped-up an old edition of Grey's Anatomy, the first step on my route to a medical career, or so he thought. To please him I pretended this other person's life was mine. I kept it going for a good few years, until it became too unbearable and I lashed out with the truth. "

Keith Henderson appeared pleased with her story; so she dropped the epilogue. The books return to the Grainger never got told.

"We're damned if we do and damned if we don't live up to their expectations. Now would you like another half."

Peggy watched him move through the crowded bar, his back straight and shoulders broad. She found it difficult to imagine being disappointed by Keith Henderson, but she was uncertain how he felt.

The pub heaved with men dressed in rough-knit sweaters and wild hair. Heavy work boots outnumbered the Oxfords and Brogues. While women appeared to favour the more delicate ballet pump or Roman style sandals that strapped high on the ankle. I could fit into a place like this she found herself thinking, and so could Keith. In the far left corner sat the band: an interchangeable number of fellows, who stood-up from the bar, then melted back into the crowd when their piece was done.

It was the absence of any particular uniformity that struck her. Beside Keith in his seersucker jacked stood a hulk of a man dressed in a denim work jacket and a cabin boys peaked cap. Men who could have been accountants or bank managers talked with shabbier types. Accents collided, plumy vowels danced with an Irish lilt. A North London twang combined with a flat northern. One or two black faces were scattered amongst the white; West Indian or African, she had no way of telling. She quietly thanked Keith Henderson for taking her to such a place. Thanked him for fitting in as well as he did, and for being the kind of man who flipped a coin in a beggar's bowl.

Mairi was glad to be making the journey alone. All the thing's she'd left behind would be waiting for her back home. The black and white certainty. The shipyard buzzer calling a population to and from work. Slicing up the day into predestined portions. Men teeming through the yard gates. Running fast: making their escape, weighed down by haversacks full of tools. She knew the scene:

    The washing spread across back-lanes and women polishing doorsteps. Then out to the furthest reaches of town; where houses peter-out and fields stretch on-and-on. Where the smell of horse manure replaced factory smoke and bone yard. Where Wagon Way paths criss-cross and the ghosts of coal trucks pass from pit head to staiths at the rivers edge. She recalled rainy days sheltering in bus shelters and coffee shops. Boredom enveloping days; weekends and holidays. Arguing with Judy until exhausted they lapsed into silence. Slow wet kisses, snatched then discarded. Blisters, sunburn and midge bites. Dock leaves and stinging nettles. Her first taste of cola from a bottle. Cinder toffee and Kendal Mint Cake. Shops selling buckets, spades and fishing nets. A pilgrimage to Lourdes. An escape South – where there were no memories, just expectations.

    There are particular things that make a place special. That forces it deep into the soul. And it takes guts to leave such a place and never return. The alternative is to stay and never leave. But there is third type of state, where people can neither stay or leave: instead they tear themselves inside out, until nothing is left of them- a fate she knew would be hers.

The driver turned on the radio and Mantovani filled the coach with sickly strings. A cigarette found its way from handbag and pocket to mouth. She smoked it down until it's heat burnt her fingers; then crushed it's remains in the metal ashtray.

On the morning of her leaving there was a smell of breakfast wafting from a Haymarket café. The sadness of soot-stained stucco. The smell of kidneys frying. Mantovani became Ray Conniff, became Acker Bilk. Became a Sunday afternoon in the back of a stranger's car. She'd met him not long after losing her party at Victoria. He looked Italian but spoke like a London native. He gave her the story that got her out. Free of the guided tours and boring afternoon teas. His friend riding in the passenger seat. A woman named Margaret by her side. They were doing sixty skirting Regents Park, the window open, headscarves billowing. Talking a mile-a-minute. He turned to look at her, taking his eyes from the road.

"I've got a little surprise for you," he said flashing a wicked smile. And she stared wide-eyed into his. Light danced and shimmered on their dark brown surface, suggesting nothing of his scheme. And the pleasure centres of her brain, wanted him there and then. Transplanted from their speeding car to a bed, four walls and a locked door.

Naked and warm, wrapped around her body. Engine with tailfins and electric indicators – pulsating ON and OFF.

The girl beside her begins to apply makeup. Synthetic perfume leeches through the car. She inhales deeply, taking in the light headed smell of seduction; a cheap and beautiful high. A hand mirror and powder puff move from left to right. Each movement is accompanied by a pause; a moment of examination, before the process begins anew. There's a hardness to her beehive hair, a lacquered French-polished finish that renders her crowning glory inert. She feels like touching its brittle surface just to see how hard its set. The pizzicato strings of an Adam Faith song plays on the radio.

They drove into the entrance of Eden Court, a nondescript mansion block, down a side-road. They passed through a small cloakroom, and handed in their coats. Then moved into a beautifully bright dining room. It's light pink walls lifted her mood, and she found herself smiling spontaneously. He dealt with the business of securing a table in the packed dining room, slipping the Maître d' a note and ramping-up the charm. It was at this moment that any nostalgia for Willington and her side of the river evaporated. There was no grand plan, just the need to be gone. Really gone.

Sleekly dressed diners, centuries older than her, were attended to by equally old dinner-suited waiters.

"So what do you think," he said as they were seated. And all she could think of was how overwhelming the restaurant felt. His, greasy friend saved her:

"I'm speechless, bloody speechless. What a marvellous place," sounded honest. Someone like greasy would love a place full of creeps she though; he was right at home.

"Now tuck in the grilled grapefruits getting cold," said Margaret. Waiters fluttered about a corpulent man who occupied a window seat. She was on the outside looking in, sitting inside a goldfish bowl. Scrutinized by a bunch of snooty people. The clank of dentures accompanied the smell of the money and expensive food.

Mairi took in the dining room: the fat man with his daughter, mistress or whore. The group who must all have been eighty years old, celebrating a birthday. The lone jolly looking man, who looked a bit like Robert Morley. The business man, the accountant, the solicitor and the surgeon. The man who had made his money, manipulating the joints of the great and the good. They were all so much older, but that hardly mattered.

She ordered Holsteiner Schnitzel, because she wanted to hear those preposterous words out loud. And with no direction and just a smattering of French, she chose something that sounded as ancient and pompous as the restaurants clientele. He meanwhile stared away from the waiter and ordered a Steak Diane.

Her head floated, still unsure of how to deal with the whole experience. Over in the corner an empty table was being readied for a new party of diners. All men; five of whom were no older than her. The sixth man was a little older, possibly thirty. All were dressed smartly, but there was something theatrical about their appearance. She looked away when the older man caught her eye.

THE HUM

McMenemy scanned the doctor's waiting room. A small child sits with it's mother. The child has blond curly hair, and its skin has the ethereal quality of the chronically sick: yellow and translucent, alien in its perfection. There is something too perfect about this creature, too perfect for Willington. On the opposite side to the child sits a middle aged woman, who performs the type of frantic mime adults suppose children like. And with each distortion of the woman's face, the child draws itself closer to the mother. But he or she, can't help glancing from behind the shelter of its mother's sleeve. The simple entertainment of a gurning human face, reminds him of old variety acts, of sideshows at the Hoppings; of childhood amusements too strange for television.

McMenemy pondered: Willington in late November is not a place to be ill. The permanent wind blowing in from the North Sea could cut a man in half; turn a runny nose into full blown flu. Force even the hardest of characters to despair. Winter chills to the bone when all the heating you have is a coal fire and the warmth of another human lying close. It's something to be endured, to survive.

Yet children played-out in the snow, wearing short pants and Wellingtons. Feet frozen into blocks of ice; their mittens sodden from rolling snowballs, they remained outside until called. McMenemy in his cashmere overcoat and fur-lined gloves, tried to imagine the cold of his childhood, but all that remained were impressions: a sledge hurtling towards the burn stream. Men warming their hands on a brazier. The smell of moisture evaporating from damp dirty coats.

The mother ignores her sickly Childs head, as it nestles catlike into her side. She lights a cigarette, smokes it quickly, then reaches for a magazine. She's no beauty, but has a pleasing face, the type of face men would be happy to greet after a hard day's work. Her trews are tucked into fur-topped booties: she could have stepped from the ski slopes of Switzerland. Wrapped-up warm in a thick woollen coat, scarf and fluffy hat.

A small two bar electric fire, tucked into a neat ceramic fireplace, barely penetrates the rooms frost-bitten air. Its glow matches that of the young mother's coat, burnt orange. The middle aged woman continues her pantomime, making rabbits ears from fingers, and nibbling her teeth. When she breathes a frozen trail of moister passes into the room. The room hums like an idling train. An existential hum. A hum of confinement...

On a troopship, or a train; in the gents when the coda of glances, and long lingering pisses spells out dot-dash, dot-dash. In bars, where men stand at the invisible line separating compliance and violence. And in the bedroom, where a wife, brother or uncle sleeps; when their breathing becomes shallow, and movement is still.

McMenemy pondered. The hum made him feel alive; it was everything or nothing. He moved to another space: the small outside nettie at number 142. Aye that was something – an oasis of calm. A place of meditation and safety. Raw brick, cast iron and porcelain. Cement darkened by smoke; that he scraped away sometimes to reveal the cream colour it had been when newly laid. And when he was older, it was a place to read books and think about life outside. Indoors there was always someone rattling about the room; disrupting the silence with their sound. In the nettie, there was nothing but space.

The surgery door opened and the hum wavered: it disconnected with a jolt. A smell of pipe-smoke and cigarettes mingled with that desperate smell unwell people give-off. The young mother turned a page of her magazine. Old Doctor Coopers pipe tobacco lingered; his final imprint. He'd kept all of Willington's ailments in his head, and on small indecipherable index cards, meticulously mis-kept. And he died suddenly; his great brain, the repository of all medical knowledge, became a living room for worms.

A new patient entered the room. Stout, vertically challenged, in the sort of heavy overcoat favoured by poorer women (first generation Irish and as hard as nails). He knew her and she knew him, yet there was not a flicker of recognition. Nobody wants to be ill, it's a thing you don't want to share. The most private of things – because it's part of you that's going wrong. It's nobody's business but your own.

The dust settles as it always does when a new person enters the room. And air adjusts to their dimensions. He hears the sound of an organ, but it's just the hum shifting its pitch. He grabs a copy of Life magazine and buries his face. Cooper liked America, although he'd never travelled further than Northern France. But he'd seen the countries vast expanse. Those wide Midwestern plains and deserts baked white by the sun. The palm trees of California and the strangeness of so much space. He'd seen it all at the cinema.

The new doctor would eventually clear the old mans distinctly masculine magazine collection. Life, sat atop a mix of Vintage Car Monthly, fishing and DIY magazines. The occasional Peoples Friend was the only evidence of his housekeeper Mrs Edwards. Cooper had smelled the way men smell when they lack a woman's touch; not quite clean, yet not quite dirty.

He opened the magazine at a spread featuring the Kennedy's at home. Kennedy with his young family. Kennedy is a saint who walks the earth, the living embodiment of all that god created in his own image. His straight, white teeth are angel's teeth; proof that he is no mere mortal. And the light that surrounds him exposes the seediness of ordinary Politicians. The issue dates from the summer months; there's no hint in the ex Presidents healthy

248

tanned face of what's just around the corner.

McMenemy listens to the hum; it sounds like a sprawling theme to a western, something like Big Country. He scanned the pages of Life looking for something to match the young President, and he hovered over sail-boats and expensive bottles of booze. Amongst the perfectly rendered slogans, he found a big hollow emptiness.

And he wondered if the men and women who worked in the offices of Life Magazine were anything like the people gathered together in Doctor Coopers waiting room. If they moved unnoticed and unappreciated down the big avenues of New York. If sometimes in that city full of Jazz and action, they found solace being alone; being blue.

A lost in thought McMenemy, was called twice by the new Doctor, who asked him to extinguish his cigarette as he entered the room. She pointed towards a No Smoking sign. Coopers bare smoke impregnated walls, had been given a lick of magnolia. A new pot plant, failed to add life to the room – a room with the pallor of death.

"So what can I do for you today Mr...," she consulted a large black desk diary,

"McMenemy."

The hum had not quite broken-off. Her words sounded like a faint echo; not quite in the hear and now. She looks down. He can't see what she's reading, but he can guess.

"Take a seat Mr McMenemy, "she says.

Inside the consulting room, Coopers pipe odour is diminished. Doctor M Percy has won the war of smoke. She's added a plain ticking clock to the wall, for measuring out her appointments. She's younger than he imagined, younger than him. Her hair is a bubble of black and she has eyebrows that arch. She smiles revealing a gleaming set of teeth. And the hum splinters like a mirror. Before him sits Jacqueline Bouvier Kennedy. She has an aristocratic air, that he finds unnerving; she reels in all those staunch conservatives, with her society connections. Takes-out a whole row of lacklustre political wives with one shot. Bang!

Dr Percy's upper lip quivers when she speaks; a Marilyn Monroe without the flakiness and stupidity. And he felt like talking about ordinary things, not doctor patient stuff. But here he was, and there was she: studying a letter, attempting to decipher old Coopers scrawl.

"It says here you went to the RVI for tests."

"That's right Doctor."

"And...and...and..

I can't read Dr Coopers notes, but I'm assuming he let you know the

hospitals findings."

"Yes Doctor, it was a few days before his sudden demise."

He could see she had no idea what these results were, and guessed she would ask him to explain what was happening. He saw the confusion, left by Cooper, in her eyes.

250

It was distressing and unfair, and he wanted to comfort the woman – to cross that Doctor patient divide.

The boy stands head-down winding tape on his fists. He can see the intense concentration in the little guy's eyes. He must be thirteen or fourteen, only moments out of the cradle, but already battered by a hundred fights. He has none of the mock toughness or the swagger – that's just a coward's camouflage. No he is still, still as the wind on a summers morning. Each and every cell, sinew and muscle is under his control; they do his bidding.

And he's thinking of only one thing, the other mans weakness: his soft left, the eye that cuts easily, the legs that won't hold-up over four rounds. It's a war of attrition out there and it's the last man standing who wins.

McMenemy adjusted his gaze. In the other corner of the dressing room stands the opponent. Tall, beefy, not an ounce of flab. He jerked his neck from side to side, as if trying to relieve an itch. McMenemy knew the whole thing was an act – stolen from some Hollywood boxing film; Kid Galahad maybe.

Fists like hams, that's what he had. While jerking his neck, he lovingly taped those great joints; swaddled them as if they were his children. He's jerky, and nervous, and he's probably going to loose.

"So what's the odds on titch."

The bookie looked disappointed, like he, like

McMenemy knew the outcome.

"The odds aren't very generous for that one," he said.

"Well I'll put a Guinea on him, and collect my winnings over at the Coach and Horses later. "

The bookie palmed McMenemy's bet, and both men returned to their respective seats on opposite sides of the ring. He closes his eyes and hears the hum once again. This time it's pulsating rhythm eradicates every sound.

JUDITH PEMBERTONS AFTERNOON

When she's there, she's there:
The phrase sat in her head, refusing to shift. It was Clarke
Gable talking about Marilyn Monroe; it was his way of
excusing her not always being there. And maybe it was an
error in circadian rhythm that caused her to take all of those
pills, and maybe she didn't want to die, but the rhythm, like a
perfectly choreographed dance routine, did not falter.

Snow has seeped through shoe leather and stockings;
sending chill messages to skin and bone. Her feet lock into a
pattern of steps; first learnt at Kane's Dance Studio, then
practiced in her bedroom and on sprung dancehall floors.
They follow an outline of footprints traced on paper: Going
one, two, three-a-four, five and a six. Left foot step back,
right foot in place. Then Chasse - three-a-four, five and a six.
A million daydreams join the whooshing slush; a zillion
particles of mud shift beneath the headscarves and
umbrellas.

Judith Pemberton sits on the bus, on her way to work.
People jabber and stare out the window with docile eyes. The
smell of horse manure begets factory fumes and bone yard.
Thick air, on the top deck, is full of perfume and tobacco
smoke. She puffs away, along with everyone else. She

retrieves a lost brolly from the floor and shakes it out: *today is her lucky day.*

The road takes her through places where memories of Wagon Way paths criss-cross. Where the ghosts of coal trucks pass from pit head to staiths. A shipyard buzzer sounds the Willington serenade. The Skyline shifts from grey to burnt orange to grey, and pastel cranes droop on the horizon. It begins to snow again.

St Vincent's spire still points toward the sky. The Ranch, where cowboy pictures played all week, is scheduled for demolition. The Royal, The Queens, and The Gaumont, all have predeceased Monroe. Among the bingo halls and car-showrooms only The Ritz, continued. Showing horror films, foreign films and old films. Films that championed dubious morals; that are saturated with sex, and frequently outrage according to the Gazette.

As they pass the Boys Club a girl begins to apply makeup; spots are carefully erased. A hand mirror and powder puff are produced. Her stop may be minutes away, but this girl wants to be ready and fresh. She thinks of Marilyn lying on a mortuary slab. She will never be late for work again. Never have to apply makeup. Never smoke a cigarette, kiss a fellah, fuck and be fucked. Or take a handful of pills and wash them down with booze. The Starlet sandwiched between a sailing-boat advertising vacuum cleaned tobacco and frosty Ovaltine; taken prisoner by the Hollywood life. The girl who took up acting, because the real-world was kind of grim. The eleven year-old who had grown-men honking their horns at her on the way to school.

According to the Town Hall clock it is just past nine. She's late for work. It's night in California, day in England, and somewhere - someone is wishing they were someplace else.

You'll be late for your own funeral Judith Pemberton. And if you're unlucky the boss will be sitting at his desk, counting down the minutes. Each of those sixty second intervals will be marked by a low, thunderous, thunk. By the drum of his fingers on mahogany. By two frown lines, lengthening. And what if you were a soldier, Judith Pemberton, would you be late for a nuclear war?

Hail falling like small daggers. The wintery High Street hums with activity. A third wave of workers, pedestrians, young mothers, and grandmothers – flow from right to left. She hoists her stolen umbrella above the head of a passing woman, who exchanges a hello without breaking her stride:

Mary, her age, her height, but head and shoulders ahead of her in attractiveness, is looking tired. The mound beneath her chequered coat has grown. Her hat droops down. *Oh the luxury of not having to work!*

There are precisely five more shops and one street junction before she reaches her office, slotted between a Travel Agent's and Woolworth's. Faces from mass; from sixteen minus five years of school; from two of work and four of dances.

"Hello Mrs Henderson," I see your Keith's grown so tall. I wonder if you'll be kind and let him know I will never be interested in marrying him or any other spotty youth for that matter.

Steam jets rise from Marchetti's Bar and Grill, emptied of teenagers. The pinball machine at the café's rear waits expectantly for the insertion of a penny, and the pull of its lever. The silver espresso machine, dispenses frothy coffee. Old Giovanni in white jacket and black moustache, is at the window. She hears a snatch of Come Outside, and feels the pull of lazy work-free days:

Where girls dream of falling in love, and excitement. And the thought of settling down is furthest from their mind. Suddenly, at the age of nineteen, she feels old. Caught between the Mary's, who have a home, husband and children; the Mairi's who upped and left and Peggy, barely out of childhood. *Spinsters Purgatory.*

Giovanni gets a waggle of her umbrella, and the clock above Boots moves to a quarter past. The Travel Agent is offering coach trips to the Yorkshire Abbeys; to Lindisfarne and the Farne Islands; to Lourdes: *ah Lourdes.* But that's the trouble with excursions you always end up back in Willington.

The Ritz is showing a double bill: Some Like It Hot and The Apartment.

When she's there, she's there:

Whirled about her brain again. And then she's few feet from the cinemas shabby entrance. The ticket booth is empty, but she sees from a billboard the first show begins at ten. Time enough for a cappuccino and a smoke.

PICTURE PALACE

The slow winding back of a red velvet curtain, trimmed with gold brocade. Torchlight cutting through darkness, and the projectionists beam. The adverts begin:

A motor scooter skirts the narrow coast road, it twists and turns. Sheer cliffs fall down to the sea. Impossibly tight corners appear to have been designed by a madman, a lunatic who longs for the sight of mangled flesh and shredded smoking metal. Down below the sea crashes against jagged rocks, promontories, stone and wooden piers. Tiny figures dance in the surf. The shimmering sun, falls like a beaded curtain across the landscape. A priest passes in the opposite direction, riding an ancient bicycle; he sounds a bell as he negotiates the blind corner.

The music is upbeat, sweeping like a bird above motorcyclist and passenger. Their heads are uncovered. His, a raven black mass of curls; hers long, blond and windswept. The unseen eye tracks the two as they round one corner after another.

They are sleeveless, with tanned skin, unencumbered by clothing. Her sandaled feet rest close to the exhaust pipe. Her arms surround his waist. He turns to say something, and she responds. He points an arm in the direction of some far off thing, and she nods her appreciation.

Judith sucked all this in with one great slurp of orange juice. The picture exploding like a thousand orange suns inside her head. The boy, the girl, the motor scooter. The boy, the girl, a blanket, a beach. Her in a bikini, he in skimpy trunks. She traced the outline of his penis. His hand on her thigh; hers on his. There were no others on this tiny rocky outcrop. Just them and the seabirds, and the unseen eye tracking their every move. And the music sweeps them into the sea - crashing white foamy surf against tanned brown legs.

Her hand strokes the velvet armrest, and she imagines another texture, another place. Where could they go now, with their scooter parked high and dry on the cliff above? But that was already taken care of. The two were now dressed; their clothes expensive and Italian. The boy once again spoke into the girl's ear. The unseen eye swoops higher and higher, and shows them as part of a group of three or four couples. All Similar; doppelgangers, on a terrace, leaning out to sea.

People fly in hot air balloons, high above the party-people's heads. They watch the action down below through Eighteenth Century Telescopes, and they're decked out in wigs and finery. They drop rose petals that fall like multicoloured rain. And the screen is filled with colour; bathing the whole cinema with a warm glow. The party people are drinking and laughing, throwing their heads back in the way only film people do. The women wear long evening gowns, and the men have slicked back hair, white shirts and open bow ties. Like the evening was drawing to a glorious end. In the warm afternoon advert sun, she sucked on her straw and imagined a tea that did not include luncheon meat.

After the show she goes home. Home of course is not home at all. It's her grandmas in a privet lined road. A two story, three bedroom, Edwardian terrace. A kitchen, and a scullery. A front room and a back room. A brown front door. A patterned glass inner door with a shower of balls descending from its top left corner. Blue carpet on the floor. A brass picture rail, running along the walls. An orange sofa bed, with wooden arms. A cocktail cabinet, with whisky and advocaat. A writing bureau, and a coffee table. A stereogram. Records: Jazz, Show Tunes, Irish traditional, Frank Sinatra. In the parlour there's a Rediffusion TV and radio. An armchair, a small dining table with three chairs. A sideboard. The sofa is against the window, the dining table against the wall. A picture of a fishing village, hangs: all harbour and fishing boats. Some books, the readers digest, newspapers lie next to the sofa. The fire is electric, surrounded by a fireguard, intended for flame.

Grandma is in the kitchen; the oven is on. Grandma has her back to her, when she moves across the hall and on to the stairs. The first step creaks, but the remainder give silently. She sits at Grandmas dressing table, beside the heavy wooden double bed. The bed that dominates everything. She is used to her Grandma or herself tucked under the sheets, before and after sleep. At other times, the room is abandoned, only Grandads photo and a silver backed hairbrush, suggests occupancy.

Judith sits at the dressing table; sunlight comes in from the street and past the high headboard. Everywhere else people are in suspended animation. There are no sounds except for the ones she makes. And her thoughts start first with her mother in the hospital. The white metal bed, the nightgown borrowed from a dead patient, the tip of a hypodermic weeping fluid.

Her thoughts then change direction. Splintering off with the sunlight, in the direction of the mirror. Inside the mirror are a collection of lights, small twinkling lights, like a city viewed from the sea. And inside the light, she finds her face, her skin, her blond hair, diffuse and translucent. There are no more blemishes; no horseshoe scar at the side of her eye. She runs a thumb across each eyebrow, and they arch. A brush of her hair gives it body and length. Lip-gloss and a subtle colour on her eyelids come next, and her fingernails sprout a polished alabaster white. And she arches back her head and laughs. In her hand is a drink with a cherry floating at it's centre. Underneath the soft folds of her dress, she is naked. A warm Mediterranean breeze buffets her legs and arms. Anita, as she is now, leaves behind the dead skin of

Judith Pemberton.

It's just before six and the people are expecting her at eight. She has two hours to get ready. Two hours to learn the habits of this new person, to fill their space with her, to say *hello*, just like she would. Anita's feet are the same as hers, and they slip so well into expensive sandals. They fit perfectly, so when she walks as Anita, her movements are light and feathery. Outside the day's heat is giving way to a warm humid night; where the smells of rose petals infuse with citrus and cigar smoke. Boats bob on the harbour, their human cargo below deck, taking a siesta before the evening's hubbub. Crewmen busy themselves, washing away the sand and sweat. They sit smoking cigarettes, coiling ropes round polished brass fittings. Flags flutter for every nation that has a class of such people.

The chop, chop of preparation is happening behind waterfront cafes. Where Michele and Gregorio, their fingers smelling of lemon and olive oil, pull in the day's catch. Boxes flop with fish dripping salt water. Great wide-eyed sea bass are stacked top to tail. Gregorio takes a handful and throws it at Michele, who responds with a wave of his knife, and the shake of a fist. Wood smoke permeates the air, and the chink of glasses sounds on a single waterfront table. Tourists drink off the long hot afternoon, in white linen and pearls. Anita sighs for no reason in particular, and continues to brush her hair. She feels like listening to music, and calls for the maid, who obliges with a nod of her head. Her villa is fitted with speakers in every room. A continuous loop of music never ceases, until she decides. It's the music of adverts and films: anonymously accompanying the roll of ice cubes, the soft sensual sounds of the sea rolling in. Every mood catered for with an on or an off. This world has many dimension's: A bedroom, the Villa, a moped with a hot engine, waiting. Inside she's the same; organs, brain, the way blood circulates slowly to her extremities. Anita had no father or mother. No job. No history. No eight o'clock mass. No Sunday Dinner of shepherd's pie, Yorkshires, roast potatoes and sprouts.

On the harbour at night, boats rest and small round lights twinkle. Gregorio grills squid on a charcoal oven; Michele dresses plates with salad and sauté potatoes. Two others tend boiling pans, while a boy washes dishes. From her villa window she watches the kitchens activity, and paints her nails. A lazy old-fashioned bossa nova plays. The maid brings a second martini, and lays out her dress on the bed. In a silver spice holder, purchased in Marrakech sit two blue happy pills. Anita will take these before she leaves at ten to eight.

Already the motor scooter is being polished and the day's dust removed. Antonio, Gregorio's brother, will see the engine is turned over. There's a smell of gasoline and wax; of citrus and the cigarette she has left burning. Her red lipstick marks the filter; it matches the lip imprint on her glass. Antonio sounds the scooters horn, and she takes off her dress. She stands naked looking out into the kitchen,

263

watching squid bake and pasta boil. All this is contained within those wide rolling tears, flowing to the edge of her mouth. Accumulating on her chin, like salt morning dew. And on the tip of her tongue are the words, *Calamari Fritti.*

THE NEW CHURCH

You're either on the bus or off.

In the distance artificial lights twinkle. They hang from cranes and the hulls of half finished ships. Everything is oversized, except for the men who scuttle about like ants. Occasionally an oxyacetylene arc rises and falls. There are small pinpricks of light; cigarettes being puffed. Everything else is black and tan. The river is dark and still. Pressurized hammers pound rhythmically. Men see-saw across hanging wooden gantries.

They sit down by the waterline, legs swinging over its edge. Watching the night-time theatre. A crate of beer by their sides.

"I love the modern world: Port Talbot Steel Works, Canvey Island Oil Refinery, Dagenham motors and the Windscale Power Station. They're the new Cathedrals, where the Bishops carry slide rules and white coats serve as vestments." Said Maurice McMenemy, who flipped a bottle top into the river; it disappeared into the blackness, with a silent splash. Jim Flannery raised his bottle:

"To the new religion," he said. Beside him Keith

Henderson sat smiling. The alcohol was goading him to laugh, but he knew McMenemy was serious. He also knew that Father Flannery, no matter how drunk, was dead serious too. And if he were to interrupt their solemnity, with a laugh or a mocking phrase; the game would be up. They would dismiss him as some young Kid, who was not serious, not suitable for their business. So he too raised a bottle and toasted the ESSO tanker with a shaky hand.

"To technology."

The Priest gave his shoulder an affectionate squeeze; while McMenemy showed his appreciation with a non-verbal sound. In the distance a gas flame moved in the breeze, like a slender bodied dancer it swayed from side to side. Maurice McMenemy saw the young Fred Astaire, cheek-to-cheek with Ginger. Jim Flannery saw the flicker of a Roman oil lamp, carried through the Villa that was now buried beneath a slipway. And Keith Henderson, he saw a bank-robber cutting his way through strong room doors.

He was so close to those foot-wide slabs of metal. Close enough to feel the steely cold. To feel the thermal lance heat as it turned metal molten. There were smells; the singeing of flesh and burning of wood and paper. And then the smell of money, stacked high like a pools win. He could smell the money evaporating through the skin of Maurice McMenemy. He could smell it despite Jim Flannery's sweet smelling aftershave.

The crackle of McMenemy's cigar, matched the pop

of industrial fireworks. Another bottle top flipped from the businessman's lap. There was a guzzle and a slurp; then the sound of a low belch.

"I'd like to propose a toast to…"

Another beery belch was followed by some incoherent rambling. Then McMenemy appeared to revive.

"And…excuse me Father for I have sinned. I'd like to sing their praises to the high heavens. And drink beer from their dainty little shoes."

Keith Henderson pulled another beer from his crate, and caught the eye of Flannery. The Priest raised his eyes to the heavens and shook his head. The danger of insulting McMenemy with a wrong word or misplaced laugh was now past – he'd achieved total drunkenness. Instead of giving the toast a name, McMenemy's head sunk deep into his chest and he began to snore loudly. And a giddy atmosphere of relief replaced tension. Flannery said nothing, but his face had taken on the countenance of a much younger man. Meanwhile Keith relaxed. He slouched, and managed to dribble some beer on his tie. He thought of his small house and of the time when his dad was first taken ill. Then the relief had crept up on him like a new love; until one day it hit him like an express train. And he had sunk into his dad's chair; fearless, happy and alive.

And he thought of this time as an interlude; because his dad did return from the hospital, and he did start shouting again. But he was weaker, and he grew weaker fast.

So this time was the beginning of a new beginning. The fearsome man, became an old man. Who was buried, minus his gold signet ring, that he now wore. He rubbed the rough edges of the ring and looked at the wavering flame across the water. A fat genie with the face of his father replaced molten strong room doors. The genie smiled, revealing dark worn-down molars, and he waved, just before disappearing.

McMenemy is sleeping, and dead to the world. Dead as the trees that decomposed to make the coal and the gas. He lit a cigarette and inhaled deeply, offered one to the priest; cradling a light in his hands. There was little wind, but the cigarette took its time catching fire. Flannery's hand lingered on his for longer than was necessary, but he let it pass. Putting the arm round his shoulder, and the occasional body contact down to drunkenness.

In the morning McMenemy would remember nothing of his unfinished toast. He may remember the evening before St Vincent's closed. He may even remember his drinking companions. But everything about their time down by the waterline would be open to interpretation. The soundless grunt he gave, could well have been an invitation. With a little imagination and some help from the genie of the lamp, anything was possible. Father Jim Flannery had also seen an opportunity, and held on to it like a seasick sailor.

"Thanks for the smoke Keith."

"That's ok Father."

"You can call me Jim. I think we've drunk enough to

dispense with the formalities."

He removed his dog collar and tossed it towards the river. The gesture was supposed to appear spontaneous, but he'd been rehearsing it long before McMenemy went under. Just like he'd been contemplating how McMenemy managed to imbibe so much and still remain coherent. Practice he supposed. And he supposed young Keith was teetering on the edge too, despite his steadiness and a lightness in his eyes.

"I see where my offertory money goes."

"Now where would that be Keith?"

"To your ecclesiastical outfitters I suppose. If you throw away clothes every time you're drunk."

"What makes you think I'm bladdered?"

"Who else would be sitting down here, past midnight. Watching the yards at work while McMenemy snores like a walrus. "

"You got me bang to rights," replied the Priest; putting his hands up in surrender. There were ten bottles of beer remaining. So if the object was to drink Keith Henderson into submission, he'd better slow down thought Jim Flannery. They talked about Willington, seeing both were immigrants to the North East. And both men made a conscious effort not to disturb the sleeping businessman. Every so often they both glanced over at the snoring man. He could see the pound signs in the young man's eyes; smell the greed coming off the boy. It had the same shitty, polluted smell as the river. At quarter past two the Keith Henderson's eyes began to glaze.

"Hope this one's not the straw that breaks the camel's back," he said. Passing another bottle to Keith; secretly hoping the good looking camel would crumple into his arms. And when the only response came as a loose-necked nod, he knew the camel was bending.

Jim Flannery liked this part of the game; the most exquisite torture. With the boy immobilized by booze, there would be no possibility of him walking away. No chance he would become disinterested and bored. The trick was to keep him conscious and a little unconscious simultaneously. Pissing in a puddle and avoiding being splashed.

"When I came to Willington this is what I first saw. A great mass of men." Flannery's arm made a sweeping gesture; encompassing the dry docks and slipways, engineering firms and half built ships.

"I remember wondering why it was so light after midnight. It took me a week to discover the river, and another six to realise everyone I knew had family who worked down here." Said Keith. Who despite his glazed expression, and the full crate of beer he'd drunk, still sounded coherent. But it was his composure that surprised Flannery. Here he was sitting with an unconscious Maurice McMenemy acting like it was an everyday occurrence. Smoking cigarettes, sipping beer and shooting the breeze with his parish priest. An everyday occurrence. The boy was unflappable.

"Here Keith have one of these, Maurice won't notice."

"Better wait until I've finished this one first Father. Appreciate the offer though," said Keith, shaking his half full Double Maxim.

There was something easy about the boy's conversation; it crept round you like a seductive tune. He imagined the lazy way he spoke being a hit with the girls. He thought of a young Robert Mitchum, rolled an indecent thought round in his head, and returned the bottle to it's crate.

Flannery made a pillow with his coat. He moved the head of Maurice McMenemy down gently, like it was the delicate scull of an altar boy. Keith Henderson, spread his coat over the sleeping mans shoulders, who stirred for a moment, then returned to his dreams. Among the cranes and machinery; the metal and the brick, birds sang the dawn chorus. And the brightness of the shipyards dulled as natural light replaced man-made.

"I used to swim in the local river as a boy. It was clean and alive with fish. It was a small river, and I was the biggest fish. I knew everyone in the village and they knew me. There was no such thing as privacy. I thought it would be possible to get lost in a place like this. But it's impossible, in this uniform."

He tugged at the place where a dog collar normally sat, rumpling his shirt in the process.

"A quarter of the men over there know my name, and the rest have an idea who I am. "

He could see how the Priest may mistake Willington for somewhere bigger. It had an oversized reputation for its size. And it had people like McMenemy, who were not afraid to talk-up their small town; until Venice of the North became a reality; not just a politicians pipe dream.

"I saw a picture of him in the paper. He was walking over some bombsite, covered with rubble and bricks. Behind him strode an entourage of suits and hacks. The place looked bleak, and primitive. It might have been raining, or an out of focus photograph. I remember the wind had blown about strands of his hair. His suit was a bit crumpled and his face puffy and unhealthy looking. But the way he talked about his plans for Willington; the certainty, made me stop and think. And when I finished reading, my food was stone-cold. But I wasn't bothered, I'd found something better than food to sustain me. Passion, that's what this funny man has."

The man in question had risen from his slumber, unnoticed by the Priest and his disciple. Pushing himself up from the improvised pillow and blanket.

"I'll have less of the funny Henderson," he said, grinning into the surprised faces of Flannery and Keith. McMenemy's car driver slept upright. But a tap on the shoulder re-animated the man.

"Charlie can you take me home, drop Father Flannery first and Mr Henderson after me. And if Henderson lives in Timbuktu, make a note of the mileage, so I can send his employers the bill. "

Once the Priest was gone, McMenemy got down to business.

"I've been watching you all evening Henderson. You hold yourself well for a man who's downed half my booze. And you handle Flannery well. He can get half of Willington on your side, and that's better than having them against you. People don't like change, but a man in a cassock can sweeten the pill."

McMenemy lived in a house overlooking Willington Dene. Built of timber and glass, it rose from hawthorn and poplar trees. A collection of clean lines amongst the rounded shapes of nature. And the house, like the man was a performance; with a porch big enough to accommodate a family. In the driveway a white sports car was haphazardly parked. A garage light had been left on, and the drivers door, left ajar.

"Wives," was all that McMenemy said, before fumbling at the front door with his keys. Henderson caught a glimpse of figures in the hallway, then the garage light switched-off. The front door closed; the day was done.

MCMENEMYS PARTY

The Maurice McMenemy who greeted his guests on New Years Eve was no different from the man of 1962 or 1961. No different from the man of 1958 who'd decided to show off his newly built house by way of a lavish party. He'd even wrangled special permission from the Corporation to hold a private fireworks display. Nobody had done such a thing outside November the fifth, that's what he was told.

He was a few pounds lighter this year, but people said it suited him. They said he looked youthful, vigorous and healthy. A new man, all agreed except for the doctor whose opinion he'd discarded along with the Christmas wrapping. And with each compliment he became emboldened, shaking-off the doubts. The doubts he'd managed to hide from everyone close to him.

The plans he made with Judith Pemberton, they were real. As real as the glass of whisky and water in his hand. She would move, on January 8th, into a small flat close to his office. And the plans for Willington, they were fixed in the handshake that greeted the Alderman.

"Welcome," he said to the Alderman and his wife. And although he didn't mean it:

"I'm pleased you were able to come, "slid off his

274

tongue in a glorious impersonation of bonhomie. He
appeared unchanged to Keith Henderson, who attended the
party alone.

"And where's the lovely Peggy," indicated he'd
forgotten their drunken conversation about his fiancée
travelling to London for a Beatles show. He was glad her
liking for the latest teen sensation was forgotten.

"Oh she's visiting relatives in London," satisfied
McMenemy's curiosity. There were other guests to greet,
other conversations to he had.

Henderson soon found himself divested of his
overcoat and scarf, and standing in a large room; furnished
in the Scandinavian style. There were impressive views of
Willington Dene through floor to ceiling plate glass windows.
And an impressive array of people; some he recognised from
St Vincent's, others were total strangers. Young and old, all
appeared prosperous. Some even looked important, like the
Alderman who he recognised from the Gazette. He had no
interest in exchanging pleasantries with the great and good
of Willington; so just in case one of then cornered him, he
kept moving.

The drink he was handed tasted like sherry. A
waitress circulated, handing drinks to those without, and
taking empties from the remainder. A temporary bar was
situated in the corner of the room. Here men congregated in
groups, holding tumblers filled with drinks of a different hue.
The Alderman had collected the largest following for himself.

He held fourth, gesticulating with his glass. Whilst Father Flannery had acquired his own little clique. The usual suspects from Mass. The readers and collection takers. The boring types who lived clean and boring lives.

A large L shaped sofa occupied the rooms centre. That's where the women mostly sat. He recognised Mrs McMenemy and the Alderman's wife, because she too appeared in the local paper. They were drinking sherry and nibbling snacks from small bowls. But some of the younger women had resisted this segregation and were striking out on their own, mixing with the men and forming small groups away from the sofa. Everyone appeared to be deep in conversation, except for him. He moved again, making for a plate glass door that appeared to be open. Getting closer, he could see figures standing outside. It must be freezing he thought, although nobody outside was dressed for the cold. The mystery was solved when he stepped through the door. Scattered about the terrace were small electric heaters, glowing red at people's feet. It was still cold, but a tolerable cold. The darkness made him feel anonymous, less self conscious. He could see the crowd was younger and having fun. McMenemy had piped music to the garden, a mixture of Jazz and standards. Unobtrusive and inoffensive, perfect for a party.

Judith Pemberton could feel goose bumps rising beneath her stockings. Her toes pricked a little with the cold, and her

276

fingers felt welded to the glass she'd been handed. And she chain smoked to keep her right hand occupied. McMenemy had insisted she come. It was important he said. Even so she had to wait to be spoken to, just so Mrs McMenemy didn't get suspicious. Like a fool she'd accepted his invitation. Accepted his request to wear something nice, which really meant don't show yourself up. And now she found herself on the wrong side of his double glazed French Windows, hiding from his wife, and freezing cold.

She'd let him dance her round the room of an empty show house, as compensation for not having one at his party. A consalation prize. She waited for what, she didn't know. There were millions of girls like her who'd fallen for married men; who believed the promises that things would work out. That a scandal could be avoided by moving away from Willington. And, and, and the thoughts just kept on coming. Why am I here she wanted to ask him, but speaking without being spoken to first just wasn't allowed. Why does he want me at his house, when all they could do was glance at each other across a crowded room. A room containing his wife, but thank god not his children. That would be a travesty. The pretence made her sick and so did the cold which was biting through her clothes. Flat or no flat this was no way to treat a girl you claim to love. And then she remembered it was her decision to escape the claustrophobia of indoors for outside.

"Fancy meeting you here, "said a voice that took her back to a previous life. It belonged to Keith Henderson, who looked just as lost as her. Most of the men were decked out in black and white evening dress, but he obviously didn't own a dinner suit.

"Move a little closer to my fire you look freezing," he said, stepping aside to make space for her.

"I am cold, thanks Keith."

"So how did Judith Pemberton get herself invited to Willington's bash of the year."

"I was just about to ask you the same thing."

She was glad when he answered first, it gave her time to concoct a plausible story. He made it sound like an accident, but she guessed there were other reasons for him spending New Year's Eve with a bunch of stuffed shirts.

"Where's Peggy," she said, hoping to divert the conversation elsewhere.

"Well she's not here. She's somewhere in London."

"London?"

She thought of Mairi and her sudden disappearance. She was somewhere in London too.

"The Beatles Christmas show."

"Lucky girl."

He couldn't resist making a face, but in the poor light it went unnoticed.

"So now you know the sad details of my life, how did Judith Pemberton get herself invited to such a posh do. And how come you've come alone."

"Who says I'm alone."

She watched the ebb and flow of people through the plate glass windows. It felt a little unreal. Like she wasn't really present, and the evening was happening to someone else.

"So do I have to play spot the fellah."

"You can if you want," she said. Playing out in her head the part of the game where she identifies McMenemy as her fellah.

"But I wouldn't bother, I came alone."

"That's brave of you."

"I wasn't feeling very brave before you came over. Leaving is what was on my mind."

She surprised herself with her honesty, but immediately followed it

with a lie.

"You see it was Mairi who got the invite and I was coming along for the ride. She knows the Alderman, who knows McMenemy."

"So what made you decide to come alone."

"The truth is a little sad Keith."

"I don't mind sad, that's what New Year is for, melancholy and men crying into their pints."

"I thought Mairi might make an appearance. I've heard nothing since she decided to stay in London."

"She sent a Christmas Card to us, but there was no letter. I think she'd just had enough of Willington.

Did you two have a falling out?"

"Not really Keith, we just drifted apart once school was over."

Judith was now regretting the lie, missing Mairi, and feeling very alone; She hoped he wouldn't notice.

"I expect she's having a ball in London."

"Just like Peggy."

"Yes just like Peggy."

They fell into silence, their thoughts elsewhere.

"Come on let's play spot the fellah anyway," he said, trying to lighten the mood.

McMenemy moved sleekly through the room; a panther stalking his territory. He made brief entrances into conversations that were not his, before moving on. Assembled in the room were people he considered important, necessary, elemental – without whom he would simply evaporate, or become an ordinary, commonplace man. Beside these elemental beings stood the escorts and concubines; associates invited to keep someone other than himself company.

Padding through his thick pile carpet. Smoking a cigar. Taking hungry draughts from a whisky and water. McMenemy floated. Out on the veranda he could see his mistress talking to the boy who would one day take his place. And he saw they were totally unaware of how the future would unfold, but he knew. Everywhere in the room he could see the future unfolding.

"I have great plans for you in 1964," said the Alderman. Squeezing his shoulder.

"1964 is going to be your year McMenemy."

And even though he knew that was not so, vanity, alcohol, delusion, allowed him to bathe in the moment. To still the ticking clock, to be immortal for one night; one sodding night. Or maybe this was what revenge felt like. Sweet and heady, a drunken swing that connects with a nose, an eye, a chin. He wanted in that moment to beat the man, to beat out all his corruption. But tightening his grip round the glass was all he could do. McMenemy raised his drink and flashed a smile, and went upon his way. He caught the eye of Father Flannery who looked at him with a beckoning eye. Under a Priests gaze it was impossible to sustain the pretence. He would be forced to surrender to the gaze, and confess. And so the party would be nothing more than a memorial, a living wake. There was time enough to make an acquaintance with death. Time enough to decline and go. He raised his glass, and bowed his head, and moved on. Eyes met his and burned into him like bright suns. Glasses reflected light. Christmas decorations sparkled. People smiled.

Keith Henderson touched her arm, he guided her round so they both faced the window. With the touch came a tingle; an unexpected surprise.

"Tell me Keith how do you play this game?"

"With your eyes closed."

"So how are we supposed to spot anyone?"

"By smell."

"Don't be daft you can't smell anything through plate glass."

"That's correct, but it's a different type of smelling I'm talking about."

"You know Mairi always said you were a little strange Keith Henderson."

"Strange in what way?"

"She said you weren't much of a talker. Said you would just stare at her reverentially. Like she wasn't real."

"That was years ago, the old Keith. Now I'm new and improved."

"Come on then what's that different kind of smelling?"

"Ever heard of blind tasting."

"No but it sounds strange to me."

"It's something I saw on TV. A person tastes some food and has to give their opinion based just on taste, not how it looks."

"Now you're making me hungry – where's the food anyway."

"It's coming, look over there I can see another waitress with a tray of vol-au-vents."

"You're just making that up Keith."

"Ok I am, but now you're getting a taste of the game. If I was to say she was wearing a white blouse and black skirt, and her hair was black and beehived, then you might spot her."

"But she's not there."

"Just suppose she is, then you would spot her with my description."

"So this games nothing to do with smell, its just I spy with people."

"That's right."

"Come on then, close your eyes Keith, I'm going first."

The food arrives and is swallowed rapidly by the crowd. A small quartet assembles themselves: Double Bass, Drums, A Spanish Guitar and Trumpet. Dancing follows. Groups splinter, partners are found. The room undulates with rhythm. McMenemy dancing first with his wife, switches partners. He chooses safe women, those who would never provoke a jealous look or suspicious glance. Yet all the while he has a picture of her fixed in his mind; she's the goal he's moving towards, the only person he wants to touch – even if its just fleeting. He dances well, a smooth and sensual mover.

"Come on Keith let's dance," says Judith Pemberton.

Her mind shifts from one man to another. As McMenemy supposed, she spots the only opportunity to make contact. To talk without speaking. And so they wrap themselves round the room. McMenemy slowly making his way to the space occupied by Judith and Keith – the youngest people in the room by a country mile. The music segues into a Beatles melody, and Judith laughs. She thinks of Peggy, all screamed out and happy. The cacophony of her evening compared to theirs. She feels a pang of jealousy. Instead of the real thing, they were being served-up a middle aged facsimile.

There's a pause in the music, the Alderman cuts in with an "excuse me." He whisks Judith away as the next song begins. Leaving Keith Henderson partner less and McMenemy thwarted. The Alderman is one of those men who can't dance. His minds preoccupied and protoplasmic, too busy for the intricacies of rhythm and grace. He's full of thoughts and images, and the sensation of holding a young girls body close to his. And she in turn is stiff and unresponsive. Her mind churning through excuses to get away. She knows what he'll try on next; on some pretext he will have her alone in a distant room. Then his hands will move more freely, snaking inside her clothing, pushing with fingers, making contact with flesh.

"All this dancing is making me hot, let me go and freshen up, "she says as the song ends, and the Alderman loosens his grip. She has no idea where to go next, so makes for the nearest woman.

"Do you know where I can find the ladies," she asks – still a little breathless from the dance. The woman says she needs to go too and escorts her through a side door and down to the basement. No one follows. All they can hear is the music's muted tones, and the hubbub from above.

"I don't blame you wanting to escape that awful man," the woman says as they enter a large bathroom. She bolts the door, and in a stage whisper says:

"He's just about the worst man in Willington."

"I know," she replies, her voice strained with tension.

"I was hoping you didn't know; he's a spoiler of innocence. But don't worry he wouldn't dare follow us down. But be careful when we go back, is there someone who you can be with."

"Only Keith, and he's young like me."

"So not much of a match for that dirty old man."

In that moment she felt powerless. The man she was supposed to be with; had to think of his wife and the good people of Willington. Keith in comparison was a boy; a nobody, no match for someone like the Alderman. He could rely on the Police, local Magistrate, and just about anyone who was anyone to take his side. Whatever she had to say, would be dismissed too. And McMenemy, to save face, would do nothing.

"I think you'd better stay with me, until that man finds another young girl to bother. Its his wife I feel sorry for, she must know. I'm Jane Stephenson by the way, my husband, for his sins works with Maurice

McMenemy."

"Judith Pemberton," she said. Not really knowing what to say next, save for a genuine "thank you."

She was safe now, protected by a group of middle aged woman. At midnight they assembled on the terrace to watch McMenemy's fireworks. That's where Keith found her, and took her hand.

"If we leave now, no one will notice," he said.

His offer sounded right and proper, and the only option for her. McMenemy had not said a single word to her. All he managed was a sheepish glance in her direction. He'd failed to protect her from the Alderman, a known pervert. Failed to make her evening even remotely enjoyable. Outside McMenemy was playing master of ceremonies. He lit the first touch paper.

"Thank you," she said to Jane Stephenson before making for the cloakroom. And then they were out in the cold night air – running down the hill towards Willington town. Laughing with relief. Hardly aware of where they were headed or what they would do.

There was nothing ordinary about the marriage of Keith Henderson and Peggy. Only the ceremony, a sparsely attended affair at St Vincent's Church followed by a cold buffet at the parochial hall, fitted such a description. Keith and Peggy were destined to be together; it's just that nobody saw it coming. Even McMenemy, who contrived to know everything about Willington and its inhabitants, was caught on the wrong-foot.

To some Peggy appeared from nowhere; ensnaring the poor boy with her white-bread charm. To others she was a perfect wife, whose church going and home making complimented Henderson's imperfections. Floating about the edges of his ego, silently dusting away anything unsightly. A neutralizer of bad odour, the sort that rises from those handicapped by sweaty ambition.

At this stage in his life Keith Henderson was no more than an office boy. But she'd spotted something else on that trip to London; self contained she would say when asked to describe her fiancée. Yet such a vague word hardly accounted for them departing as strangers and returning home with a cheap engagement ring. And what had happened on that five-day trip was all together stranger than the gossiping tongues of Willington could concoct.

Father Flannery was seated beside Peggy on the first leg of the journey; he slept most of the way. While Miss McMenemy, a spinster relation of the businessman, sat beside Keith. She too contrived to sleep all of the way south; her false teeth chattering along with the engine.

These sleeping chaperones were blameless in the eyes of those who wished to apportion blame. Or by those who envied the clever transition from total strangers to the owners of a newly built home. The fact that Keith now worked for McMenemy and had moved into a house built by one of his business associates, was beside the point. It was the arrogance of that Vesper Motor scooter, parked outside at a jaunty angle, that raised hackles. And the way Peggy tended to their tiny patch of garden; dressed in Capri pants and sunglasses.

Ordinary was not a word used to describe the Henderson's. After all their extraordinary coming together was a topic of conversation for weeks in the living rooms and lounge bars of Willington. Then there was the scene outside St Vincent's and the way he towered over tiny Peggy like the Colossus of Rhodes. There were rumours too about a New Years Eve party at McMenemy's, and a certain Judith Pemberton. All very unordinary.

Their coming together began with a darkened hotel corridor, and the shuffling of cardboard suitcases. He just happened to choose the room next to hers. Bodies separated by paper thin walls; two to a room. A grimy hotel in Mornington Crescent; surrounded by pubs spilling out Irish navvies. Bodies that met and slept together, and fell in love.

New Year brought with it changes. Keith became serious; he put away his boxing gloves and buried the memory of Geordie, with one last visit to the poor mans grave. The headstone of his parents and younger sister was joined by his. In Willington's windswept cemetery – abutting the coast road, he'd said his goodbyes:

> "Sorry Geordie but I can't be as certain as you. I'm fallible as the next man, which you never were. And I've turned into a chancer, sorry. Let me be, because I'm not as strong as you. Let me make my own mistakes. All I ask is that you forgive each one of them. Put them down to youth, ignorance and stupidity. Ambition is as corrosive as sloth. Two sides of the same coin, you used to say. And I'm stuffed full with it. So long old friend, say a prayer down there for me. "

A winter wedding is what they called it.

"Two paupers not quite twenty," is how McMenemy put it.

"We'll have to find the Henderson's a home," he'd said, laughing at the rhyme. Nobody asked them why they were marrying in such haste. But his mother appeared happy, she began to talk of lodgers when he mentioned

McMenemy's offer. And Peggy's folks, they just smiled benignly, like the Pope had canonised them both. Although beneath the smiles he sensed something approaching relief – their bodies visibly relaxed, sinking into the furniture. Her mother took to calling him Keithie, which somehow suited their friendly mood.

"Has someone started dosing your folk's tea with opium," he'd said after a particularly luxuriating evening.

"Don't be daft Keith, they like you that all," was Peggy's reply. And he had to admit it felt good being the favourite son in law.

In the bedroom where she dresses is a painting of Lindisfarne Castle; it's a bedroom she never enters, her parents room. All dark brown wood and tobacco leaf wallpaper. A place that smells of toilet water and ancient human sweat. Her room is occupied by bridesmaids, teasing their hair into lacquer sculptures. She sits at the dressing table, alone momentarily; the painting is reflected in its mirror. Old ghosts circulate, then her mother enters and spell is broken. She holds a brush and veil. The hairspray is already there, ready to be used.

Prenuptial flutters were smoothed over the previous week. Keith had asked to add Geordies widow and daughter as guests – she'd objected, the numbers had been sent to the caterers and it was her family footing the bill. She responded a little too quickly, a little too harshly.

"Don't remind me of that, I suppose you expect me to be grateful for the rest of my life," he'd said. His voice matching hers in volume and tone.

They faced each other in silence, both incapable of finishing the argument. And then her dad entered the room, wearing a look of concern:

"You can always back out if you have second thoughts Keith, and that goes for the bride too." He said, stretching out his arms as if to

separate a pair of angry prize fighters. Although he said it with a simile, his voice sounded serious. They said nothing, too stunned to respond.

"Now that's better, a bit of peace and quiet. Save your arguments for the honeymoon and the years to follow. Marriage is a serious business, don't walk into with your eyes shut. "

This time there was no smile. The silence broke as the door closed, and they both laughed until tears of relief streamed down their faces. Nothing more was said about who was paying for what. An invite was sent out, and there were no more arguments.

He tenses the muscles of his stomach and exhales until the gagging reflex has him gulping in air. Sit-ups follow press-ups; follow one hundred expansions of his Charles Atlas

Chest Expanders. And when he's done, he relaxes. Sitting naked on the side of his single bed, eye to eye with Monica Vitti.

He lights a cigarette and inhales rapidly; burning down the Embassy to its filter. The radio noise rises upwards through floorboards and rug; distorted and metallic – the sound of circuits and diaphragms, and distant other worlds.

On the morning of his wedding, he laid his suit, shirt and tie out on the bed; the way he always did. Clothes are his signal of intent. A message that travels faster than the speed of sound. Triggering a sonic-boom through any ballroom or wedding congregation. And in a roomful of relatives and strangers, he chose to stand-out. He chooses to be seen by the McMenemy's, the Pemberton's and Henderson's.

When Rocky Marciano was learning to fight his trainer, Charlie Goldman tied string to his feet. Keith Henderson felt like someone had done the same to all of his limbs; locking them together in a stiff suit. Constricting his toes in an ill-advised pair of winkle pickers; that looked good on Jimmy, and felt comfortable enough in Timpson's, but hurt like hell walking. A flight of stairs, down into his mother's kitchen, drew on five years of boxing training to manage the pain. In China they bound girl's feet to make them dainty, in England a man cripples himself for fashion.

"You look lovely Keith," said his mother, repeating her well-worn compliment.

Keith Henderson sandwiched between his mother and Best Man listened to the rise and fall of voices. The renewal of acquaintances. The direction of altar boys, and guests being greeted by ushers with a hymnbook and order of service. He watched the brides party take their places to the left. Wood and leather, Fancy hats and stiffly fitted shirt collars. Lace mantillas. Half St Vincent's regulars, half strangers – but strangely familiar. At the very front he sat, the husband-to-be. He held himself with a mature dignity; not a million miles away from a heavyweight boxer. He leaned into his mother and whispered.

"Keep your voice down Keith," she hissed.

"Save your voice for the vows."

More guests arrived, adding to the density of noise within St Vincent's. Every so often his mother would turn and say the name of a person she recognised. Maurice McMenemy and his wife preceded the Gallagher's who preceded Martin Henderson, his bachelor uncle. Soon the church came to resemble the sparsley attended eight o'clock mass on a Sunday. Except the congregation were better attired.

At twelve O'clock precisely Peggy married her man, exchanging vows and rings. A sigh passes through the congregation. Father Flannery flashes a beaming smile at some unknown recipient in the congregation. The newly married couple take communion, Faith of Our Fathers follows Hail Queen of Heaven, the Ocean Star. And they all file out to a reprise of the Ave Maria.

"A nice lad, but he always gives me the impression of being a little preoccupied," said Judith Pemberton's grandmother when they'd moved a sufficient distance away from Keith Henderson.

"What do you think Judith?"

"The poor boys out of his mind."

"Oh Judith, please."

Peggy cranes her neck to gaze into her man's beaming face. A suffocating crowd draws near. The Daimler pulls-up, its bonnet festooned in white ribbon. The bride throws a bouquet that's caught by a young girl.

A sickness nestles in the pit of McMenemy's stomach. The sort that can't be settled by medicine or rest. A loser's sickness; despondent and incurable. The body's way of saying you're beaten, before you beat yourself to death. Peggy was happy, happier than he'd ever seen her. But all he wanted to do was wipe away that smile and erase every single person who stood between him and Judith. Erase in a Soviet style purge, with woodland burial pit and machine guns mounted on either side. Then ride off with her into a forest mist, leaving behind gunpowder smoke and the glint of a discarded wedding ring.

Time slowed to an aching waltz. A journey along the Coast Road. Uncles Martin and Anthony following. He shoulder-to-shoulder with his new bride. Grey skies give way to blue. A high summer gleam settles over Tynemouth, giving the town a magical tint. Way above the clouds Telstar 2 completes its elliptical orbit. Seabirds dive at the ocean. The Long Sands are empty. Shuggy Boats are stilled. Striped windbreaks, children building sandcastles, swimmers and paddlers, are all abscent. The gleaming white Park Hotel sails into view; a landlocked ocean liner on a sea of manicured grass.

"Keith remember to mix," his mother says as they stride ahead of the two uncles. A pageboy and young bridesmaid stand beside a woman, decked out in a floral hat and polka dot blouse. They pose stiffly while a photographer aims his camera. As they pass a small cabal of dark suited men he catches a fragment of their conversation.

"Hiring this place must have cost a pretty penny..."

He recognised Maurice McMenemy and one of the Gallagher's. The Gallagher brothers were prominent within and without the parish - middle aged and aggressively self-made, they'd accumulated money by turning animals into glue. And with them came the stench of the bone yard. McMenemy, a foot taller and resplendent, looks bored. Keith has no idea what his boss has paid for the expensive suit, but whatever the cost he fancies a slice. Their eyes meet and both nod. For a moment he's in McMenemy's world. A place smelling of calf leather driving gloves, expensive cars and money: oodles of money.

He steps into the Art Deco hotel entrance. A pianist

plays a jazzed-up version of Mairi's Wedding:

"Step we gaily ....," sings his mother.

A drink from the bar gets him relaxed. A sour taste of the days first pint; one cigarette followed by another. He listens to the tone and rhythm of voices as their chatter spreads throughout the reception. The pianist changes pace; tapping out the chorus of You're Driving Me Crazy, before segueing into the more sedate Portrait of my Love. The Marciano crouch and Matt Monro croon: one he could never get right, and one he couldn't stand.

Perfume mingles with the odour of clean bodies and freshly cut flowers. His mother circulates, more dogfish than shark. Voices cracked and cackled; a cacophony of words such as *bonny*, *lovely* and *lucky girl* rose above the practical business of male conversation. There was nobody there who didn't seem to be having a good time. He takes a scoop from a nearby bowl and fills his mouth with salted nuts.

"In Willington they say you're only fifty feet away from a blood relative. But here, I make it five inches. "

He turns to find a smiling McMenemy occupying the bar space next to his. Close-up the suntan appears deeper, the teeth whiter, eyebrows arched – a la Sean Connery. A selection of drinks, mostly wines and spirits, are accumulating – as two barmen service his order.

As far as he knew there was no bloodline between the McMenemy's and Henderson's. But there'd been a family connection that faltered at his generation. No argument, no estrangement, just a parting of ways that happens sometimes.

"Weddings are strange beasts," continued McMenemy.

"A year in the planning, a day in the making and thirty odd years, if you're unlucky, in the undoing. And everyone will raise a glass to the bride and groom. We'll wish them well, while secretly wondering how the hell they managed to pay for a do at the Park Hotel. "

McMenemy pointed at the assembled guests, sweeping his arm to encompass the room.

"Curiosity is what keeps all these cats alive."

He took hold of Keith's upper arms and turned him, so they both had the same view.

"No need for padding there. Got shoulders like your old man...Each one of these is also wondering how a poor girl and her man from who knows where managed to pay for all this booze. They're not complaining though. Just curious."

He held on, burrowing fingers into material and muscle. Glasses chimed behind them. New orders were shouted across the bar.

"Take Rumpelstiltskin over there. Who's he with, what's his connection. And who goes to a wedding in Teddy Boy regalia. Someone should tell him The Beatles have just killed off Elvis."

Next to the rocker was his wife, welded to his arm by an oxyacetylene torch of love. The king of the Ted's and his virgin bride.

"I take from your silence you have the answers Keith."

"People will just have to remain curious, Mr McMenemy. I've taken a vow of silence."

"Well if you want to make yourself useful, before getting smashed to smithereens, pass me some nuts."

The barman called over, his order was done. With that McMenemy was on his way; trailed by an overladen waiter. He shouted:

"Catch you later son," before snaking his way into the crowd. The world turned and he rolled with it. Tanned and urbane, a cigarette in one hand, a drink in the other.

MCMENEMYS BLUES

Nobody notices the etiolated person, who bends and bows in the breeze; who prays for an end to his journey. A safe passage, accompanied by St Bede the Ferryman.

On a cold night in '64 McMenemy sang his blues:

"Judith the cards are stacked against people like you and me. We struggle and try our best, but a simple twist of fate can unravel everything. Take away our livelihoods and our homes. Smooth the path from semi-detached luxury to doss-house. And no amount of praying to the queen of heaven, the ocean star, will make things better.

There's a man down there in The Salvation Army, raggedy like all the rest of them. And he drinks too much, like the rest of them. He smells of putrefaction and decay. And once he had a wife and a couple of kids, and a home not far from the Colliery Houses. He had a job in the shipyards and had worked on the Mauritania, god rest her soul.

But the depression put an end to all of that. Brother can you spare a dime, followed him about like a theme tune. It took him from Jarrow to London; where the great and the good opened their flies and pissed all over those poor and desperate men. And someday the grandsons of all those grandees will pull down their zippers and piss over you and me, and we will be powerless to do anything about it.

When workers united, they sent in the army and those who'd never done a day's work in their lives, pretended they could do decent men's jobs. They talked about how easy such work was, when they'd only done it for five minutes. When the next meal for a family never depended on their labour. When they'd never had to face twenty or thirty back breaking years, only to end-up dead, in an early grave. Or in the case of Jack, our resident of the doss-house, enduring a living death. They will never face the prospect of redundancy; have skills acquired over a lifetime, rendered useless.

A movement of one point on the stock market sends a hundred or more to the Labour Exchange. A signature by some Government lackey, cancelling an order, puts an end to the hard work of thousands. Work is not virtuous or dignified, such words come from those who have never had to work, never went hungry. And if you complain, like Jack did. They make your life a fucking misery.

He sent his kids to school with no shoes on their feet and their teacher lit a fire to warm a classroom full of small frostbitten toes. And it was at school where they had their first and only meal of the day. The teacher was a small slim woman with short bobbed hair. She had no children of her own because female teachers were not expected to marry. And she supported her whole family, five or more brothers, on meagre teacher's wage. She had compassion in spades, and despite her own suffering, she always had time for others.

While all this was going on, the great and the good partied like there was no tomorrow. They drank champagne, and got up late. They slept in warm luxurious houses and they ate three or more meals a day. Around their dinner tables they dismissed the working man as lazy, and not a patch on his foreign counterparts. They revelled while others starved.

The teacher saw the effects of unemployment on the children's thin and undernourished faces. The more people like Jack suffered, the more their sons and daughters did. Falling asleep during lessons. Unable to concentrate. Clothes full of holes, mocked by richer children for their poverty.

Jack tried to move away, tried to find a job to feed his family. He went to Manchester, to Hull and London. But everywhere was the same story. He slept on the street and in doss houses, because he had no money for lodgings. And all the while his family went hungry.

One day down at the Labour Exchange he was told his dole money was being stopped. He was not trying hard enough to look for work, he was not deserving enough. A clerk in some back office had singled out his name; added his to a list of troublemakers. He after all was one of the Jarrow marchers; men who'd set about embarrassing the government. Poor men, who were given too much publicity.

The clerk of course was only following orders, the way the spineless types who implement the policies of others do. Some work-shy Civil Servant, had him jumping to attention; while he in turn had done the same when called by his superior. At the end of this chain is a man born into luxury, who thinks more of his dogs than the common man.

That simple twist of fate had Jack destitute, and his family readying themselves for homelessness. Things did not improve. Jack resorted to begging, to stealing coal, to hunting for scraps in the rubbish of others. And his wife, out of her mind with worry, joined the wives of other desperate men – down at the fish-quay.

But not every man can face his wife becoming a prostitute, or accept the money she made from other men. Jack was one of those men. He turned instead to the bottle, and drank away her hard earned money. So they were back to square one, except this time it was worse. His wife had to take the casual abuse and rape, the lot of a waterfront prostitute. She tolerated the indignity and humiliation, until one day her period never came.

When one month became two she decided to do something about the situation, in the only way possible. She died a terrible death of septicaemia and Jack drank himself to oblivion. His kids never came back to class; they were sent to separate children's homes.

When the work came back during the war, Jack was too far gone to get his old job back. He was too old for the army, and too unfit for work.

He's an old, old man now, hardly aware of who he is or what he was.

But I'm certain the man who signed Jack's death warrant is living comfortably in retirement, sitting atop a big fat pension. Complaining about the power of the unions.

We are all a step away from being Jack, all except those born into privilege. Never vote Tory Judith, they are the enemies of hope. "

SEASONS OF PEGGY

Another Green Day:

The morning, when it comes, comes in pieces. Monochrome jigsaw shapes, slowly moving together, pushing out a Technicolor dream. At the puzzles centre is his body, suspended on a set of springs and soft cotton. His nakedness reeked of the nights sweat and bodily excretions; and there's a fresh indentation, where Peggy had slept.

An Italian Actress had come to him during the night; secreting herself under the eiderdown. Blowing him like a Captain Horatio Hornblower. She left behind her name and his heart racing. She left him wishing the infidelity was real. Monica Vitti with her almond eyes and fleshy lips, buzzed around the edge of his consciousness. She followed him to the bathroom, where he shaved, morosely.

"Monica Vitti, Monica Vitti," whispered Keith Henderson, as he peppered the Armitage shanks with black beard-dust. Black as her Kohl rimmed eyes. Pieces of a stone-grey morning fused together. The sound of Peggy at work, preparing his boiled eggs. Body soap, chemically enhanced; a toothpaste zest stinging his tongue; and the day's first cigarette, smoked while his bowels moved.

A breeze blew in through the small bathroom window,

rattling her thermometer in its cup. It wafted her sanitary belt and underwear, drying above the bath. He pictured the calendar she kept by the bed, and its colour-coded markings. A light crimson would now give way to duck-egg blue. And in a week, with the danger over, there was an emerald green. Green for go; for copulation without consequences.

Monica Vitti has green eyes and blond hair. She wears black, and folds her arms in that distinctive way. Her look is pensive and distracted, and when she meets his gaze, there is a perfunctory exchange. Peggy's face is superimposed onto the actress.

To sharpen-up the day's rough edges; he pops an orange and black pill. Drops a dash of Optrex in each eye and lets out an uggh sound from deep within his chest. The veneer of civilization momentarily slips. He bares his teeth at the pristine man in the mirror and summons-up the actress again. She scratches him with sharpened fingernails; bites his lip until he bleeds. In her almond eyes there's a reflection of his damaged face.

"Your eggs are ready love," calls his wife and the blue day reassembles.

The buzzer sounds; calling Willington to work. Peggy's voice is accompanied by the smell of cinnamon toast and a radio playing a Jim Reeves song; Adios Amigo. On the stairway is a print of a bloodied Christ, a crown of thorns with crimson droplets streaming from the puncture wounds. Further down another wedding present, a marriage blessing from the new Pope Paul. He experiences a flicker of irritation, as small as flea bite. It's added to all the other irritants, accumulated since their wedding.

WILLINGTON SQUARE

The town leers like a black-eyed drunk; imposing itself on fragile suburban borders. Making mischief where there was once, two hundred years ago, a rural order. It belches, slow and dirty; leeching effluent into tributaries. But when it smiles, that higgledy-piggledy smile; when the carcass of a ship is brought to life. When children maraud through its parks and burns, and laughter rises above the cacophony of work; ugliness is dispersed - filtered through a prism of Easter Sundays and Whit Weekends. Where men recline on deckchairs; dressed in formal suit trousers and shirts, rolled-up at the sleeve. Where on pleasant sunny days, they bask uncomfortably. Smoking pipes and cigarettes; sipping from warm bottles of ale, while families congregate at their feet.

Willington is a town between river and sea. A landlocked place. Where the winters are severe, and summers cooled by a steady North Easterly breeze. Where a dissonance hangs in the air; like the twelfth day of Christmas when paper decorations begin to wilt.

"A penny for your thoughts," she says. But he just carries on staring out of the window; waiting for the second coming. For the rain to subside, for Willington to magic itself into someplace else. The tap-tap of her typewriter begins again. She sets to work on invoices and letters; on the discourse that underpins McMenemy & Co. He in turn watches from the corner of his eye. The rise and fall of her breasts, the twinkling of light as it bounces from her horn-rims. The rat-a-tat-tat of her fingertips as they precisely needle the Olivetti's keys.

There's a correctness in her posture, like a female acrobat preparing to take the trapeze. An economy of movement. A Sophia Loren smile, wide and full. Her teeth protrude slightly; which on an ordinary girl would be considered goofy or buck. But the girl carries them off. Every so often she lets her tongue pass over those pristine molars. If they were to sleep together, he would insist she wear the horn-rims. A vision of her flashed through his mind; she does that thing with her tongue before latching protruding teeth on to his foreskin. The image lingered, like an unfinished conversation.

"No work today Keith," she says. And for a moment he is flustered, caught in flagrante. She continues her tap-tap tapping, but her eyes look at him with expectation.

"Just admiring McMenemy's rainbow," he says.

The rainbow straddles a large empty plot of land at Willington's centre. The rains have set to work on the soil, turning it into a muddy quagmire. Dirt spills out onto the pavement, giving it a murky grey hue. A large sign lets everyone know McMenemy has plans for this land. It supposes a universal agreement with his scheme. And for the most part it supposes right. Her gaze remains steady and unflinching.

"Just pacing myself, the planning committee meets tonight and McMenemy wants me there. Another sixteen-hour day, another dollar."

He attempts a sort of world weary smile; but already her attention has drifted. The ping of another carriage return and the ratchet sound of paper being ejected, replaces conversation. The plans for Willington Square sit before him.

McMenemy's rainbow shimmers; then slowly evaporates. Sheltering shoppers emerge and go about their business. His mood lifts, and he takes hold of the Quantity Surveyors report. There's a quick hint of a smile from behind the typewriter.

Drainage: The clay soil is prone to water logging. Special consideration needs to be given to the construction of basements and other underground structures. It is recommended the plans for an underground car-park be revised.

The report continues, like the drone of a persistent shower. He feels damp and a little uncomfortable. There's a hint of dissatisfaction, secreted in every sentence. He pictures the Surveyor, scowling behind a theodolite. Sinking into the mud of Willington Square, unable to contain his distaste of this unlovely plot of land.

But at every disappointing turn, Keith Henderson mentally rights the Surveyors depressing narrative. A clay soil, leeching water, prone to the peculiarities of North Easterly winds; is also an ideal location, situated at the towns centre. Workmen returning home from the shipyards will stop for a pint at the Squares hostelry. Young mothers, pushing prams, will congregate round its central piazza. On a sunny day, the scene will be no different from a one being played out in Sienna or Rome. A little piece of Renaissance architecture imagined in breeze-block and concrete.

At six McMenemy returns. He makes his way slowly to the mezzanine; clutching a large rattling box. A minute or so later, the girl is summoned. His eyes follow her swaying behind, as she ascends. She carries with her the reports he's supposed to have digested; while he in turn returns to the window. Keith Henderson looks out into the future. At a Willington, transformed. An Edwardian parade of shops becomes a modern shopping centre, a self-service supermarket, a bowling alley and entertainment complex. The towns industry, is tastefully hidden; shopper's eyes are directed inland rather than towards the river and it landscape of ships and cranes.

The modern man moves about by car, unencumbered by the drudgery of busses and bicycles. A notch above his predecessor on the evolutionary scale. Dirt no longer resides below his fingernails, and smart shoes replace seg-heavy boots. Computers direct traffic lights, and a silver telephone kiosk is a feature of every street. In this future bad weather has been irradiated, and the sniffles of winter colds, cured.

And there's no need for him to imagine the clean lines of the new Willington. The white balsa wood model sitting in McMenemy's office has captured every future detail in miniature. From Traffic cops to pregnant mothers; from space age ice-cream men to a new coastal motorway.

Keith Henderson paused to survey the blotter. His scrawl was perfectly legible, executed in a neat, if rather ornate hand. It resembled the automatic writing touted by Spiritualists. If he was truly possessed, he would be ready for the planning committee. Ready to spread the gospel according to the man on the mezzanine. McMenemy for all his faith in the modern world, thought of himself as a Renaissance Man. A healer of rifts and an unofficial confessor to his protégé. It was McMenemy who listened like a wise uncle, when he was thinking of leaving the yards. Over a pint in St Vincent's, he was offered a job, on less pay, and with little in the way of prospects. The only thing his new employer could promise was a chance to join his crusade.

"I'm going to build a new Willington, and you're going to help me finish it," sounded less ridiculous after three pints of Exhibition.

He watched the miniaturised people of Willington move through their white balsa wood shopping city, lost in a future reverie. At the top of the mezzanine two figures move behind a partition frosted glass. They perform a shadow play, which on first glance, looks like any other office. Two figures pass papers between themselves, one is seated, the other standing. Then they kneel, their hands are clasped together. A medieval monarch and his consort at prayer.

"Let us pray for the success of tonight's meeting, "says McMenemy.

Their heads bow a little lower in unison. The girl thinks his little rituals silly and superstitious, but she continues with the pretence. After a minute or so of silent contemplation, the shadows rearrange.

"It's your turn now," she says. But he remains oblivious to her presence.

"It's your turn now Keith," she says again, emphasising her point by dropping the papers on his desk. The crack of heavy paper wakes him from his daze and he turns, startled.

"Turn, what turn."

"Your turn to go upstairs," she says, pointing helpfully at the mezzanine.

"And you can leave these here, the're for the meeting. Just bring your body and brains Mr McMenemy says."

The smell of the mezzanine and its heavy oak presence reminds him of an old ship. A Persian rug covers bare floorboards. Pictures of buildings fill the space behind McMenemy's head. New York's Chrysler building twinkling in a black night sky, competes with the Guggenheim. The Lawn in Harlow New Town and St Mark's Square, Venice – vie for attention. An English country house is juxtaposed with a pitman's cottage. An interior shot of the Johnson Wax building shows its moulded Perspex roof, held aloft by giant concrete lily pads. Falling Water and Cragside merge into the natural landscape. Buildings hang like acquisitions, like stuffed animal heads displayed by a big game hunter.

"Take a seat Keith I won't be long."

McMenemy slipped out from behind the oversized desk; and rummaged about in the box he'd carried in earlier. This was McMenemy's way. To keep a person waiting, while holding court on the telephone, or scanning an important document. Every so often, he broke off from his activity and gave a conspiratorial nod. Somehow he managed to make the person feel involved, when they were in-fact passive observers. He made eye contact with Keith Henderson. Whatever he was doing with the mysterious box, was somehow Henderson's business too. His boss was letting him in on a secret; it made the hairs stand up on the back of his neck.

McMenemy's head emerged from two cardboard flaps.

"My secret weapon's Keith," he said. Holding up a bottle of Johnny Walker Black Label in one hand; and Hock in the other.

"I got a taste for this stuff in Germany, and I hear its Lady Councillor Sullivan's favourite tipple. The same little bird has it on good authority that Austin Davey is partial to a little brandy. She also tells me that

314

Laird, the non-conformist smokes Cuban Cigars. "

McMenemy pulled out   more bottles from the box; each had an associated councillor's name.

"It pays to be impartial Henderson; you don't know who's going to get in next." The possibility that these were bribes never occurred to Keith Henderson, who happily, accepted a cigar and glass of Irish. "Let's wet the baby's head," said McMenemy.

"To Willington Square and all who sail in her."

"To Willington Square," chimed in Keith.

"Every spirit builds itself a house; and beyond its house, a world; and beyond its world a heaven. Know then, that the world exists for you: build, therefore your own world," said McMenemy, standing stripped to the waist like a circus strongman. A shaving razor hung loosely from his hand and a towel draped over his shoulders. He spoke Emerson's words to the bathroom mirror. He spoke above the TV noise, playing in the next room. A cigar stub smouldered in an ashtray. The unique smell of rich Cuban tobacco and soapsuds, mingled with cologne.

"Are you calling me Maurice," she shouted from the adjoining room.

"Just rehearsing my speech Judy."

"Can I Listen?"

"I'll be out in a minute, do you mind pouring me a

drink."

Until recently the flat above his office had housed an overspill of filing cabinets and plans for buildings, never built. It served as a dressing room, when he needed to freshen-up; and a place to catch the occasional cat-nap. It also stored imperfect copies of McMenemy & Co.'s ledgers; stashed in boxes under the bed. The flat had never experienced female company; nor had its kitchen or the contents of its drinks cabinet been particularly well stocked. A second hand settee, a radiogram and an old TV were its only comforts.

"The thing about Keith is he's reliable. I don't need a Billy Whizz who's going to steal all my ideas, and leave with half my business. I need a machine to help me make money."

"A machine that sleeps on the job and stares out the window for half the day."

"Judy he just needs training. The lads a fighter not a thinker, he'll be useful later."

"Later?"

"Let's change the subject love. I can't imagine Burton and Taylor have such mundane conversations."

"All right Maurice, I'm ready for your speech."

LUCKY KID

Mairi left for a Praed Street Clinic, from her shabby apartment on Brecknock Road. She took with her a three-inch scar, crimson and white – stretching the width of her forearm. There was the book she'd read on the bus to London and the vibrant green of Hyde Park. The good spring memories of when her feet first walked on the Heath. Up to parliament Hill, behind mothers and fathers pushing children, directing their shaky progress on pushbikes without stabilisers. That first weekend in the city, with the sun shining and inside the beginnings of his child.

There was no room in her head for tomorrow or the day after. Only room for the meal she ate in South End Green. The cinema, showing I Could Go On Singing. The café, where old men played chess; hanging on to it's bohemian past like background players from La Boheme.

There's the music of lunchtime chatter. A gentle burr of sound, detached from city noise. Taking her to the chequered table and a hand written menu. And to her mind emptied of everything but the taste of chips, bacon and eggs. Her first meal, without a job or promise of one. The beginning of a new beginning, accompanied by the sounds of knives and forks, and her enunciating *rumbaba*, in that northern patois she spoke back then.

She counted the steps up to that first apartment. One, two, three, an uneven thirty-seven. Wooden and without carpet, a lick of crumbling cream paint on either side. Indented and discoloured by a thousand and one footsteps. For three months she creaked up and down, down and up until her luck changed. And she traced a polished banister down the red spiral of velvet - down to the Executive Club. Karim worked behind its long chrome bar, decked out in black trousers and white shirt. There was an empty leotard waiting for her, and silver drinks tray if she wanted it. And two hundred pounds a week, crisp rolls stuffed down her bra.

After South End Green she walked south, south until she hit the river at Hungerford Bridge. She watched the dull grey Thames pass her by, and thought about suicide, as one of three options. To consign her body to the murky depths, where river policemen would scoop her out. One would make notes: Female, between 18 and 30, pregnant; distinguishing marks – a scar on the left forearm (recent). And when no one claimed her, she would be buried by Westminster or whoever ran the stretch of river where she washed-up. Buried in a mass grave in some municipal cemetery while people at home saw out their dotage. And there would be no mention of her in his house; she would pass into heavy silence.

Her name written in an appointment book, then crossed out. In a rent book, then crossed out. On letters accumulating in the hallway she had long since left. And in time the room would be re-let and her bag of things put in the loft. And like a hundred tenants before, her name is removed from the letting agents book. She would join all the others who had gone away without a forwarding address.

Option two had walked out in front of her on Parliament Hill, tucked inside a great-distended belly. It said:

"mummy mummy mummy,"

it said "daddy daddy daddy."

It was loud enough to pull her eyes away from the river and demand her attention. Her baby, the one Jim knew was his; after all it was his money paying for everything. It was going to pay the clinic in Praed Street, and keep her on painkillers, until she felt better. And then she was supposed to carry on like nothing had happened.

Standing on the Hungerford as people filed back and forth from the South Bank, she contemplated option three. Suicide was just the type of defeat he would have liked. His dirty little secret consigned to the rivers bottom. A baby would always be a constant reminder of him. A reason for her to make all the wrong decisions. And that baby would not only look like him, but it would grow to be him. A living, breathing eating, defecating accusation. And her only excuse is:

"he was married to someone else, he never wanted a kid."

Her imaginary child is a boy, with a soft mess of a face, and an awkward body. Standing at bus stops, head low;

shoes the size of ocean going tugs. A blank, without any connection to her but those tiny double helixes, twisting elegantly inside their million cells. This unformed boy would eventually be twenty years old. A man, her age.

But this kid is going to be a lucky kid, not born, but conjured up on Hungerford Bridge, and killed off as she walked to Embankment tube. The picture of Hungerford Bridge dissolved into a collage of broken images. Her head stuck down the toilet at number fourteen Brecknock Road. The green bile, the acid taste. Morning sickness on the morning of her abortion. When that lucky kid of hers passed into a container labelled medical waste, and started off on its journey to the incinerator.

Was it really so long since her life had been altered? Three or four months, she could barely remember.

"Hello new lady, my names Karim, flat two," wafted down the hall at Brecknock Road. His dark face is hidden in the under lit gloom; reduced to a shiny set of pearly whites. What she supposed was an ugly gap, became a shiny gold crown when he depressed the light button. While the formless shape of his head, became a thick mass of dark hair. Karim: a short , slight man, who could have been Turkish, Greek, or Italian. He walks towards her, carrying a Carpet Bag - giving him a touch of the Phileas Fogg's.

"I've just moved in, top floor flat. Just the other day. You're the first person I've met here," she trailed off as the stomach acid hit her throat, and her mouth clamped closed to contain the rising puke. The uneven thirty-seven steps, felt like a thousand and ten as she raced to her door, and somewhere down the three floors, she could hear his voice, then the slam of a door.

Karim came back later, or she supposed it was him. The creak of floorboards, the sound of breathing then footsteps retreating. And there was she, lying on her rented single bed, watching the wood-chip as it undulated. Inside her was that lucky kid, who'd forced out her dinner. And at the back of her throat, was a dry after sick taste.

Jim Stark dressed in a second hand mohair suit and tasselled loafers – gliding across the dance floor. She in a tight pair of Levis turned up at the bottom – a quarter inch of light blue. Crimson red socks, and a mans suit jacket. Nothing like a real Modernist – but different enough to raise an eyebrow in the bar at Club A GoGo.

Smokey Robinson singing Shop Around. French Blues, swilled down with lager and black. One moment followed another, and the consequences of one never impacted the other. A man older than her – married. Encumbered with a wife and a house and a job. Clubs were a standoff of wives and girlfriends and people like Jim who had told the missus they would be elsewhere. Memphis Tennessee. His short dark hair, contains tear shaped droplets of sweat, poised to drip onto his forehead and nose.

Moisture runs down his cheeks, making his face glisten in the dark.

And she cried for all of that on her little bed in Brecknock Road; while the person she assumed to be Karim, slammed the door somewhere down below. That sick feeling in her stomach transformed itself into sleep. Sleep with the bare white flex and forty-watt bulb, dangling naked above her head. Sleep with a hundred thousand others separated by plasterboard and brick; fragile as balsa wood. Doors, flat numbers, peepholes, crumbling excuses for water heaters. Absentee landlords, making money from the R.E.M. sleep of others. One long collective intake of breath, a thousand cries, strange names muttered a flat away, one hundred thousand sets of eyelashes – fluttering like butterfly wings – eyes open – eyes closed – staring wide and new.

Mairi she's somewhere else now, where there's warmth and salt air. She sits by the sea; waves lap, and her eyelashes, bat for one millionth of a second. Between her fingers, an olive, soaked in lemon juice. Her skin is a golden brown, her hair – lightened by the sun. Between bites she sips from a glass of white wine - it's fruit flavour frozen out by immersion in ice. She can taste its dry acidity on her tongue. The bottle is on the table, half drunk, and she is alone, the only customer of a small harbour side restaurant.

Waiters stand talking at the rear; lights hang above their heads, shining like halos in the dusk. A hundred and one twinkling low intensity stars. Looking out to the harbour she sees blue black and the glow from boats already out at sea. Lights from moored craft, leeching out of portholes and cabins. Keeping alive card games, and sex games. Shining on the pages of diaries and books half read. Powering the application of lipstick and aftershave. Of soft cotton shirts, and weightless shift dresses.

Mairi is early today, or the others are late – she can't remember. She's numb, impervious to anything but the sensation of being in the circumference of skin. She bleeds B negative red. She feels the effects of two blue happy pills as they diffuse through her body; the sensation envelops like a cashmere coat. The appetite she had a moment ago evaporates. She desires movement, activity, a hilltop – sea-drop road. An engine driving too fast, a foot on a hot exhaust. She signals to the boy who sits astride her motor scooter, flexing his muscles. Caught in freeze frame his vanity appears ridiculous – but a necessary companion on their journey. Then he shifts his pose, like a pouched bodybuilder, and she sees beauty, a night holding onto his hard flesh.

On the road, they stop by one of the small shrines, that litter the hillside, and he plucks a flower from a wilting bouquet. When she touches his muscular arms, he talks about his daily exercise. He prefers the early morning, before the sun rises and the heat begins. He prefers to be alone, not joined in congress by the sweat-drenched bodies of others. Sit-ups and crunches, are his warm-up. He describes the black leather gloves, fingerless, cracked from thousands of repetitions. Softened by sweat, worn thin by friction.

She can see the gym, a mirror running the length of one wall. Weights neatly arranged on metal racks. The discrete door that leads down to its basement entrance. At the stairs bottom is a counter, where an old man takes money from paying customers. He distributes towels, rough as his own skin. A silver dish sits on the counter – it always contains a few coins – an incentive to others who may wish to make a contribution.

The gym was once a wine cellar, and has vaulted ceilings. Some say they can smell the wine – they can taste the acidity of the grapes while their lungs gasp for air. And the air is as thin as a whisper, in this hot cramped place, where ten men and more can pump iron. She allows her hand to rest against his chest. She can feel the moisture on his shirt, and below, his heart beating.

Mairi wakes; a damp film covers her body. The small town of Willington is two hundred and fifty miles North. She has slept the sleep of the discontented - emptying her bladder twice that night. Each time she is disorientated and finds it difficult to make the journey from bed to toilet without hitting unexpected objects. The debris of these collisions are strewn across the small bed-sit floor. Nothing is broken, just rearranged, like a quiet burglar has been at work.

She has two hours to wake and feed herself. Except this morning no food must pass her lips. No coffee, no tea, just plain old London tap water. A taste of putrefaction and old lead pipes; inert, lifeless, nothing like water. She sees an image of Jim – rising from her bed – the day he impregnated her. The look on his face is that of a satisfied man, not the face of a man who had just procreated. She sees the young mothers pushing their children on Parliament Hill.

Mairi hears the sound of people leaving, slamming doors. It's the beginning of the working day for those who do, and a brand new day for her. On this brand new day, she will do everything for the first time. On an empty stomach, she will negotiate the rush hour. Stand shoulder to shoulder, close enough to smell a stranger's breakfast, read their novel, their morning newspaper, and take a dip into their lives for the duration of a stop or two. A brand new day, with the sun shining high over Hungerford Bridge and Battersea Power Station; over Regents Park and Edgware Road.

The offices and cafes, the shops selling gaudy clothes and strange smelling food. Cafes with old men, puffing on hookah pipes, like downtown Bagdad. The clinic on Praed Street where she will have her first abortion. And inside her purse, Jim's money: saved for a holiday, and the new sofa, his wife was not going to have. Money that if she chose, would pay for a thousand things she did not have. All she had to do was keep on walking right past that dreadful clinic. But for girls like her, there were rules, authorities had to be avoided, expensive Harley Street Surgeons were never an option.

If Jim knew her real age on that fateful night, he was a bettor actor than lover. He faked concern when she mentioned the missed periods, but her true age got a reaction. He looked crestfallen, like a child who's just been told Santa is a myth. And his face went through a transformation; into the elegant equation of his life, she'd thrown in an unknown. A situation he never imagined would happen - having a child, with a girl not far from childhood herself. And she watched as a million calculations ran through his mind. Like a fighter with one punch left in him, he swung his haymaker. It was good enough to floor her; to have her counted out. Where did love come into this; the love he had quietly declared. She'd felt it flow from him to her, and now, like a cruel magician, he made it disappear. Her tears of defeat were wiped by him, as he laid out his plan. The money, the clinic; it came to him fully formed, no holes and no ambiguity. He was full of surprises Jim, turning on her that last night, his face an angry blur of red.

"How can you do this to me," he barked, when her reluctance to go along with his plans, showed through. When she suggested keeping her baby.

"For what, so you can play house, you're twenty years of age girl, you conned me into thinking you were older, and now you're thinking about parading this about town for all to see."

He'd moved round her, with the low gait of a predator, in his hand a glass. Liquid spilled as he moved, but that caused him no concern. The glass she could see was an extension of his rage. She thought about giving his money back, running to her bag and handing it over. A peace offering. But there was something about his face that reminded her of an angry dog. A vicious, barking beast, who responded to no one's command. And if she were a man, with hands as big as his, she would take a chance. Chance that the glass he was holding wouldn't be broken and pushed into soft flesh.

But she was out of her depth. So she assumed the position people take when they're about to take a beating; she curled herself up into a tight ball, with arms protecting her head. The sound of breaking glass followed, it silenced her tears. And she found herself calling out "No, no, no, please no." But Jim had only heard the pounding in his head, a sound without language or morals; a sound without pity.

Curled up in her ball, she felt the thump of a small heartbeat; and for a wild moment she imagined their baby's tiny heart, bursting out of its chest. Sucking in all her fear through its umbilical chord. With her head pressed tightly to her knees, she listened to the pulses rhythm and the sound of staccato breath circling the kitchen. And when he struck, it was over quickly and without words.

Her body barely registered the wound he'd inflicted, that pain would come later. All there was inside her ball is the sound of a tiny heartbeat, and his deep sobs, flooding the kitchen with self-pity. He cleaned her wound with a tea towel. In silence she accepted the kiss he gave her forehead, and the arrangement - a waiting room where last months' magazines mingled with contraceptive advice. On that morning in Praed Street, she read about Judy Garland. She read about the rumours and the men and the drugs. There was a photograph of her looking gaunt and unwell. On that morning in the Praed Street Clinic, there's a receptionist, who asks her to extinguish the cigarette she's smoking. And when it was time, her name was called out, and those tiny fingers of that lucky kid slowly uncoiled from her hand.

THE PLAZA

Easter Weekend: Cold, dull and wet. Drinking tea at the Tynemouth Plaza. Briefly remembering Her Majesty's visit in 54' - when there were years stretching out to the horizon. On the Long Sands a diaspora of sea bathers and shuggy boat riders. Old men sit in deckchairs in their Sunday best; with sleeves rolled up and shoes neatly stored below. Large family groups spread out behind windbreaks, candy striped and blowing in the breeze; a firmament of grey above their heads. The hum is now ever present, an accompaniment to everything, including sex. Sex should be enjoyable, but now.....

McMenemy sits alone, a Newspaper lies open at a story of teenage Mods and Rockers, complete with apocalyptic predictions for the nation's youth.

I fear for the future, says a Brighton based Cleric.

He turns the paper until its at the sports section. Stories of penalty shoot outs and goalless draws. Of winners and losers. Nothing grabs him. He sips some more tea, but still his mouth tastes of sandpaper and gravel. There's a feeling of detachment, and of sickness; tiredness rules, from morning through to night. He's aged ten years, presenting a worn out face to the world. Dressed for winter in an overcoat and heavy woollen suit, that appear to envelop rather than fit his body. Down by the sea, dull and overcast, a bitter north east wind blows.

Yet still she's passing through his mind, an undulating wave. A mirage down at the shoreline, collecting shells, bent over in a summer dress. He takes Judith Pemberton from behind; takes her for ride at The Spanish City, and they play the one arm bandits until all the pennies are gone. Another life; someone else's.

Half a mile out to sea Turbinia passes, its small funnel pumps out grey smoke. He blinks and the boat is gone. Back to the Hancock Museum, and children playing in Exhibition Park. One two buckle my shoe, three four knock at the door.

With the end of his cigarette, he lights another. The flame burns intensely bright and the cycle begins again. In his mind's eye he sees the new Willington. The centre of town now has the look of a Florentine Piazza, a Roman Forum - with a modern system-built twist. At the developments heart is a small public area, with a copper Henry Moore style statue, beginning to turn green. It's supposed to represent an ordinary shopper, a woman laden with bags. And it stands on a raised speakers platform, where he imagines spontaneous public events will occur. Firebrands may use the space as a platform for radical new views, energising the town. Remaking local government. Democracy without corruption. Like Rome during the

Republic. The statues plinth has a simple carved inscription: This stone was laid in 1964 by Maurice McMenemy, architect and town planner.

"I built this," he whispers to himself.

"I will be remembered for it, if nothing else."

Funny, now he could barely remember how the derelict site in the centre of town became a shopping mall. McMenemy's Mall. But he was certain it was only through his hard work, that this daydream had become reality. His eyes close and open, he's back at The Plaza, sipping tea. Cigarette smoked down to the butt. Another already removed from its packet.

There's an unusual feeling passing through his body. He feels translucent and clammy, and is shaking ever so slightly. *If only I could give up these bloody things; if only I could lie down.* A crackle of burning tobacco and the hiss of saltpetre. The toll of a bell. Twelve uniform figures trudge through the surf. The leading figure carries a hand bell; behind him six carry a sarcophagus. The remainder walk in procession, following St Cuthbert's bones. In the distance, he can hear the sound of roller-skates; the heavy noise of ordinary souls at play. Cheap music, beat and string laden pop sonatas. Girls chew gum and boys circulate. The stench of perfume, tobacco, and oily pomade drifts over on the breeze. Synthetic bottles of cola with a dollop of ice cream. Zoot suited peacocks resplendent with zits. And the bump and grind of perpetual motion.

"Would you like another cup of tea," asks a waitress. He shakes his head and looks out across the sand, teeming with family groups, and brave sea bathers. The memory of swimming causes him to shiver, so he pulls his overcoat tighter. His eye falls on a large extended family, a father, grandfather, sisters, children. The adults occupy deckchairs, the children play. A small boy digs a hole, his face a mask of concentration and contentment. Forty years ago, that was me; a child with a spade and a hole, nothing else mattered.

Now there's a tightness in his chest, it's been squeezed by a giant vice. He says a prayer to the Queen of Heaven, The Ocean Star. The pain as time passes becomes bearable, no worse than a bad case of indigestion. Yet he can't stop the tears. A girl approaches his table, she's out of focus, a blur with light coloured hair. He can't tell if she's the waitress or just a passing stranger.

"Maurice what's wrong, you look awful," she says. But he can't find the words to reply; the language is gone. So instead he smiles through a grimace.

"Maurice tell me you know me; please, please."

"God help me," he cries as the pain becomes unbearable. And then simply:

"God."

FRIDAY

The shipyard buzzer sounds, and just like every Friday afternoon, men sprint from the exit. Like overdressed whippets, they negotiated the steep bank in overalls and steel capped boots. Older men wear cloth caps; the younger workers prefer an uncovered head. The sound of segs crunching against cobble and tar-macadam merges with the buzzer to make a deafening roar. Some of the men push bikes up the steep hill, or make for the ferry landing, and a journey across the river. Seeing this is a particularly cold April, the coldest since 1911, a scarf or a woollen hat tops the old Sunday suit jacket worn by those who feel the cold. And among them, the occasional raincoat worn by the office boys, who counted pennies and drew plans; who poured over wiring diagrams.

Keith Henderson looked down into the human river. Just as he'd managed to swim upstream against the tide, McMenemy had gone and died. Extinguished on Tynemouth Longsands. The promise of a future was undone in an instant, and so rapid was his transition from trainee architect to standing outside his old employer cap in hand, he'd barely had time to adsorb life's sudden backswing.

The noise of the yards dampens, between five and six,

the dayshift is gone and the nightshift slowly rumbles into action. In the distance he could hear the sound of compressed air machines.

"All quiet on the Western Front," he said to no one in particular.

He'd kept the whole sorry mess from Peggy; the pay cut and mortgage hike. And there was still McMenemy's funeral to do. Although he wasn't sure if he could face another grieving widow, or another church full of crestfallen people. McMenemy was never supposed to die. People like him lived forever. Heart Attack is what the doctor said. But there was a muttering around town. Everyone thought it was something else that killed him. A someone not a something. Geordie would have known where the blame lay:

That Alderman, he sucks the blood out of the living for sustenance. You have no chance against people like him, because they have one subtle advantage, they're hollow inside. No heart, no soul; just a carapace so hard its tough enough to withstand anything you hoy. Don't get mixed up with people like him if you can help it.

Geordie would have known...

And Peggy knew he needed a job. Money was getting tight. Small luxuries, well they were gone. Expectation had morphed into desperation. Any interview would do. A one that happened after all the office workers had clocked off at five fifteen, that would do. But as he entered the empty drawing office he realised the late appointment was not for his benefit, but theirs. They weren't going to give him his old job back, they were going to let him down easy. It was not going to be a public execution. Out of respect, he supposed. He was already well and truly in the shit, all of Willington knew that.

There would be no witnesses; all the benches were covered and emptied of draughtsmen. Below the office, a freight train idled. Smoked seeped through the wooden floor. A fine black film of soot began to settle. Now he knew what it felt like to be dead, to not be among the living. Stuck in Purgatory; punishment for kissing the Alderman's ring he supposed.

A door opened at the far end of the office and a voice called:

"Come in Henderson, we're ready for you now."

When he entered, instead of a firing squad, he found a squat, bald man puffing furiously on a pipe, offering a small hand:

"Norman Vickers, Mr Vickers to everyone who works here, Mr Vickers and the jobs yours."

"Mine?"

"Yes we have an opening for you Henderson."

And that's how the conversation went from there.

"We need someone whose trained with the best so to

speak. That way you can improve on what we have here. Not that the boys here aren't very good. Some are excellent marine draftsmen. But you young man are something quite different. You'll shake this place up a little. Rouse these dullards from their stupor."

Had him disliking the man intensely. He'd learned a few things from

McMenemy. So he smiled and laughed when he was expected to laugh; and he got through the whole excruciating process with some of his soul intact.

She'll think I've landed on my feet. She'll pour me a drink at the day's end, and one for herself. She'll cook dinner, wash my clothes, and offer perfunctory sex. The girl who'd been a wonder in London, was dull in Willington. A void had opened up between them; now he lay in bed beside her, getting hard-ons that were never used. There was something incomplete about life with Peggy, but it had taken getting married to find that out.

Marriage is something women chatted about, and men ignored, is all his old friend had to say on the subject. And the only person in the whole of the world he could speak to about his marriage was a priest, last man on earth he would confide in.

No one would see him bowing and scraping to someone like Vickers. Except for the ghosts of Geordie and McMenemy. The notion of deferred gratification was something both men agreed with. He guessed McMenemy died owing nothing to nobody. Or maybe he'd left the planet before things got messy. People talked. Night watchmen pretended to sleep.

Vickers described the type of work that he'd be expected to do. Everything from electrical drawings to great hulls, drawn like dinosaur skeletons, stripped of cabins and engine rooms. And he saw in an instant there was no room for manoeuvre in the daily work of a shipyard drawing office. The repetition was going to kill him, but he needed money fast. Beggars can't be choosers, he thought as they shook hands.

Men soaked up the end of the working week with a pint at The Ship, and he chose to join them. He let his thoughts run over the heads of those at the bar, into the encroaching night. Somewhere out there was a woman who would be available for him. A warm woman, with open arms, and lips ready to join his. A thought, an idle piece of fantasy. A basic form, not too dissimilar from .... her, the one who occupied his mornings.

In the morning he said his new workmates had taken him for a drink, one pint had led to another. And she accepted this like she would a change of shirt and tie. She looked at him, not with wonder, but with an ordinary, everyday eye.

"I'm pleased for you Keith. You're tough, I like that," was all she said. As he ate his toast and drank cool weak tea, he waited for the questions. But instead she switched on The Light Programme and busied herself with nothing in particular.

He had a week before the new job started; a week to bury McMenemy. A week to forget that Friday night in The Ship; when a barmaid had once again responded to his charms, and he had taken her to the coal-house. A repetition of a night when the stars aligned differently in the sky.

"You know this doesn't normally happen," he'd said to the disinterested girl. And she'd told him:

"to go back to his wife."

And as he looked into her eyes, he saw no knowledge, no secrets; just the acceptance that people come and people go. The ordinary and unimportant; people like him.

POLKA DOT AND BLUE

It was the moment dark brown earth, hit the polished brown of Maurice McMenemy's coffin lid. When he joined the dead of St Vincent's, singing the halleluiah. And those looking down into the precipice, considered their own mortality. The moment lasted a minute, but within it's limits, her lungs exploded and out came a banshee wail. A strange, primitive sound, that reminded some of funerals in far off places. Places where the wife dutifully leaps onto her husband's funeral pyre. Or takes a vow of celibacy and a black dress to see out her days. And those old enough, recalled the great funerals of their youth; where mourners stood fifteen feet deep, resplendent in black plumage.

But for those without history or anthropology. There was the smell of damp clay, and freshly laundered clothes. The mumble of their Parish Priest, and a breeze blowing flowers about well tended graves. There was the sound of grass being cut in a nearby field. And the wail of a woman, with a face ruined by channels of black mascara. Positioned in a nowhere place, between family and friends. She clutched a bunch of white lily's. Crushing out chlorophyll, until it ran green on her hands. And her mouth, opened as if a great aria would follow. But instead there was silence, and the sound of broken flowers hitting hollow wood.

"Now at the hour of our death ...amen," finished off the scene nicely. With family and friends all joining in with the amen.

All except Judith Pemberton, who left quietly, halfway through the Hail Mary. Her hands sticky and smelling of death lily's, fingered the smooth round rosary beads. While in her mind any thought of father, son and the holy ghost passed to a place reserved for father Christmas and four leafed clovers.

Over in the Catholic section of Willington cemetery, the funeral continued. Mourners remained motionless, like cockroaches frozen in daylight. A cloud of incense drifted over their heads. Behind them, gravediggers, scratched their backsides slowly. And another cortège passed into the cemetery, as smoke drifted from the crematoria chimney. A ghost danced past her, dressed for dinner, making for the exit gate. And she followed the dancing figure, until it led her out, into a breathless Keith Henderson – late for the burial of his old boss.

He looked different, in his crumpled work-suit and battered briefcase. Beads of sweat dripped from his temples, and his hands were clammy when he touched hers.

"Look I'm so sorry about Maurice, I know you two were close." He said innocently, as if her great secret, was public knowledge. And she felt a pressing need to correct Keith Henderson. But he was gone before the lie had left her lips. Leaving Judith Pemberton feeling, disorientated and foolish. She had hardly noticed Keith Henderson's embarrassment, or that of the other mourners. Now some of the looks came back to haunt her. Snatches of the day were played back, in glorious Technicolor, with the sound turned down. And underneath the perfume, and incense, she could smell the hatred, as it crept back down church pews, and through open hymnbooks. As it followed her from St Vincent's to Holy Cross cemetery. And she could feel Maurice McMenemy's disappointment, pouring out of his still heart, through black Sunday best, up from clay and timber. And finally, there was the funeral announcement, which read:

By Invitation only. No flowers or cards.

And she'd kept her grief at bay, right up to the day of his funeral. Right up to the time next doors radio hum, passed through brick and plaster, and into the tail end of her dream. Where the radio joined a chink of cups and plates, footsteps, then a back gate slamming. The scrape of a metal latch as it fell, and the noise of heavy work-boots, scuffing cobblestones. It joined the cries of children, coming from backyards and back-lanes. As she was released from sleep, came the realisation that day was about to start without her.

She heard Maurice McMenemy, purring in her ear. Saying:

"everything will be fine Judy, you'll see."

341

And everything that morning felt far from fine. With him lying stiff as a board, half a mile away. He would no doubt have a rag tag band of the Catholic Woman's Guild, finishing off their vigil. Putting away rosary beads and prayer books. Attending to his corpse like concubines. She could see the cotton, stuffed up his nose, and his hands forced together in supplication. And his little wife, arranging his hair, so it fell just so.

But something stopped her from imagining any further. Maybe it was the silence of the street, now emptied of workers and schoolchildren. Or the thought of his wife, touching dead strands of hair. Having a moment of intimacy, before the coffin was sealed. Maybe that's what sent her downstairs, to the drinks cabinet.

A glass of whisky would steady her nerves she thought. A second, take away the sound of his voice, seeping out of the sofa and sheepskin rug, and anyplace associated with last Saturday night. A third glass, brimming with iced water – sent her to the radiogram. Where his favourite long player lay naked, its cover, upturned. The fourth, fifth and sixth, were a mistake.

But after the seventh, she passed the point of no return. She cooked a haphazard breakfast of eggs and bacon. Washed down with strong black tea. She thought of the word femme fatale, as tears roled down her face. As the astringent smell of soap, wafted up to her nostrils. And while she collected together her clothes; she secretly thanked god, there was no man, no husband, observing. As she fell off the bed, tangled up in stockings and shoes.

And all the while Matt Monro serenaded her meanderings from bedroom to bathroom. His mellow vocal chords accompanied the scraping of cold cream, and debris from the corner of her eye. He crooned through the evacuation of ten whiskeys, a pack of Ritz crackers and a breakfast of eggs with bacon.

Softly as I leave you, permeated every last morsel that poured out of her. And when she was empty, Judith Pemberton cried, wide rolling tears. She cried as cold water washed away her yellow-brown residue. And when it was gone, all that remained was grief, breaking like giant twenty foot waves.

And the sound of a needle, travelling back and forth through it's play-out groove. Synchronised with her heaving chest, and the flow of tears, soaking into camisole. And after a while, it's slow rhythm took her to a calmer place. Where a drummer brushed his skins, through a lazy Bossa Nova. While dancers criss-crossed, cutting their way through air and lightly oiled parquet. She dressed like a dancer, following the rhythm. Covering her body with a white and blue polka dot blouse, and the navy suit she had worn for a wedding. And her mind filled with Saturday nights at St Vincent's, where men and women, engaged and disengaged – with precise, preordained grace. She followed a living Maurice McMenemy with her eyes, as he swept a hundred women off their feet. And she watched herself, step onto the floor. Where the new leather of her shoes, slipped; and without a table or chair to hold onto, where she fell.

Where Maurice McMenemy had picked her up with a hand and a smile. And stayed beside her until the evenings end. Where later, when the Henderson's and everyone else, slept, he was inside her. Filling her up with love. Tearing and shouting, while the needle hit the play-out groove, again and again. Beating a steady bu-bum, bu-bum. Like the sound of her heart, pumping below the polka dot and blue.

She reassured herself, with the thought of black shadows at the back of church. Where she would light a candle, and pretend it was for someone else. She could leave before the service was over, and be at the graveside, before they all arrived. She drank another glass to take away the shaking. And the stylus kicked for the last time, sliding out of it's groove with a scream, like a woman, out of control. Then her house was quiet, and she felt like a stranger; who'd stepped out of her skin, and was looking at the world with a fresh pair of eyes. On the bed lay her nightdress, draped like a carcass, over disorderly sheets. And she sat down, next to the dress, stroking its damp fabric. Taking it in her arms, pressing it close to her chest. And for a moment she could feel the beat of another's heart, against hers.

BENEDICTION

The chalice rises, theatrically, its gold edges catch the light. A
rumble passes underneath the fine Italian marble floor. The
seven O'five on its way to the coast. Flannery could be
Gregory Peck if she squinted, or suspended disbelief.
Benediction on a Monday evening is invariably a negotiation
with the cold, whatever the season. St Vincent's congregation
stand, kneel and sit; their movements are dislocated and
shivery. Father Flannery raises his arms, like a pair of
magpie wings. Time is suspended at the moment of
benediction. Peggy narrows her eyes, so the priest becomes
her only focus.

She sees the black and white bird take flight; and
imagines her body, small and scrawny, holding onto its back.
Through the stained glass, they fly out into the Willington
sky. The monstrance glows, illuminating St Vincent's and its
environs; lighting their way.

"Like what you see," says the bird as it flies over
fuming smokestacks. But her eyes are clouded by blue-black
pollutant. Behind them Willington recedes from view as they
hit open country. The Great North Road twists and turns
below, following the costal route.

She can see the stone walls of Bamburgh Castle, a

great hulk on the landscape. Long Northumberland beaches stretch out luxuriantly. The soft foam of the sea, laps in at high tide. They pass over hamlets, glowing with human occupation. Solid houses, with small windows, built to resist the cold.

"Over there is Lindisfarne and the Farne Islands," said the bird.

"I know that," she wanted to say. But when she opened her mouth, the wind took her words away. Then just after Bamburgh they shift direction and head inland. Shes sure there's some double-backing going on. But shes also sure the bird knows where they are headed.

"I'm going to take us down soon, hold on tight, and please feel free to scream," says the magpie.

As the ground approaches she feels fear for the first time, and buries her face deep in his feathers. Her grip tightens round his chest, and she can feel the steady beat of a man's heart.

The smell of thick incense mingles with damp earth, wood and buttercups. Father Flannery swings his thurible; the odour intensifies and overwhelms all that is natural.

"We must hurry Peggy; there are animals in this field that do not take kindly to trespassers. Come, it's not far."

He pointed towards a church steeple in the distance. "Just over there."

There's no time to ask how a priest could become a

magpie, or why they had set down in a Northumberland field. Flannery quickened his pace. With arms moving back and forth, he maintains a steady sway; while his thurible belches out an incense cloud. And all she can do is follow.

"Hail to the Northumberland night, "sings the priest as he negotiates fences and cattle grates. Until finally there is one more field between them and their destination.

"Jesus is never far from places like this. He stays away from the city and its horrors. He's easy in a place like this, where the destruction wrought by man is hidden."

But words continued to elude her; like a will-o'-the-wisp, they fly out into the night and evaporate.

She first sees Milburn Hall through a gap in a privet hedge. Suddenly the wilderness of grass and fenced-in enclosures open out, becoming the roll of a perfectly flat field. Manicured lawns, and an ornamental lake. A stone humped back bridge, that serves no structural purpose. Meandering thickets of man-made greenery, giving way to a gravel path. And then the hall's first outcrops, delivering dark wood-burning smoke to the atmosphere.

Again the words won't come. So she silently follows Father Flannery as he edges around the halls perimeter fence.

"Be careful Peggy it's electrified," he says when her hand reaches out to touch it.

"There's an opening a few yards down, we can slip through without much danger to life and limb. But for god's sake, avoid any contact with the wire."

An inch away from her nose, the fence hummed. It's power, pulsating, threatening, drawing her close like a magnet. Then a heavy hand gripped her arm, and she was dragged clear.

The residents of Milburn Hall announce their presence with screams and groans. Some press distorted faces against barred windows. While it's more silent members, rock soundlessly, in quiet corners.

"We are invisible to these poor souls. But they can feel us, the way you can sense electricity."

Flannery took Peggy's hand and guided her through an open side door.

"Normally this would be locked, to prevent escape. But magpies, as you know, are expert burglars and gentleman thieves."

They enter a treatment room. A girl's arms and legs are bound with leather straps. A piece of wood has been inserted in her mouth. Her body is shaking beneath a flimsy floral dress. Silver electrodes are taped to either side of her head. Peggy counts five standing people in the room. A woman in nurse's uniform attends to the strapped-down girl, while the men give their attention to a silver radio box. There is very little conversation; just nods and glances, and empty pauses. Then the procedure begins.

Three men and the nurse take positions, either side of the girl. The fourth man adjusts his radio dial. A sound more animal than human issues from the girl, while her body shakes. The attendants hold down the girl's limbs, as her spine arches. It's all over very quickly, leaving the girl still. Her pretty floral dress looks beautiful; it could accompany a walk in the park or a visit to some costal promenade. And her face is serene and untroubled, as if the fifteen seconds of extreme violence had never occurred.

"There for the grace of god," said the priest as he led her from the room.

"Fifteen more patients tonight, another fifty thousand in England by the year's end. The modern world is a strange place Peggy. We have Sputnik and Telstar circulating the earth, nuclear power and television - but we can't fix people like these. Instead we invent drugs like thalidomide, to make matters worse. "

She wondered if Father Flannery was gearing up for a sermon, but instead he switched to twenty questions.

"Teratology, any idea what that means Peggy?"

"Studying something Father, "she felt weirdly elated hearing her voice. But it had somehow detached itself from her body and floated, disembodied, in the room.

"Your close Peggy, it's from the Greek teratos,

meaning monster. Teratology, the study of monsters; our true business of the evening. Now that you've found your voice we can proceed," he said, rolling up his sleeves. And she detected a certain pleasure in his tour of Milburn Hall.

"Sometimes we hide things away Peggy, like the people in here. Nobody wants to see monsters on the street. Drop a penny in the crippled boy's box, yes they will do that. Feel a little sad about the callipers on his legs. But out on Willington High Street they only want to see people like themselves."

"What about the woman having shock treatment Father, she looked perfectly normal."

"She's a fine looking woman, I grant you that. But the horrors inside are hidden, only the curious like us choose to look."

One hollow corridor merged with another. Door upon door of locked rooms. A mural on one wall showed mountains, not the Cheviots or Pennines, but stylised alpine peaks. Below the artist's signature, someone had scrawled The Mountains of Giant Turkey, using a child's crayon.

"Father I feel like I'm going mad," she said, as they arrived at the children's ward. The priest studied her face, as if he was looking for signs of insanity.

"No Peggy you're perfectly well, only the sane would voluntarily choose to visit such a place. "

They stand at the door for an impossible length of time, his hand poised on the handle, his eyes scrutinising hers.

"Now close your eyes Peggy, our visit is over."

Father Flannery takes the monstrance into his hands and with it makes the sign of the cross. The congregation kneel in silence, all except Peggy who weeps silently into her hymnbook. Keith takes the book from her shaking hands. The low drone of St Vincent's organ precedes the evening's final hymn. With the Blessed Sacrament, back in its tabernacle, the priest slips quietly away.

"Everything will be just fine Peggy, everything will be fine," says her husband as they exit.

ENCHANTED

There are mornings when he wakes and his life has returned. And then its July. The old year, the one that started so well, is half over. A thick scum has formed on top of a perfectly good year. The months following Peggy's decline felt like a kind of enchantment. A time when he was sleepwalking. July is hot and sticky in the draughtsman's wood and steam enclosure: his sleeves are rolled high and are moist to the touch. The roll and click of drawings taking shape – fills the room. Tables are ordered like school desks. The shiny bald head of Vickers, glistens as he wanders through the office on one of his random inspections.

With Peggy away he'd taken to drinking on Friday nights and spending Saturdays in St Vincent's. Living the life of a romantic, without romance. He'd swapped his motor scooter for a car, and sunk deeper into debt. On Sundays he drove out to visit Peggy, and walked her through the grounds of Milburn Hall. She rarely spoke, but when she did, insisted on calling him Danny.

As one month stretched into another, her conversation moved backwards. She was a girl again, and with each visit her backwards story became more elaborate.

352

None of it made much sense. And nobody explained to him what was exactly wrong with Peggy, but with each visit the person he knew receded. Occasionally she jittered and stuttered – a broken record, trapped in a word or phrase. The only way to get her out was to fix her eye and sing. She said he had a good voice, that his singing took her to another place.

"I can still hear the lapping of the sea,
Fare thee well my hinney,
Fare thee well."

Took her from the trance, and for brief snatches of time, she was his wife again. Then the curtain would draw, and she was gone:

Dreaming when he should have been....wrapped in the movement of the earth – pulled down by gravity, one of life's prisoners. The clock is slowly making its way towards five fifteen and his release from dreamtime. Already an unspoken arrangement has been made, and with a nod of his head he was in on the plan. The same arrangement they had every week; a different type of enchantment. Where with senses dulled by alcohol he became someone else. And the part of him that always hoped the raven haired barmaid would make an entrance is gone. Part of a past that will never be retrieved.

Home alone and depressed, the melody of his life segues into minor key. Minutes, hours, days evaporate. One evening he returns home in a stupor, decides to look through her things. Maybe find a clue to her decline – something that can bring her back from Milburn Hall. A cure. A piece of magic to break the spell. She keeps a suitcase in the loft. Her things:

"old things," she'd said.

"Nothing important, only to me."

The suitcase is locked, but he has her keys. He jangles as he walks up to the landing. The trapdoor. The loft. An open suitcase neatly packed with belongings. A child's weight card, Family Allowance book and small items of clothing. There's a letter, written but not posted to a person called Danny, and a small pile of photographs – tiny prints barely larger than a postage stamp. They're duplicates, showing a small baby, bound tightly in a christening robe. On the back she has written Danny.

And he knew in that moment about the thing she was missing. The lost child. He read her letter, expecting love, but instead found sadness. A remembrance of times past.

The clock on the drawing office wall shifts to five past five. Already shoulders begin to relax. Some hands have stopped drawing and are beginning to tidy-up. Others are deciding what to finish and leave unfinished. Vickers will come at ten past for his final inspection. He won't keep anyone late because he also likes to be out of the door at quarter past too. But he'll make their life hell if their desk is untidy or their work is sloppy. His inspection takes a matter of minutes, giving everyone including Vickers time to put on a jacket. There is a rule, jackets on outside – no matter how hot the weather is.

On this particular Friday, as sweaty sleeves push through armholes; he thinks of cosmonauts in capsules passing through the burning outer atmosphere of earth. And of downing that first pint, it's like landing in a cool sea. Work is washed away - a blessed moment. He thinks of Peggy, of New Year's day 1964. It feels like a hundred years in the past, not the beginning of a year two quarters through.

The colliery wheel is turning, and a new shifts beginning. The river is dark and polluted. Toxic with ships and effluent – fresh and untreated. Some said that mercury from up river had killed the fish. He runs with the effortless ability of a former athlete, familiar with the slap slap of pavements. With dreams of lost cousins. A shipwrecked marriage. A crystal clear reason to clear out and clear off.

Haversacks full of tools bounce on backs powering homeward. The noise must be tremendous, but all he can hear is the sound of his own breathing. The road becomes flat as it passes The Ship, already crowded with men greedy for beer. He passes under the railway bridge; squat and functional, a part of the industrial landscape. It reminds him of an old girlfriend, no longer loved.

On High Street West the sound of traffic and people, mixes with construction noise. Work on McMenemy's Roman Forum is underway. The world is getting on mightily fine without his old boss. There's nothing much to see when he peeks through the hoardings, only foundations and pipe work. McMenemy is absent; there's no mention of him anywhere. No hint that this was his project. Another firm from out of town finished the drawings – McMenemy's plan has died with him. When he'd gone to see the final plan displayed at the Town Hall, nothing was left of the old design – save for the basic site outline. Custom features had been stripped out and replaced with pre-cast concrete. With grey bevelled panels, unremarkable and plain. But they'd kept the square and statue. Even the dedication was preserved, except McMenemy's name was replaced with another's, The Alderman.

At the cemetery they'd huddled together like people sheltering from a storm. There was something about it, something about the passing away of one life and the beginning of another. A life already spinning dangerously out of control, edging towards the precipice. He recalls her fingers, stained green; and the black mascara stains on her cheeks. She looked insane, yet he knows she's not.

"Judy there are things I need to tell you."

"Judith please."

"Because that's what he called you."

"Yes, because if it's about him, I already know everything there is to know."

Is how their conversation began, outside the

cemetery gates one windswept afternoon:

"He was a bastard McMenemy, he didn't tell the truth."

"What makes you say that."

"I know you looked up to him, but he wasn't nice when you saw him close-up. And I saw him magnified. Like The Queens with its massive screen."

"You mean..."

"He fooled you all including The Alderman."

"I think it's the other way round with The Alderman."

"Maurice played that greedy pervert like a violin. But he also turned a blind eye too. The man deserves to be locked-up."

"But instead he gets a dedication at the new shopping mall."

"Well your old boss was just as guilty because he let it happen. And I was too love struck to notice. But then he went and died."

"So you found something, some papers, a letter?"

"No, I had a visit from a Solicitor who works for The Alderman. He came around the day after the funeral and gave me a warning. "

"What was that?"

"Any repeat performances and I would be sent away."

"Look this isn't Stalin's Russia, people can't be disappeared."

"No but they can become unemployable and a social

leper – it's well within The Alderman's powers to get someone blackballed."

"So that's when you realised the type of characters McMenemy was involved with. "

"No I guessed the working class hero was a bit of an act, long before that. But he was good, he never dropped it with me. I believed him, just like you did."

He'd not thought of them as kindred spirits. They were neither in love or great friends, but there's a like to like attraction. A bond. She'd always been there, but on the periphery. Mairi then Peggy had blotted her out, and there'd been a chance at New Year, but he'd walked away. One of those memories that replay over and over, never to be resolved. And he'd walked away again, after that brief meeting outside the cemetery.

"Come on Keith," he said to himself. They are there at The Ship, sinking pints. McMenemy's shopping centre will still be there in the morning. Along with his hangover and empty house.

DEAR JUDY

Dear Judy

If you're reading this letter, then I'm very happy. If you've stuffed it in the bin, I understand that too. You see I never meant to just leave, but London sucked me in. I was swallowed, or maybe that's the wrong word. I've got a picture in my head, from my favourite children's book, Pinocchio. Geppetto the woodcarver is scribbling away in the belly of a whale. He's made a little home from home, with a washing line, writing desk and front door – a bit like me. I got so caught up with my new life, I forgot about the old one. I let you and Willington go. Watched you all sail away. I forgot about the important things. Selfish, that's what I was. Old Geppetto had no choice, he needed rescuing, me I have no excuse.

But news has a way of travelling south. Or rather a certain Priest bearing news, hitched a ride with the Knights of St Columba. Your old friend Father Flannery took time out from his trip to look for me. He chose the most obvious places to look; where young people like us get washed-up. You know, bright lights, music, nightlife and men. He started with an A to Z of London, opened on the Soho page.

He found me by the third street. Well he found someone who recognised my photo – pointed him in the direction of the club where I worked half a lifetime ago. And the club foolishly mistook him for a punter (I expect he left the dog collar at the hotel) and let him in. You'd laugh if you saw where he found himself. Squeezed into a red velvet bucket seat, drinking overpriced wine with a girl who needed his money, more than he did.

I've heard he even paid for a personal strip show in an upstairs room. And all the while he was waiting for the opportunity to mention my name. The wine must have given him courage, because before the bottle was finished, he asked for me. He was lucky, the girl could have given him the brush off, but she knows me and guessed he wasn't the usual type of punter. She didn't give him some story, she told him the truth. It was not my night off, and there was no chance I'd be back, because I was working The Two Jacks in D'Arby Street.

I was working when he turned up the next evening, so he waited until the end of the night. Which was a long wait, my night ended at four in the morning. And he was cutting it fine too, his coach trip to Canterbury was leaving at eight am. We had half an hour together, long enough to persuade me that you needed help. He told me about McMenemy's death. How you had taken it badly. Upset a lot of people, including the poor mans wife. He didn't say how you were living now, or if there was anyone other than

360

me who could help. And I didn't think to ask. He was gone before we had time to talk about the important stuff, but I'm not stupid – if half the congregation of St Vincent's are playing guessing games about your love life, having any sort of life in Willington is going to be neigh on impossible.

Remember the Club A Gogo , I spotted you in there with him. Part of me wanted to warn you – instead I left you to get on with it. Maybe it was jealousy, I don't know. But I suppose I'm saying that part of your mess is down to me. If I'd been a better friend, I would have tried to help, but instead...

Please if you've read this far don't stop !!

Please come to London, stay with me. We can sleep top to toe until I find a bigger place. Please, you can be happy here.

Lots of love
    Mairi xxx
PS.   Go to Keith if you need help, just say I asked.

She was outside looking in. A child with its face pressed up against the glass of Fenwick's Christmas window. She walked the streets of Willington at dusk and in darkness. She felt ashamed; nothing was normal. And when he first contacted her, she knew Mairi had written to them both.

361

He found her at early morning mass, the eight o'clock
– the one nobody but the waifs and strays went to. She sat on
the dark side, where a baptismal font and a Christmas time
crib were secreted. She wore a headscarf and dark clothes.
Widows weeds he thought, while slipping into the pew
behind her. And she could sense his presence. In the old days
she would have turned round and smiled, maybe even said a
few words. But on this occasion she kept her eyes focused on
the altar. Father Flannery was there already, standing in
silence, looking out at the empty spaces of eight o'clock mass.
After mass Keith followed her home, trailing at a reasonable
distance. They met at her door, when she turned to face him.
She let him in, taking him upstairs to a small front lounge.
Neither of them mentioned the letter.

"I thought I'd see how you were doing," he said as she
laid out cups, biscuits and a small pot of tea.

"Mairi always said you were nice. You know you're
the only person who's come to see me since the
funeral. April feels like a lifetime ago."

He was going to make up a lie about meaning to. But
it wasn't true and she would know. He told her a truth, that
Peggy was in hospital, and their Marriage was done.

"But..."

"I know it's been six months, hardly time to get used
to sleeping in the same bed. Anyway that's another
story, and I'm here to see you. "

One magnolia tinged day drifted into another. Every one of them began in the same way. Gravity pulled him down deep into the mattress. Part of him wanted to know about what it felt like to be a baby in the womb – cut off from the trials and tribulations of the world. But in that route lay oblivion. Because there'd been no happy homecomings, no greeting Peggy like Elvis in Blue Hawaii. A garland round his neck, a guitar in his hand. Singing I Can't help falling in love, because that's what his problem was, the reason he was in-bed dreaming.

And falling out of love happened so suddenly, there was no way of predicting when it would strike. But it always did. He'd agreed with Mairi for old times sake. She could have asked anything and he would have said yes. Yet despite her physical absence, Peggy is there at home with him – its her furniture and wallpaper, her choice of colours. A wedding photograph, taken outside St Vincent's, sits on the mantelpiece. Another on her dressing table. A brush still contains strands of her hair, and the laundry basket, items of her clothes. They are still together in the eyes of the church, only they don't sleep together. And they don't love the way newly married couples do.

As he sinks deeper into his mattress there's a vision of Judith Pemberton on New Years day. With tinsel on the ground. It's freezing outside, but he's drank enough to keep out the cold. They sway towards the park, and a hill that will give them a clear view over Willington. She slips and breaks

one of her stiletto heels. He finds himself breaking off the
other heel so she can walk. They kiss, slowly in the cold.
Willington is ablaze with light. Lights hang from cranes, they
burn as streetlamps, and glow from inside peoples houses.

When August came there is already a chill in the air. They sit
and smoke, sombrely. Talking in whispers. She asks him
about Peggy and he answers truthfully. He smells of beer
again, the sourness leeching through his skin. Lately she'd
begun to feel uncomfortable, when the anger and frustration
he's feeling tears through. He's electric in those moments, a
heartbeat away from violence. Living an accelerated life.
Caring for an infirm wife was gloomy and miserable, and
pulling him apart.

August becomes October. The're sleeping together.
Snatching brief respite from their lives. She begins to talk
with him about moving away from Willington, and he
doesn't object. He's remembering Miles Davis's Kind of Blue
and a drive through the London suburbs. Then there are the
bad days when he'd come pounding at her door. At the
beginning of November, the claustrophobia of months spent
inside made them venture outside. First to the cinema,
where they joined other anonymous couples in darkness.
Then to pubs a car ride away. In towns where they were
unknown. Yet there was something unsatisfying about hiding
out in public. They didn't belong, and the regulars no matter
how friendly, always knew too. She supposed most people

thought they were having an affair, getting out of town so as not to be caught. And it was the wanting to be caught that drew them back to Willington.

She said nobody would notice. But they would know, and that would be magic – the secret ingredient missing from those sad drives out of town. She said it would be more thrilling than sitting in a dank Lounge Bar. And he started to think of her dressed up for a night out. He would watch her, and she him. Then later they would tumble onto her bed in their best clothes. She said it would be harmless. But he knew it would do a lot of harm if they were discovered. So he planned their escape, the way people plan a murder; and he waited until November became December.

DECEMBER

They were stopping off to admire the scenery. Making one last pilgrimage, before the arc of their journey headed south. Fragments of the intervening years lay scattered on this barren Northumberland beach. And they had time to climb the dunes and revisit a few glittering memories; he with a bottle of vodka, she with vermouth. Round a makeshift fire they drank, while the ocean chipped in its chorus of moans. On a night like this, with the full moon risen: Lindisfarne and the Farne Islands were visible. Ghosts of long dead monks followed wooden crosses along the waters edge, carrying the thousand-year-old bones of St Cuthbert to safety. And the cries of seals, flapping their flipper arms; and seabirds ever present, scavenging for scraps. And the smell of a makeshift fire; burning driftwood, smouldering. She could see his face illuminated by the flames. Pushing out of the darkness, like a study in light by Rembrandt or Caravaggio.

The details are important to her, his Sacred Heart lapel badge, the shine of his grey Tonik suit. His hair; long at the back, curling and unkempt. A large gold signet ring that had belonged to his father; it had rough edges that scratched. He has a dimple on his chin, like Kirk Douglas; but that's where the resemblance to Spartacus ended. He was no champion of the underprivileged and underfed, he was the champion of him.

"How are you," she wanted to say. But instead she concentrated on keeping her legs still. They started shaking under the table at St Vincent's, while drink after drink poured down her throat. People had noticed her, and she could feel a rumour circulate through the dance floor and bar. See it pass from mouth to mouth. A sideways glance here, a stare from above the foamy head of a pint.

And she wanted to tell him to stop when he began to sing, the way men do when they work. But the threat of violence, lurking round a familiar collection of notes sent a chill through her. She saw hammers and chisels, tenant saws and butcher's aprons – stained a carcass red. She tried to push past the vision of herself, looking up at his great head, applauding with all her might. And whatever was left of her reason, scavenged for excuses.

A new beginning is what this was supposed to be. An escape from Willington; once and forever. He made it sound so easy, so matter-of-fact, that it sounded like something people did every day. And he'd shrewdly left out all the complications. And there was no question there would be complications. She could hear them rattling in the wind. They were over there in Seahouses, emptied of day-trippers; they were inside his wallet where a picture of his wife still lived. Circulating, black carrion birds; waiting to pick the meat from their bones.

The details are important:

He made her think of strong dependable men, who washed well after a hard day's work, and held open doors for women. The type of men who were not afraid. Who gave themselves, without complaint. Who created a relief map of the moon on her kitchen door, rather than her face. Who made her think of sex and pleasure, and naked summer afternoons.

Square men and hollow men:

Men smelling of sweat and paraffin. Men sprinting from the ship yards exit. Negotiating the steep bank in overalls and steel capped boots; in caps and old suit jackets. With segs crunching against cobble and tar-macadam, making a deafening roar. Pushing bikes up the steep hill, making for the ferry landing and a journey across the river.

The sweet smell of bruised fruit, rotting on her table:

Willington's skyline shifting to burnt orange and spring yellow. Painted cranes, unnaturally bright. A child blowing bubbles in a back-lane. He looked at her once again through the flames. Lighting another cigarette, taking a swig from the vodka and then the vermouth. He always preferred a mixer, never a straight drink.

He touches her hair, moistened by sea air and flaked with debris from the wind. He smiles a wide open grin; a flash of happiness before the heartbreak. And he begins to sing once more.

Oh the sharks.....

Printed in Great Britain
by Amazon